TANGENT

CAROLINE GOLDSWORTHY

For Pippa

CHAPTER ONE

Josie shivered, pulling the thin jacket tighter around her slender torso. Earlier rain gave the streets a metallic, just-washed scent; the cold turning the damp pavements icy. Frost sparkled under the streetlights. Looking down to admire her new scarlet suede ankle boots, Josie wondered if they matched or clashed with the jacket. She stamped her feet and tried to shut out the chill breeze. Suffolk winds were lazy, they didn't bother going around the body, they went straight through. Josie knew this, but she still turned out in her best outfit. Not ideal for winter.

The itching started again, and she scratched her thighs furiously. It had been too long since her last dose of heroin and the side effects — her friends called it *clucking* — were kicking in. A runny nose, stomach cramps, prickly skin. She shoved her fist into her belly, trying to ease the pain, and wiped the back of her other hand across her nose. Looking anxiously up and down the empty street, she forgot about her nose and stomach and began to rub her arms, forcing blood into her fingers.

Oh, come on, someone come soon. I need the money. I'm

1

fucking freezing. I don't want to be here. I just need me fix. Come on!

A car's headlights turned into the street as if on command. *Yes!*

The car drew up beside her. The electric window slid down. Forcing a smile, she leaned in and spoke to the driver. Someone she'd seen cruising the streets before. Even better. A regular user, like herself. Only the product differed. He'd know the score. No quibbling afterwards. Do the business, take the money and go. She struck a deal, opened the door, clambered in and secured the seat belt as the car pulled away. The night's trading had begun.

'I've seen you before, haven't I?' he said

'Yeah, I guess so. I often work that corner.'

'What's your name?'

'Scarlett.'

'Sure, of course it is.' The man laughed. 'Do any of you girls use your real name?'

'Nah, not normally,' Josie replied. She fluffed up her shoulder-length blonde locks, hoping that the dark roots weren't too obvious.

He nodded as if he understood. Josie looked at him. His pale eyes studied the road as he dragged a large hand through fair, wispy hair. He seemed deep in thought.

'Where are we going?' she asked, as he indicated and slowed.

'A flat just off the main drag. A friend lets me use it when he's away.'

'Cool. Remember though, it's extra if you want me in the buff.'

Josie hoped the flat would be warm. Dank, chill nights

played havoc with marketing the goods: punters weren't turned on by goose bumps, although some liked a cold mouth on the cock. In the main though, shagging someone with a layer of permafrost was an overrated pastime.

The car turned into a narrow road, the closed shop fronts and sheltered doorways barely lit by a sad line of weak streetlamps. The driver concentrated on parallel parking between a van and a liveried taxi. Josie wondered if she was meant to be impressed, as there were easier spaces further along. He turned off the engine and she made to get out, but he signalled for her to wait. She frowned, but sat still while he got out and walked around. She looked up through the passenger side window, wondering what he was doing. Then he opened her door and stepped back.

Josie gave him a genuine smile. He didn't have to do that. She was a sure thing without chivalry, but still, it was always nice to be treated well.

'Why, thank you,' she said.

He looked through her and locked the car. She waited, trying to suppress the shivers from the cold and the withdrawal. He took her elbow and guided her across the street to a hardened security door squeezed in between graffiti-covered shop shutters. Once again he stepped back and held the door for her. She stepped into a narrow, damp hallway with a single flight of stairs ahead of her. She began to climb, the heels of her suede ankle boots clicking out against the bare wood. She knew he'd be following close, getting a good look at her short skirt and what lay underneath. On the top landing she stood next to the only door and waited for him to find the right key from a bunch he was jangling in the half-light cast by the landing's bare bulb.

· · ·

'Drink?' he said, pushing open the battered green door.

She followed him down a grimy hallway and into the main room. He flicked the light switch, but the energy-saver bulb scarcely pierced the darkness. As it warmed and grew brighter, Josie took in the surroundings. The arms of the shabby brown settee shone with the grease from a thousand dirty hands. In front of the sofa lay a frayed rug, pockmarked with cigarette burns. A fine layer of dust coated every surface. Josie sniffed at the stale air, wrinkling her nose. She turned to look at the man.

'What ya got? Some vodka would be good if you've got any,' she said.

'Let's see.' He shuffled the bottles in a laminate topped sideboard around and pulled out a clear one. 'Yep, you're in luck,' he said, pouring generous slugs into glasses that he had blown the dust from. He passed one to her.

'To business,' he said, raising his glass.

'To business,' she replied, raising hers. It looked clean, but she sipped hesitantly, rolling the liquid around her mouth. Some punters thought they could get away without paying by spiking a drink. Josie was a two-year veteran of the streets. No one was going to do that to her!

He sat down on the settee, switching on the widescreen as he did so. He opened his flies. Commando, she noticed. Looking at her intently, he pulled out his cock and started to stroke it.

'Start sucking, love,' he said.

'I thought you wanted the full doings, not just a blow job.'

'Yeah, but just a little something to get me started, eh?'

She tossed back the vodka, removed her jacket and set to work. She felt him growing harder inside her mouth.

Suddenly he pushed her away. 'On your hands and knees!' he hissed.

He moved in behind her, dragged her skirt up and her knickers down. He entered her roughly. She grimaced and focused instead on what was happening on the screen. Typical porn, she thought. Doggy fashion, same as he was doing. His hands grasped at her breasts, her shoulders and her neck. He was pushing harder now. Grunting. Close to climax. She looked at the television again. There was something familiar about the actor. Then she realised the man on the screen was a much younger version of the man now behind her. Josie watched as the performer slipped a scarf around the girl's neck. She saw the look of horror on the actress's face. As the shock of what she was seeing struck her, Josie struggled for air, realising too late that soft material had been slid around her own throat. She choked as it tightened, gasping for breath, wheezing and bucking against him to release his grip, unable to use both hands without falling flat on her face. Bracing herself with one arm, she scratched at him and at her neck with her free hand, desperate to inhale.

As he ejaculated she blacked out, unable to feel his weight on her as they collapsed to the ground. Nor did she feel him pulling the scarf tighter around her neck, forcing the last vestige of life from her body. Her eyes, bulging yet unseeing, stared directly at him as he lay beside her until his panting subsided. She didn't see him pull away or squat on his haunches to stop the hidden camcorder. Her sightless gaze didn't register him plugging the camera into the TV or sitting back on the sofa to rest his feet on the arms.

While her lifeless body lay where it had fallen, he stroked his flaccid penis and assessed the film he had just recorded.

CHAPTER TWO

July 1981

The boy woke with a start. His pulse racing, nerves jangling. The door handle made a barely audible squeak. Through the thin, ragged curtains, the sodium glow of the streetlamp shone into his room and he saw the door opening. A small crack of dark appeared between the white of architrave and door. The boy heard the man's breathing and smelt his distinctive musty aroma of beer, sweat and cigarettes. He screwed his eyes shut, silently begging mum's new boyfriend to go away.

'Bill, is that you?' his mother called from down the hallway.

The boy shuddered with relief as he heard her voice. Bill Travis muttered an oath and closed the door as quietly as he'd opened it. Not knowing if he was truly safe or if it was just a temporary reprieve, the boy decided to take no chances. Grabbing his teddy bear and duvet he shoved the dirty clothes and clutter aside and took refuge under his bed.

Sarah Jenkins was thrust into the new day. The alarm clock buzzed by her head; she silenced it with a thump and rolled over onto her back, glaring at the ceiling. Half asleep, she reached across to the far side of the bed. It was empty, as it had been for several months. For a moment she wondered if, at thirty-two, her romantic life was at an end. Before the tears could start, she squeezed her eyes shut and willed the temptation of a few more precious seconds of sleep to overwhelm her. She snuggled in the duvet, wrapping herself in its warmth. Her two-week Christmas break had come to an end and Sarah was not looking forward to a January filled with sifting through the backlog of stories, searching for the glimmer of a lead. There had never been time for that type of nonsense on the London paper, always something new to go for. Scratching and whining at the door made her lie-in a non-starter and she pushed the duvet off and swung her feet to the floor. Bad move. She winced at the pressure in her head, pushed the brunette hair off her face, rubbed her eyes and tried to focus. Shuffling into slippers and a dressing gown, she pulled back the curtains. The dark winter morning echoed the gloom of the bedroom. Sarah fumbled her way to the kitchen, flipped a few switches and the space flooded with fluorescent light. The aroma of fresh coffee from the filter machine wafted across the room as Sarah rifled through cupboards in search of painkillers. Danvers thrust a wet muzzle into her hand, and she fondled his glossy black ears and tan snout before opening the patio door to let him into the garden.

After letting the dog back in, Sarah sat at the breakfast bar sipping the black coffee and coughing on her first cigarette of the day. Neither made her feel any more human and she regretted her decision to open the second bottle of red the night before. Sighing, she looked at the glowing tip of her cigarette and reflected on the fact that, these days, she was making a lot of senseless choices.

Danvers sat at her side, gazing up with trusting dark eyes under his tan eyebrows. It restored a little piece of her self-worth. Sarah slipped off the stool, stubbed the cigarette out and swigged the rest of the cooling liquid. Trudging up the stairs, she threw on the clothes which had been lying in a heap at the bottom of her bed.

'Come on, boy,' she said, and they left the small end terraced house just as weak, winter light broke on the horizon.

Sarah and Danvers wandered through the village as it slowly came to life. Being situated far enough away from town planning and clean air laws allowed people to light fires in the winter. Wood smoke drifted over the rooftops as the residents woke and prepared for the first working day of the New Year. She headed for the woods and, once past the kissing gate, unleashed the dog who bounded off into the undergrowth. Sarah wandered down the footpath in no hurry to go to work, enjoying the fragrance of the damp earth and the crispness of the air. Sounds of Danvers crashing through the shrubs and bushes drifted to her ears, until sharp warning barks woke her from her daydreams. Groaning at the noise, she moved quickly towards it. The dog stood on the stream bank. He was whining now and trying to paw an object in the water. Panting as she approached, Sarah saw a floating mannequin.

Exasperated with the dog and fly tippers alike, she tried to drag him away. Danvers refused to be pulled and Sarah peered more intently at the dress shop dummy, bending down to be closer. The blonde hair with its dark roots was so lifelike as it floated in the fast-running stream. She gasped as she realised with horror that the doll's arm was floating too. Sarah recoiled from the naked body of a woman who had been dumped with all the dignity afforded to a fast food wrapper.

Pulling her phone from her pocket, she hesitated, weighing up who she should call first. This was the story she'd been looking for. It would recharge her career and boost her reputation at the local paper. Sarah took a deep breath, hit speed dial and spoke to her editor.

Only then did she call the police.

CHAPTER THREE

Detective Chief Inspector Ronald Carlson eased himself
from the passenger seat. Time was when he would have leapt
out the driver's side, but he was younger then and a junior
officer. Rank has its privileges, he thought. He pushed the
door shut, reluctant to leave the warmth of the car, and
headed into the mist, adjusting the waistband of his suit
trousers as he walked. He'd not worn them since the funeral,
and the material had cut into him whilst he sat in the car.
When had they got so tight? he wondered, I'm sure I should
have lost weight, not gained it. He shuffled reluctantly
towards the perimeter tape, struggling to pull his jacket close
around his chest as the seams strained around his broad
shoulders. The blue and white tape fluttered in the breeze,
twisting the wording.

Police line, do not cross.

A flash of his ID card prompted the uniformed officer to
lift the cordon for him. Carlson signed the officer's log.
Come on Ronnie, get a grip, he told himself, and taking a
deep breath, he strode to the inner cordon where Kirsty

Russell, the crime scene manager, was organising the CSI team. She turned, smiled, and waved a greeting.

'Hey Ronnie, good to see you back. How are—?'

He raised a hand to silence her and bowed his head. This was going to be harder than he'd thought. Facing the compassion of colleagues. He couldn't decide which was worse, the silent sympathy or the enquiries after his health. Not for the first time, he wondered if he should have come back to work at all.

'What have we got then?' he said.

Kirsty replied briskly, 'According to your first responder a dog walker made the discovery at 06:47. As it was a body a double crew was sent, and they were here at 07:13. They secured the scene, but the sodding dog has been all over the place as has the owner. She's over there. Oh, and Ronnie?' Kirsty said. 'She's a reporter.'

'That's all we need,' he said. 'She's not taken any photos, has she?'

'She says not, but we seized her phone. That was a challenge in itself.' Kirsty gave a tight-lipped smile. 'She wasn't going to give it up. Your new sergeant soon sorted her out. Anyway, we'll clear a common access path to the girl's body and then we can get a better look at her.

'The guys will photograph as they go,' she continued. 'The path might meander a bit if they find any worthwhile footwear impressions, but they'll mark it out and we can move closer.'

Carlson dug his hands deep into his pockets, a silent but impatient observer as two CSI technicians cleared the route to the body. One placed a rim around a section of wet grass, filled it with plaster of Paris and placed an aluminium protective plate over the top. They worked slowly and methodically, marking the official access route with yellow tape. Once they reached the girl, a third technician walked forward through the marked path and erected the incident tent. It just touched the far side of the brook but at least it protected her from prying eyes.

'Looks like I'm up then,' said a voice.

Carlson had not heard the pathologist approach. No one ever did. Creepy Kilburn, the younger detectives called him, although not in earshot of DCI Carlson.

Dr Kilburn and his assistant, Dennis, followed the path to the incident tent, ducked inside and closed the flap behind them. After a few minutes Kilburn reopened it and beckoned Carlson and Kirsty. By the time they reached the tent he was knelt by the girl and leaning perilously over the edge of the rivulet. He did not turn around as they entered.

'Dumped but probably not killed here,' he muttered. 'Likely to have been in the water around a week, maybe longer. The stream runs fast here so I'm not sure how much evidence Kirsty will be able to pick up. The body would have been washed further downstream if her feet weren't caught in those roots.'

Kilburn and Dennis recovered the girl from the brook, laying her gently on the plastic sheeting. Dennis placed plastic bags on her hands and feet.

'Ready to turn her over?' Kilburn asked.

Carlson nodded. Although the girl had looked little more than adolescent when face down, he was not prepared for how young she looked face to face. As the medic rolled her over, Carlson found himself stepping backwards. How old was she? Sixteen, maybe seventeen? Not much older. Probably the same age as Jade. He gripped the inside of his cheek with his teeth to bring himself back into the present, not enough to draw blood but sufficient to focus his mind. Come on Ronnie, he said to himself. Keep your mind on the job, don't think about that now.

'Hmm, petechial haemorrhaging. See here?' Dr Kilburn indicated streaks in the whites of the girl's open eyes. He then pointed to the scratches on her neck and beckoned for the CSI to move in and photograph them. Kilburn lifted the girl's arm, revealing tell-tale tracks in the groove of the elbow. 'But there are other possibilities. I'll be able to tell you more when she's on the slab.' He looked up at Carlson. 'Does she match any missing persons?'

Carlson raised a silvering eyebrow at his new sergeant. Ben Poole was framed in the entrance to the tent, filling the doorway with his wide shoulders.

He shook his head. 'No, Guv. Station have just come back to me. Nothing,' Poole said. Mist formed a halo around his short cropped afro curls. His almond-shaped deep brown eyes held Carlson's for a moment too long and then he looked away.

Carlson saw him shiver and wondered why. An unseen droplet of the condensing mist slid off the tent, past Poole's upturned collar and down his neck. As Poole raised the hood of the paper suit over his head with an imperceptible shudder, Carlson wondered if the fast-track graduate had chosen the right job. He watched as Poole regarded his highly polished shoes which, despite the coverall booties, were becoming less polished by the minute. His behaviours seemed to confirm Carlson's suspicions.

Carlson continued looking at him, appraising and wondering if he would ever be able to trust a man who was so handsome, then he turned back to the medic. 'No, Jervis. It would appear we've no reports of missing teenagers.'

Kilburn sighed. 'Well, you have now.'

'This is Gleam FM and here is the news. The body of a young woman was found yesterday in woodland near Mendlesham. So far, police have not been able to identify her. She is approximately 5' 2" tall, slim build, dark hair dyed blonde and grey eyes. She has a dolphin tattoo on her right upper back. Anyone able to assist with any information should call police on 0345 001 1085.'

Shazza looked up from her newspaper and stared at the café's radio. She had only been half listening to the news, whilst thinking about heading back to her flat. Those plans were on hold as her stomach knotted up. She thought Josie had gone back to her parents. They had talked about it only a few days ago but, hearing about the dolphin caused a bubble of bile to rise in Shazza's throat. She pulled her cup nearer and looked down at the tea. It had gone cold while she'd been idling with the paper. The milk formed a scummy veneer which rippled as a tear hit it. Shazza pushed cup and saucer aside and, grabbing her paper, stumbled to the café door and into the street. She pulled her jacket closed, buttoning it against the cold and stuffing the paper into one of its large pockets. Her first thought was to get a fix, but she'd been clean for several weeks. Now over the worst of the clucking, she'd been doing okay. It was the longest she'd ever been drug-free and yet, at the first problem, she knew she needed a hit to take the pain away. Her eyes were blurry as, battling to ignore the bewitching call of Golden Brown, the local brand of heroin, she entered the pub where she and Josie had shared a last drink.

The car pulled up at the kerbside and the window wound down.

'Looking for business?'

She was young, very young. Her light brown hair was pulled back into a ponytail, and as she spoke she curved her lips into a slight smile. She still had an element of innocence and beauty about her, but her eyes were beginning to develop that hard, dull look they all got after a while.

'What's your name, love?'

'What do you want it to be?'

He laughed and reached over to open the door. The girl slipped into the passenger seat and pulled the door shut.

CHAPTER FOUR

Dr Jervis Kilburn was on the point of starting the autopsy when DCI Carlson and DS Poole arrived. Poole scurried in, but Carlson slowed himself to a stroll, anxious not to appear like an errant schoolboy.

'Ah, there you are, gentlemen! I was just about to start without you,' Kilburn said. Carlson could see the doctor's blue eyes crinkle at the corners, hiding the white lines on his sunburnt face, although any smile, if there was one, remained hidden under the surgical mask. He stood, as Carlson had seen him so many times before, poised with scalpel raised over a corpse. The girl seemed even smaller lying on the mortuary slab. Naked and with her hair still damp, her neck was elevated on the body block, arms hanging limply by her side as if baring her breast to meet the blade head on.

Carlson and Poole put on the green gowns offered by Kilburn's mortuary assistant and tied the straps.

'Dennis and I have done the external examination already,' said Dr Kilburn. 'Ms Russell was here overnight, and she's done hers. Everything's documented.' Kilburn waved the blade at the microphone above his head. 'Photos too. As I said yesterday, it looks like a ligature, but you can't be too careful. And I don't like the look of those arms.'

He beckoned them closer as he put the scalpel down and lifted the girl's left arm.

'Mainlining, see? More passengers than a commuter train!'

Carlson and Poole looked where directed. The median cubital vein stood out against the pallid skin. Its dark purple line reminded Carlson of a map of the Metropolitan underground line. Dotted around it were hundreds of needle marks, some old and faded, others much newer, milling around like passengers waiting for a delayed train.

'Been using for a while, I'd say. I strongly suspect heroin, Ronnie. We've been seeing a few more overdoses recently. Your colleagues in Organised Crime think there's a purer opiate getting on the streets. You'll have to wait for toxicology to get an idea of what exactly, so it'll be hard to tell what our girl has been using until after that.'

Carlson nodded, wondering if Superintendent Tasker had bothered to let his Major Investigation team know or had decided to keep them ignorant of such developments. He decided that he probably knew the answer already. How long is he going to hold this grudge? Carlson thought. After all, Tasker was the one that was Superintendent now, while he was still a DCI. The timing of the interviews wasn't great but, Carlson reasoned, it wasn't his fault he'd had to drop out of the running. He sighed and then realised he was missing the conversation.

'Will you be able to tell how pure the heroin is?' Poole was asking.

'No,' said Kilburn, fixing him with the sort of stare he

reserved for his students. 'The body metabolises the opiate as soon as it enters the bloodstream. The liver tries to break it down so that it becomes less harmful to the body. From blood and urine, I could tell you the purity of what's left in her system, but not the level of the drug's concentration when it went in.'

'Oh, that's a shame,' said Poole, clearly disappointed. 'I thought you could. We'd been working on building a database of different brands, their purity levels, and mapping those to the dealers in my old force.'

'You've allowed yourself to be influenced by too much American television,' laughed the doctor. 'I'd need a sample of what she injected to tell how pure it was, and in any case, I have no idea when she last injected. I would say' — he pointed at a small pinprick on the girl's arm — 'that this is likely to be the most recent injection site, but I cannot be sure. That would be a presumption, and what do we never do here, Dennis?'

'We never presume or assume, Doctor.' It was a well-rehearsed routine. They both turned to Poole, laughing. He glowered back at them, his dark features creased in a scowl. His fists stayed by his side, but he clenched them tightly. Carlson coughed and quietly raised a single eyebrow, looking at both men in turn.

Kilburn pretended he'd not noticed and turned his attention back to the girl. 'Hmm,' he said, and picking up the scalpel again he bent to his work, making a large Y-incision running from each shoulder blade to the breastbone and down to the pubis. As he peeled back the skin, Carlson and Poole took involuntary steps backwards. Jervis glanced at Dennis. Carlson knew both men were exchanging wry smiles under their masks. He refocused on the corpse as Kilburn detached the chest plate by snapping the bones cleanly and placed it on the tray proffered by his ever-obliging assistant.

Each organ was removed, weighed and samples taken while Kilburn recorded his findings for later transcription. Eventually, he came to the stomach.

'Doesn't look like she'd eaten for a while before she was killed. But I'll test this clear liquid just to make sure nothing has been added,' he said.

He syphoned off a sample for analysis.

The core cavity examination completed, Dr Kilburn turned his attention to the young woman's head. Using the Stryker saw, he removed a section of skull, placing it carefully to one side and then skilfully separated the brain from its casing. He weighed it and brought it under the magnifying loupe lens for close examination.

'Yes, she's certainly had a good bang to the head. Several contusions in fact. We found bruising on the skull during the external exam, but I don't believe even this was enough to kill her. It would have made her dizzy and confused, however.' Dr Kilburn took more samples and Dennis labelled them as they whispered in their own private language. Finally, the medic turned to the throat.

At last, thought Carlson. Although he knew the process only too well and that Jervis Kilburn would follow it rigorously, sometimes, just sometimes, he wished the pathologist would cut to the chase.

'Asphyxiation, possibly using a scarf to cut off her oxygen. The markings are too wide to be a cord — see, here and here.' He pointed as he spoke. 'Different pressure marks indicate that something such as a belt is unlikely to be your weapon either. I will put in my conclusions that the assailant attacked from behind. The external examination showed that the crossover in the scarf was at the back, not the front. We took photographs of that and the scratches on her throat before you got here,' he said, pointedly reminding Carlson of their late arrival.

Selecting another scalpel, he made a swift incision on the girl's neck and peeled back the skin. He reached for the loupe lens again and pulled it over her throat, squinting as he stared through the lens. Dr Kilburn found what he'd been looking for right from the start — a broken hyoid bone.

'There you have it, gentlemen. She was strangled.' Dr Kilburn looked down at the girl. To Carlson it seemed that his gaze was like a gentle smile, saddened by what he saw lying before him. Kilburn coughed and continued speaking.

'She fought her attacker fiercely, clawed at him and the ligature, but there's nothing under the fingernails. One nail is ripped off, so I can see she put up quite a fight. Her assailant will have some scratches for a few days yet.

'Oh, and something else. She'd had sex. No, sorry Ronnie, no semen,' he replied to Carlson's quizzical glance.

'I surmise that a condom may have been used,' he resumed. 'Sex may have been consensual, at least at first. However, it was rough, and she has internal bruising, as you'd expect. I've taken some swabs for spermicide. But, Ronnie, and here's the thing. After being in the stream for so long, I'm not hopeful of finding any trace evidence. As I said, Ms Russell did her external exam earlier on. I've not discussed it with her in any great detail, but I think that any fibres have been washed away. I'm really sorry, Ronnie.' Kilburn removed his nitrile gloves and threw them in the bin.

Carlson pursed his lips and shook his head as if to say he knew it was not Kilburn's fault.

'So how long has she been dead?' he asked.

'When was she last seen alive? Do we know?'

'We don't even know who she is yet,' Carlson replied.

'She's been in the water at least four days,' said Kilburn. 'Taking that into account with the levels of decomposition I see here, I would suggest she's been dead for around five to six days. Dennis will type everything up and let you have the preliminary findings and it'll take a few more days for any toxicology results. We've taken her fingerprints and are running her DNA, so you may get a hit out of that yet. We'll also get an e-fit to you.'

Carlson nodded, muttered his thanks and strode from the room, ripping the gown away from himself as if doing so would remove the smell, the carnage and the waste of yet another young life.

As they stepped outside into the cold winter air, Carlson patted himself down, wondering where he'd left them. He tutted when the realisation that he'd given up five years before dawned on him.

'I need a smoke,' he said to Poole.

'I didn't realise you smoked,' came the reply.

'I don't. I gave up.'

Poole pointed towards a newsagents' shop across the road from the mortuary.

It was only as he dragged greedily on the filter and felt the smoke fill his lungs that Ronnie Carlson finally admitted that he had not come close to forgiving himself for the death of Jade. He inhaled again, realising with some surprise that he'd smoked down to the stub already. He flung it to the ground and stamped it out.

'Come on,' he said. 'Let's get back to the station and see if we're any closer to finding out who she is.'

'Right, take a seat you lot. Settle down. Settle down!' shouted DS Poole as the team shuffled into seats for the evening briefing. 'Guv?'

Carlson took his place at the head of the room in front of the white board. Photos of the crime scene were stuck to it along with close-ups of the young woman's face and the dolphin tattoo on her back.

'Okay, as you all know, the body of a young woman was found yesterday morning by a dog walker — yes, yes, I know. It's always the dog walkers. Sometimes I wonder how many bodies would be left lying at peace in the countryside if it wasn't for people and their dogs.' Carlson raised his hands for silence as the team groaned. 'Nonetheless, this was no ordinary dog walker. She was a reporter. We've seized her phone but there's no way of knowing how much she told her editor before she called us.'

Detective Constable Tim Jessop lifted his hand as if he were still in class, and Carlson found himself wondering if he was old enough to drive, let alone carry a warrant card. He made a mental note to ask Poole to make the boy get a haircut.

'Yep, you heard me. She called her editor before she dialled 999. She had taken photos and denied sending them. In fact, she had but it seems this paper has enough decency not to print them, which, I guess, is something to be grateful for.' Carlson paused for a moment and took a sip of his tea. 'Anyway, we now have those photographs. At this stage we have no identity for the victim. Vice still haven't come back to us yet. I'm not sure if they're playing silly buggers again. Tim?' Carlson looked at the eager, young DC, 'Have you still got your contacts in Vice?

Perhaps you could have a chat with them and ask what they're up to?'

Tim Jessop micro saluted with his pen, and Carlson continued, 'Tests show she just had alcohol in her stomach, no food and no drugs. She does have needle marks on her arms, but she didn't overdose. The post-mortem revealed that she had been strangled with something wide, like a scarf, and had very rough sex before death.'

'Could it have been rape?' asked Jane Lacey. She was new to the team, a transfer from Norfolk Constabulary when the two police services combined. She was keen to gain recognition.

Carlson nodded. 'That's a possibility,' he replied. 'Kirsty, could you take us through your findings so far?'

'Of course.'

Kirsty Russell was an experienced crime scene manager and Carlson knew her report would be thorough. She confidently took Carlson's place at the head of the room, looked at her notes and tucked an auburn curl behind her ear before speaking. 'We worked the scene all day yesterday and again today. Unfortunately, most of the evidence was washed away, and her fingerprints have failed to identify her as well. Which is unusual. She's a drug user so I would have expected her to be known to us.

'Now,' she said, pointing at the relevant photographs, 'what is interesting is that her finger and toenails have been cleaned.' Kirsty paused and perched on the edge of the desk, her green eyes watching whilst the team took in this latest piece of information.

'And that's not all,' she said.

The officers, who had been scratching notes in their notebooks, stopped and looked up at her. Uniform puzzlement on all their faces. Carlson saw the open mouths, thinking that they looked like a nest of baby robins waiting for their next meal.

'Her hair may have been freshly washed,' Kirsty said. 'Either by her, or it could have been her attacker, post-mortem, to remove any trace contact. Everything that we recovered from her hair was present in the samples taken from the brook. No other fibres have been found so far, but we'll keep working on the hair combings.'

A morose atmosphere settled in the room as Kirsty finished speaking. She looked around for any other questions, but there were none, and she slid off the corner of the desk into the chair behind it.

'Sir?' Jane Lacey raised her hand and looked directly at Carlson. 'She was naked.' There was a ripple of laughter around the squad room at this keen observation. 'Shut up, you lot,' Jane said. 'What I meant was no clothes, and therefore no bag or phone either. No woman is likely to leave home without a purse, keys or her phone. I don't suppose we could be lucky and he left her mobile on? Maybe his own too?'

Carlson had been thinking she had the makings of a good detective, and she was taking the ribbing in her stride, but she still had a lot to learn.

'The problem is,' he said, 'that our victim has a habit to feed. That means that she's likely to have the cheapest phone around, not something with GPS. If she had a decent phone, she'd sell it. I don't think that our guy, having taken so much care in dumping her body, is going to make a mistake like that.'

'But, if he had, then we'll all be on leave this weekend,' interjected Poole, 'But, as the Guv'nor has just said, it's not going to be that easy. If it was, it wouldn't need a team of detectives. Right, if there's nothing else?'

At a nod from Carlson, DS Poole dismissed the team, telling them to get a good night's sleep.

Ronnie Carlson sat in front of the white board looking at the photographs of one young life snuffed out before she had really lived and, thinking of his own loss, wondered if he would ever sleep through the night again.

CHAPTER FIVE

Ted Johnson hated the night shift. He left the factory quickly and took his bike from the rack. Zipping his jacket up and putting a skull cap under his helmet, he jumped on his bicycle and set off. Halfway down the road he realised that he should have used the loo before leaving, but it was too late now. Ten miles with a full bladder would make for an uncomfortable ride but, he decided, maybe he could increase his average speed. As he passed the woodland, a Muntjac deer stepped onto the lane ahead. Ted braked to a halt, putting a foot down, and whistled his appreciation of the sleek, miniature beauty. The deer caught his scent on the breeze and bounded over the road and deep into the woods. As Ted set off, the bike rolled over a stone and there came the familiar and unwelcome slapping sound of a flat tyre.

He cursed loudly, making a crow squawk as it took to the air. Taking off his rucksack and rummaging around for the tyre repair kit, the urge to pee was stronger than ever. With a quick look round, Ted leaned the pushbike against a tree and nipped further into the woods. As the flow began, he heaved a sigh of relief and started to look around. A short distance away he saw a piece of carpet dumped in a clearing.

Hey, that might do for the shed at the allotment, he thought.

Zipping up and patting himself to ensure everything was still in place, Ted strolled over to the carpet. He pulled at it to get an idea of size. It was weighed down with something, and Ted heaved to get it to budge. He braced himself for one last yank and the carpeting finally unfurled. The pale figure of a young woman rolled free, reminding him of an old film his mother had loved about an Egyptian queen. For a while Ted simply stared, trying to take in what he'd found. She was completely naked. Her hair was damp, with strands clinging to her face and neck. Her bulging eyes gazed skyward but saw nothing. There were deep red and purple bruises on her throat. Ted finally realised the importance of his discovery. He took a step backwards and then another one. Faster and faster he retreated, unable to take his eyes off her. He tripped over tree roots and knocked himself against branches, but he still could not take his eyes away.

He stumbled out into the road where squealing tyres and the blast from a horn snapped him back from his shock.

'What d'ya think you're doing mate? I could've killed you!'

Ted heard the yells but was unable to focus on the irate delivery driver. He opened his mouth, but nothing came out. He tried again and only managed a gurgle. His legs finally gave way and he sat on the wet grass of the verge. The driver pulled over, put on his hazard lights and jumped out of the vehicle.

'Here mate, you look awful. Are you sick or summat?' The man took in Ted's grey pallor and the gaping, fishlike mouth.

Ted shook his head. 'I… I…' His head swam. He was

sweating and shivering. He could feel the vomit scorching his throat.

'A body,' he gasped. 'I've just found a body in the woods. Back there.' He waved his hand in the general direction of the girl, before he collapsed to the verge. Then, spreading his knees apart, he bent his head forward and threw up.

Time passed in a blur for Ted as the police arrived amid the trademark blare of sirens and flashing blues. They taped off the road. More officers arrived; everyone seemed to know what they had to do. Even in his daze he saw a well-orchestrated machine. Traffic was diverted. A police constable stood at either side of the cordoned area; one had a clip board and was taking names. A white van labelled Scientific Support drew up, then three crime scene techs clambered out, collected kit from the back of the van and donned their paper suits at the cordon. Ted thought the suits gave them a spectral appearance adding to the bizarreness of the scene, and he sat gazing as everyone went about their business.

'How many fingers?' a voice said. Ted blinked. He looked at the hand in front of him and digits slowly swam into focus.

'Three,' he said.

'That's fine,' she said, flipping her stethoscope over her head. 'The police want a word. You feel up to talking to them?'

Ted nodded at the paramedic, who rocked back on her heels to stand up. She waved at the two detectives.

As Poole approached, the paramedic had to raise her head to

meet him face on. He didn't notice her slight gasp as she took in his dark, handsome features.

'Hi,' she said, after a moment's pause. 'This is Mr Johnson. Ted. He's fine to talk, but don't stress him too much. He's still shocked and he'll need someone to take him home.'

'Yeah, I think uniform have sorted something out,' Poole replied, distantly. He scarcely glanced at her. Turning to Ted, he said, 'Mr Johnson?' He patted his thick jacket, looking for a pen and located it in his inner breast suit pocket, exactly where it always was. 'You found the body? What time was that?'

'About eight or so. I was on my way home from work. I usually get in about half eight.'

'And you always use this route?'

'Yeah, I live in the village, see.'

Ted took Poole through all the events that led up to his near-collision with the van driver.

'Okay, we will need to take a formal statement from you. Uniform have given me all your details. You can come down to the station to do that or I can come by when I've finished here. Here's my card. Call me. Have you got anyone to see you home?'

Ted tilted his head towards a small, anxious-looking woman. 'My wife,' he said.

Poole nodded and, taking one last look at him, turned on his heel and strode back to Carlson and the rest of the team.

Carlson stood inside the incident tent, looking at the body. Dr Kilburn was making his preliminary findings.

'Similarities, Doc?' he was saying, as Poole approached.

'Now Ronnie, you know me better than that. Don't make

me leap to any conclusions before I've had a chance to examine her.'

'Time of death, then?'

'When was she last seen alive?'

'Come on, Doc, you know I don't know that yet,' Carlson groaned.

'Well, I don't deal in miracles either,' snapped Kilburn. 'Look at this.' He indicated the dark pooling on the girl's buttocks. 'She was found lying down, rolled in the carpet?'

Carlson nodded. 'So the witness says.'

'Well here we have post-mortem lividity, indicating that she was sitting up for a while after death and not reclining. Her joints are mobile now, but I don't know if that's because rigor hasn't started or if it's been and gone. If rigor has passed, then at least 36 hours. But it could be longer.'

Carlson sighed.

'Look, Ronnie, I know you're keen to find him, but don't rush me, hey?' Kilburn said, continuing to look over the young woman's corpse.

'Him? So, you do think it's the same person?'

'Now come on, I didn't say that. Don't put words in my mouth.'

'Okay, okay, but call me ASAP.'

'Will do.' With an air of finality Dr Kilburn turned to his patient. He oversaw the bags applied to head, hands and feet, she was folded into plastic sheeting and zipped into a long, black bag.

Carlson scrutinised the scene one final time and, knowing he needed to leave the CSI unit to their work, walked reluctantly back to the car with DS Poole.

CHAPTER SIX

Shazza tipped the contents of her purse onto the bar. She shuffled the coins around but, however many times she moved them, there were not enough.

'Drink, girl?' Gary ambled to where she sat, and faced her across the wooden barrier.

'Nah, not got enuff dosh.'

'Well, sounds like you've had enough already, but I'll treat you to one last one and then you can go home and sleep it off. Okay?'

She smiled at him and he placed a rum and coke in front of her. He stepped back and turned on the pub's TV.

'In local news, police say that the body of another woman has been found in woodland near Faverstone. This is the second unidentified female to be discovered in as many weeks. Anyone able to help the police in their enquiries with information about either incident should contact Gippingford Police immediately.'

Shazza stared at the screen. She could not believe that no one had come forward for Josie. 'I know the first girl,' she whispered.

'What? What was that?' Gary said, as he wiped imaginary drips from the countertop.

'That first girl. It was Josie, I'm sure of it.'

'Have you been to see the coppers?'

'Oh, yam know me and coppers,' she slurred, her Black Country burr coming to the fore. 'Anyway, I thought her parents would come for her. Didn't want to interfere.'

'Shazza, you've got to go. You've got to go now. Do you want me to come with you?'

'Nah, I'll be fine.' She got down clumsily from the stool and held on to the bar. Making for the door she fell off her heels and crumpled on the floor.

'Oh, effing great,' said Gary, grabbing the bar's keys from a drawer. 'Well you don't get out of it that easy, lady.' He pulled Shazza to her feet and dragged her through the front door.

'Can I help you, sir?' Police Sergeant Dobbs slowly put down his paperwork and looked at the man in front of him. Dobbs was not far from retirement and was taking the last few months' service as leisurely as he could. Resting his hands on his paunch, he ran his eyes over the large man, noticed the swallows tattooed on his neck, the rolled-up sleeves, and that he was sweating profusely. He had encountered most situations in his long career, but usually men such as the one here were more likely being arrested for affray rather than walking into the station voluntarily. Most of them weren't usually carrying a barely conscious girl, either.

'Yeah mate. She reckons she knows who that first girl was. You know, the one that was found in the river.'

'Does she now? You're sure about that are you, sir?' Dobbs had perfected the art of making "sir" sound like an insult. 'Doesn't look like she knows her own name at the moment.' He smiled at his own joke.

'Yeah, well, she's got herself in a bit of a state,' the man said, giving Dobbs a weak smile, 'but I thought if I didn't bring her in, she'd never come here. Look, my name's Gary Phillips, I run The Bell on London Road. The news came on and she reckoned she knew the first girl. Called her Josie. She has a mate called Josie, who's not around anymore. We thought she'd gone back home, but Shazza' — he indicated with his head — 'this is Shazza, well she thinks that girl found in the river was her mate Josie. I reckon you ought to listen to what she's gotta say.'

'Okay, let me contact the senior investigating officer and see what he wants to do. Sit down over there.' Dobbs rang through, spoke a few minutes and put the handset down. He came over to Gary. 'Someone's going to come down in a moment and speak to her. See if they can get any sense out of her. If not, she'll have to come back tomorrow. I'm going to put you in this room here.'

He helped Gary lift Shazza to her feet and corral her towards the room. Shazza hiccoughed as they propped her up on a blue plastic chair. Gary took a seat by her side and waited.

When the door opened a few minutes later, a portly, grey-haired man, suited and booted, entered, followed by a young, smartly dressed woman.

Carlson introduced himself along with DC Jane Lacey,

and Gary gave him the details of what had occurred. All the time, Carlson kept looking at Shazza to see if she was taking anything in.

'Sharon?' he said. She looked at him for a moment, her glazed eyes not focusing. 'Do you know why you're here?'

'Knew 'em, didn't I?' she slurred.

'Who, Sharon? Who did you know?' Carlson asked.

'The girls you've found. I knew 'em.' Shazza leaned forward. 'I don't feel well,' she said. Lowering her head, Carlson almost stepped back in time as the stream of vomit hit the floor.

'Damn!' he said, brushing ineffectually at his trouser legs with a handkerchief. 'DC Lacey, I'll need you to take this young lady to A&E, get her checked out. Then take her home. We'll have to get her back when she's sobered up. She's sod all use to us now.'

Carlson stood to one side, shaking his trouser leg and looking at his shoes, whilst Jane pulled the drunken girl to her feet and back to the reception desk and asked Dobbs to request a squad car. Carlson could see her face turning red, though from embarrassment or effort, he could not tell. Just as he was going to help her, the behemoth that was Detective Superintendent Jim Tasker, head of the Serious and Organised Crime team, hove into view.

'Problem, Carlson?' he thundered. Sotto voce for Tasker, since he was normally as quiet as the Edinburgh One O'Clock Gun.

'No, sir. Someone to help identify my two victims. Bit worse for wear right now,' replied Carlson, thinking that his witness was not the only one who looked less than their best.

'Two?' Tasker frowned. Despite the cool day, he mopped his face with a handkerchief grasped in porcine fingers, then ran it over his thick carroty hair. He turned to look at the detective hovering at his shoulder. 'I thought there was just one. Why haven't you asked one of my lads to have a look at her photo? I'm sure we could clear up that little mystery for you in no time at all.'

'No time at all,' repeated his lacky.

'We have asked, sir.' Carlson's jaw was already beginning to ache from the tension of keeping his voice calm and steady. 'Emailed the photos over as soon as. No response so far. Sir.'

There was silence as the two men eyeballed each other. Neither seemed to be breathing and neither wanted to be the first to break away. They stood like two bull elephants awaiting the first clash of battle, but Tasker finally spoke first.

'Get it sorted will you, Simmons?' he said. 'Can't have our colleagues kept waiting when they've important murders to solve, can we?'

DI Simmons tapped on his iPad, nodded at Tasker and they both sauntered away; the tanker hauling the tugboat in its wake.

Carlson raised a hand to his jawbone and eased it from side to side, flicked a last piece of carrot from his shoe, then turned and marched back to the squad room.

CHAPTER SEVEN

Whistling quietly to himself, the man re-ran the results of his work with the movie maker application. Where he appeared in shot himself, the image was heavily pixelated, beyond recognition and recovery. The viewer would see the girl's face and the scarf sliding around her neck. Her confusion, realisation, fear and final acceptance as her light was snuffed out.

Pleased with his efforts, he closed the program and removed the DVD from the drive. He tilted it from side to side under the desk lamp, checking for fingerprints, although he had been careful to wear gloves throughout. You can never be too sure, he thought. A smile of grim satisfaction spread across his face. Clear. As it should be. He took a label from the printer and stuck it to the jiffy bag. Sealed it. Weighed it. Checked the postage and put on the correct number of self-adhesive stamps.

'Hon, I'm nearly ready, but I can't find my house keys, have you seen them? I don't want to be late for work, so can you just take me in now?' his wife called up the stairs.

'Two ticks, sweetie. Just need to finish up here,' he replied.

He placed the package in a carrier bag and peeled off his gloves, carefully placing those in his pocket, well away from the padded bag. He decided to post it after he had dropped Rose off at the call centre. He strolled downstairs to the small hallway and saw her waiting patiently by the door.

'We've plenty of time. Don't panic. Have you ever been late? No, of course not,' he said, helping her into her coat. He held her at arm's length. 'Let's see the new coat. Give us a twirl. Oh yes, very smart. I approve. I'm glad I let you buy it. By the way, I've found your keys. You'd left them by the bed again. Silly girl.' He pecked her on the cheek, choosing not to notice her recoil, then picking up his car keys and swapping the plastic bag to his left hand, he ushered her out of the door.

Juggling a tray of plastic cups, his notepad and a folder, Poole opened the interview room door. The rancid smell of unwashed body, clothes, vomit and stale alcohol overwhelmed him, so he wedged the door ajar with his foot and stood back to let Carlson enter ahead of him.

Carlson sat down and reviewed the spectacle in front of him. Her dyed black hair was pulled back into a tight ponytail, stretching the face. As she looked up, he took in the hazel colour of her bleary eyes, the panda smudges of mascara put on over yesterday's makeup. She was very thin, worse than anorexic. He knew what anorexia looked like only too well. This girl was Auschwitz thin. She wore tight jeans and a skimpy top which in previous decades would have spoken volumes about her profession, but now so many teenagers wore the same clothes in their passive-aggressive rebellions. Hers were worn thin, shabby and not overly clean.

The over-sized jacket did not cover the knobbly wrists which spoke of her side-line and lack of self-care. Poole sat down next to Carlson, resting the tray of plastic cups at the end of the table. From the expression on his face it seemed the DS had not much concern for the wreck of a human being in front of him. Carlson wondered if he thought she was just the detritus of addiction. The dregs of a throwaway society.

Poole plonked a cup in front of her. 'Coffee,' he said.

'Don't like coffee. Yow got any tea?' she asked.

'No, I don't have any tea! It's sodding coffee or nothing.'

'Here,' said Carlson gently. 'Take mine. Do you want sugar?' He'd not noticed the flat vowels of her Black Country accent before. It took him back to his days at Wolver-hampton University and a certain barmaid in the Gifford Arms. He smiled to himself in memory.

The softness of his voice had made Shazza flinch. Perhaps she hadn't expected any kindness from police. He prompted her to talk. The small kindness was all that it took.

Shazza took a deep breath and began to tell them about Josie and her plans to return to her hometown and maybe even to see her Mum and Dad again.

'She wanted to get clean and off the streets. Her sister had just had a babby. She'd told Josie she couldn't be part of the kid's life if she was still on the game and still shooting up.'

Poole made notes and then took the photos from the folder underneath his notepad. He slid them across the table. Carlson picked them up and hid the faces for a moment.

'We're sorry to show you these,' he said. 'These women are dead, but I need to find out who they are.' He placed the photographs face up in front of her. 'Do you know them?'

Shazza nodded mutely as she focused on the faces in the photos. 'Nat,' she whispered. 'She called herself Amber. I think she was really called Natalie, maybe Natasha? Not sure of her last name. Collins, I think.' Shazza picked up the other photo and looked into Josie's grey eyes. 'This is Josie,' she finally said. 'She worked as Scarlett, you know, like that girl in Gone with the Wind. She loved all the old films, did Josie.'

'And how do you know Nat?'

'Here and there. Just seen her about. Josie, me and her, we was mates, but Nat, well, she just used to be around the same places we hung out.'

'And which places were those, Shazza?' asked Poole.

'Oh, what places do yow think?' She suddenly flared up and her eyes blazed. 'I'm a smack-head. Josie was a smack-head. We wanted to get clean, but it's not easy. Sometimes it's easier to let yourself get dragged back in.' Shazza sniffled and wiped her nose on her jacket sleeve before Carlson could find her a tissue. He watched her look towards Poole, who was wrinkling his nose in disgust at her. How familiar must that look be to her, he wondered.

Shazza sighed before continuing. 'Anyways,' she said, 'Nat did the same as us. We all worked the streets to get money for H.'

Carlson approached his front door with trepidation. For a while he gazed at the double-glazed door with its faux-stained glass, and slowly put his key in the lock. He stepped into the large hallway and hung his jacket on the rack. Keys went in a dish on the covered radiator. He called 'hi', but there was no reply.

He ambled upstairs to change out of his suit. Wallet and warrant card had their home on the bedside table, and he pondered on how the house no longer buzzed as it had once done. After he'd changed, he made his way downstairs to the kitchen where he could hear the TV, the clink of glasses and the light hum of conversation.

'Mags?' he said, as he opened the kitchen door.

His wife and daughter sprung apart as if caught in some transgression.

'What are you two up to?' he said, forcing lightness into his voice.

'Nothing,' said Marguerite. 'Aspen was just telling me about... erm... a new night club in town.' The last words spewed out in a rush. She touched her left hand to her short, brown curls. It was her tell. Carlson was surprised. It wasn't like his wife to lie.

'Hi, Dad.' Aspen rose from her seat behind the kitchen table, so she could pull at his polo shirt and kiss him on the forehead. She had her mother's figure, tall and willowy, but her blonde hair and startling blue eyes were from his side of the family. 'How was your day?' she asked. 'Mum and I have just had some quiche and salad. Do you want some?' Her voice sounded brittle. She was only just keeping control of herself. He speculated about their discussion before he'd come in. On second thoughts, he didn't need to wonder; he could guess only too well.

'Thanks,' he said. He accepted a glass of wine and ate the cardboard-like concoction on his plate, remembering a time when it would have been homemade. He wondered if those days were gone for ever as he held his glass out for a refill, although he did not miss the ceaseless arguments with Jade over her refusal to eat. Sensing that the women in his life wanted to talk some more, he strolled into the sitting room. He switched on the television and flicked through channels seeing nothing. Marguerite and Aspen stayed in the kitchen for a while and then he heard Aspen's soft footsteps on the stairs as she went to her room. That's how it was now.

Everyone kept to their own part of the house. He wondered if they would share rooms and family meals again. Eventually he heard his wife going to bed, but she didn't open the door to wish him a good night. He finished his wine and poured himself a whisky, and watched the screen figures move around pointlessly as he sipped the single malt.

Raising the glass to his lips once more, he found it was empty. He put a hand out to pour another but thought better of it and sat clutching the glass to his chest. His stomach was playing up again; he wasn't sure if it was the food or too much alcohol, but there was a constant pain. His chest too. Tightness. Heaviness. Carrying a burden that was too weighty for him on his own. Changing his mind about the whisky, he poured one more and drank until the pains had gone. Fumbling his way to the sitting room door, he crept upstairs. He paused by Jade's room. When he pushed the door open, it was as if she had just left for the evening. Mags had touched nothing. Tissues were chucked on the floor, the Bluetooth speaker still glowed in the dark. Everything was the same. Except the laptop of course; that had been thrown to the floor and had lain in an inverted V. Now it sat lifeless on the dressing table, like an innocent bystander in a Jacobean-style tragedy. To Carlson, it seemed as if she was coming back any moment. The door would slam behind her. All the lights would go on. Her feet would thump on the stairs and the whole house would pulsate in time to her music. Holding on to those memories, Carlson went to his own room and bed.

CHAPTER EIGHT

September 1981

'Hey, silly, what are you doing under there?'

The boy opened his eyes. It was day, and he could see his mother's bare feet with their cracked heels near the window. Creeping out, he saw she was pushing aside the threadbare curtains. The sun flooded her face and the boy could see she had a new bruise on her cheek bone.

'Feel safer,' he said gruffly. He sat on the edge of his bed, hugging his bear.

She nodded. Did she understand? Did she know? He wasn't sure. He could never tell. It was a secret. Bill had told him that. Their secret. Bill said to him that no one would believe him anyway. No one believed kids' tales. Sometimes he wanted to tell his teacher, Mrs Jensen. She was nice. She smelt nice. Mum used to smell nice, but not now. Not anymore. Not since Bill came to live with them. She still went out all the time. Left him at home with Bill. He didn't know where she went. Sometimes someone would come back with her. He never knew who. No one else was ever there in the morning.

'Mum?'

'Yes love?' She knelt on the floor in front of him, straightening the collar on his pyjamas. 'What's up?'

It was on the tip of his tongue. He wanted to tell her everything. All the things Bill did. Bill said it was okay, but it hurt, and it felt wrong. As he opened his mouth to speak, Bill walked past on the landing. For a moment their eyes met. Only a fleeting glance but to the boy it lasted for eons.

'Nothing,' said the boy. No, he could never tell.

Carlson sluggishly opened his eyes. His throat was sore. His mouth dry. And hell, what a headache. He staggered downstairs.

'I think I'm coming down with a cold, Mags,' he said.

'Really. What makes you think that?' his wife said, as she reached into a cupboard and pulled out a large, blue mug inscribed with the words "Hello, hello, hello". A Father's Day present from his daughters before life became so complicated.

'Sore throat. Bad head. Feel yuck.' He leaned his head against the cool door frame, but it didn't help.

'Huh,' Marguerite said. 'And do we think that might have anything to do with the bottle of red and the half bottle of whisky you sunk last night? You snored the whole night through. Honestly, Ronnie, call yourself a detective! The sitting room is littered with the evidence you couldn't be bothered to clear away last night. Well, you can go and do it now. I'll make you some coffee. Do you want any toast?'

Dutifully he cleared the debris from the lounge, brought

it into the kitchen and placed the plates and glasses in the dishwasher. He drank the proffered coffee and swallowed down the ibuprofen whilst Marguerite reorganised his hand-iwork. Their eyes met over the plate of toast she held out to him, but he shook his head and she laughed.

Using his knuckles for balance, he gorilla'ed up the stairs to the en suite and stood under a stream of warm water. Later, toothpaste, several doses of mouthwash and more coffee still hadn't removed the dead pigeon from his mouth.

'Are you even safe to drive?' his wife shouted as he opened the front door. He waved a hand in reply and shielded his eyes from the low beams of winter sun.

Poole was already at his desk, coffee in hand and reading statements from the previous day's house-to-house enquiries. He looked up at the bedraggled state of his boss and shook his head. He's not up to it, Poole thought. He shouldn't have come back so soon. Or maybe not at all.

'There's post for you,' Poole said, in a bemused voice.

'What, real post? I thought we didn't get that anymore.'

'Well, I think it's for you. It says "Chief Investigating Offi-cer".' Poole held the parcel up to show Carlson the label.

Carlson half fell, half sat in a chair and reached out for the jiffy bag. He struggled with the tape until Poole passed him some scissors. He tipped the contents onto the desk.

For a moment he stared at the disc. Poole wondered what on earth he was doing. The little colour that had been in the DCI's face had drained completely. Violently, Carlson pushed against the desk and shot the chair back into the wall.

'Get SOCO!' he shouted.

Poole was frozen. 'Wh —'

'Now!' Carlson shouted.

Poole scrambled for the handset and hit the button for the Crime Scene Investigation unit.

The face looking back at her was one she had come to hate. Skin that had once glowed was now so sallow. Her cheeks were hollow, and her eyes sunk into her skull. Blonde split ends hung listlessly to her shoulders. I hate this girl, she thought. This pathetic, needy girl. The mobile beside her buzzed and shimmied along the dressing table's surface, disturbing a coating of dust and cigarette ash like a bow wave. She watched as the girl in the mirror picked the phone up and wiped it clean. The girl sighed when she recognised the caller's ID, but she still accepted the call.

'Yep?'

'Hello, sweetheart. How are you?' Her mother's voice wafted across the ether.

'I'm good, thanks Mum. How's you?'

'I'm fine, fine. Listen, Tanith, darling, I'm not trying to interfere —'

The girl in the mirror rolled her eyes, knowing what was coming next. 'But?' she said.

'But I've been making some calls. That rehab programme you talked about; I can get you a place. I can come with you darling. Hold your hand. See you through the first steps.'

'S'not that easy, Mum, you know that.'

'Yes, I know, but I want my beautiful baby back. You must understand that, surely?' The voice pleaded, begged.

She watched as the girl in the mirror looked around the sparsely furnished room, nodded and finally agreed. Consented to an appointment. Allowed herself to hope she could make that first step to change her life around. 'Okay, mum,' she said.

'You will?' Delight suffused the voice. 'Oh darling, you won't regret it. I'll be with you every step of the way.'

'I'll try Mum, I really will. I do wanna get clean. I do wanna get off the smack.'

'That's good news.' The voice was eager but pressurising her. Coercing her. She could feel the pressure rising. She knew her resolve was like molten lava seeking a fissure — the weakest point where it could spurt forth and destroy everything in its path.

'And you're sure?'

'Yes, I'm sure,' she said, sounding less sure than she had.

'Come and see me at the weekend then?' The voice began to sound encouraged.

'Yes, Mum, I'll be there. Bye.'

'Bye, love.'

The line went dead and the girl continued to stare in the mirror. The conversation with her mother could have been worse. She had tried before. She had failed before. Perhaps this time it would be different, she thought, sighing. Maybe. She knew she wanted to get clean, to put this life behind her. Perhaps go back to school and redo her exams, get a better job. After all, anything is possible. She'd seen that once in an advert or maybe a poster. She couldn't remember. She realised she was stroking the inside of her arm. Caressing the needle marks. Saying goodbye. But one last time, hey? That wouldn't matter, would it? Before she gave up completely. She'd go out, get the money and chase the dragon just one last time.

Tanith stood on the street corner. Thick tendrils of cigarette smoke from the end of her Sovereign Superking wafted up into the cold night air. She watched them snaking up towards the streetlight. Dispersing slowly, gradually, as they twisted skywards. She remained entranced, dreaming of another life until a car pulled up next to her. She took a last puff, expelling the smoke in one vast cloud. She watched as, in contrast to the tendrils, the cloud dissolved immediately. Swallowed instantly by the chill darkness. Tanith snuffed out the stub under her toe and strolled to the car. She leaned in towards the driver and said, 'Business?'

CHAPTER NINE

Carlson leaned back in his chair. Unlike last time, so many years ago, the footage simply stopped. The screen went blank. Last time the screen had become a mass of static, buzzing, fizzing, dots whizzing around. Colliding. Sparking off each other. Grey. Black. Silver. White. Carlson stared at the blank screen, but imagined seeing the dots. However, technology had moved on and so, it would appear, had his adversary. He shook his head, aghast at what he'd seen, but other thoughts pervaded too. It can't be him, he thought. It simply can't be.

'We can get some photos taken off this?' He turned to Poole.

'Stills? Yes, sir. No problem.'

'Good. Get that girl who came forward to look at them, see if she recognises the room. Don't include any of the...' — Carlson grasped for a suitable word — 'the other stuff,' he concluded.

'Of course. Anything else? We can get the audio analysed, see if there are any markers that stand out. And wasn't there that case where they found matey by identifying the furniture in the pictures?'

'Yep, great, get all that done too. He feels safe in that room, though. Very safe, or he wouldn't risk letting us see it. Last time —'

'Last time, sir?' Poole looked over at his senior officer. 'Guv, are you okay?'

'No, Poole. I'm very far from being okay.' Carlson stood up. He'd seen the quizzical frown and needed to get his thoughts straight. It can't be him, it can't be, he muttered to himself. Aloud to Poole he simply replied, 'I need some air.'

He strode down the stairwell and headed towards the smoking shelter, standing at the perimeter, breathing in second-hand smoke and the damp air. The elements were undecided between mist and drizzle. Droplets hazed the Perspex until a rivulet formed and, collecting other drips in its path, the water cascaded down the clear wall. Carlson leaned his head against the cool surface. It can't be him, he repeated over to himself. I put him away, it can't be him. He took one final deep breath and let it out slowly. Copycat, he told himself, that can be the only answer. But how?

Shazza paused and shuddered at the entrance to the interview room. The detective, Poole, wasn't that what he was called, almost collided with her and only just stopped himself in time.

'Problem?' he said.

She watched him checking and double checking that no

tea from the plastic cup had dripped on his expensive suit. Shame he was such a prick, for he was well smart-looking.

'I don't like these rooms,' she replied.

'Look, you're not under arrest,' he assured her, not for the first time. He sighed. 'Come on, you're helping. Being a good citizen. You can do that, can't you? For your friends?'

'S'pose,' she said, and plonked down in a chair. Poole took the chair opposite, slid the cup of tea over to her and removed some photographs from the folder he'd been carrying under his arm. He spread them out on the table in front of her.

Shazza picked up the set, scrutinising each one carefully. She put them down and stared at Poole.

'Dunno,' she said. 'Could've been there. You aren't exactly teking in the sights. You just get the job done, teke your money and then get fixed up with some gear.'

'So, you've never seen this place before?'

'Nah, didn't say that either. I could've been there. I just don't know. Usually you just do it in the car or back of the cab. You don't often get invited home. Especially with the married ones.' She slid the photographs back across the table to Poole. 'And of course, a lot of the girls charge extra to go back to someone's place.'

'Extra?' Poole asked.

'Yeah, well you don't know where you're gonna get teken. It's not so safe. A punter can cut up rough when it's more private.'

Poole's nose wrinkled in disgust. Shazza noticed, smiled inwardly and continued talking, purely to annoy him. 'Yeah,' she sighed. 'It can get pretty ugly out there. A girl's gotta be able to take care of herself. It's easier to shout for help if yam near the other girls.'

She stared across the table at him, taking in his stiff shoulders and the way he would not meet her eye. She'd met enough punters on the street like that. Not that she'd ever wanted to form a bond with any of them, but sometimes, just sometimes, it would have been better not to have been treated like an outcast. Why did they always treat her like trash? They wanted her. They paid for her, yet they looked at her like she was worthless. Her temper burnt short and fierce.

'S'alright for yow,' she snapped, spitting the words out. Her face reddened, and she placed both hands flat on the table, rising to stare him straight in the face. Unable to cope with the jolt, the weak cup tipped over and her tea shot across the table. 'I expect life has been easy for yow. Well it ain't always so easy for the rest of us.'

'No one made you start taking drugs.' Poole snorted in derision, but he scooted his chair back and used the folder to sweep the drips to the floor. 'Oh Jeez, look at this mess! Wait while I get something to clear it up.'

He left the room and Shazza stared at the pile of photos in front of her. She looked at the door and back to the photos. Without really knowing why, she took her mobile from her pocket and took several shots of the stills. When Poole returned, Shazza was sitting back down. She watched him retake his seat and the disdain on his face set her off again. She carried on shouting at him as if there had been no intervening gap in proceedings.

'Yow reckon?' she screeched. 'They was outside the school gates. At the youth centres. Everywhere. It was free the first time. I never felt anything loike it. Total escape. Oblivion. Never felt so chilled. It took away all the shit of what was happening at home. All of it. And God, there was some shit going down there!' Shazza leaned further across the table at him, spraying saliva as she ranted. 'Nah, you ain't got a fucking clue. Tosser!'

'Well, thank you for your time, Miss Raby.' Poole stood to indicate the interview was over. He took a handkerchief from his pocket and wiped his face and jacket. 'It was kind of you to come in at such short notice. Perhaps you'd like to work on your rage before our next meeting?'

'Next meeting! My rage? Next time, I want to see the other copper. He's nice. I don't need to be treated like dirt. Had enough of that.'

Shazza pushed the chair backwards away from the table and wrestled with the door. She flung it open, where it hit the wall, bounced off and would have crashed into her, but she was already at the station's revolving door and pulling cigarettes and lighter from her pocket. She lit up, took a deep drag, turned to glare at Poole once more and stormed off down the street.

Poole shuddered as he watched her go. Paying for sex was anathema to him. Throughout his police career he'd done his best to avoid any connection with the junkie whores, their punters and the dealers and pimps. Yet here he was embroiled in the whole tawdry world where that special connection between man and woman was just another commodity. Traded for the price of a fix. He shook the last drops of tea off the folder but decided against putting the photos back in it. He counted to make sure that there were still ten prints in the set, then he dumped the folder in a nearby bin and walked back to the office.

CHAPTER TEN

He rinsed shampoo off the hair. Such beautiful hair. Soft, fine, almost fragile, like her. He sniffed a conditioner and chose another one. A delicate cherry blossom scent filled the room as he worked the creamy liquid through from root to tip. He rinsed that too and squeezed the water out with his hands.

'We'll let it dry naturally, shall we?' he whispered to her.

She didn't reply, but he didn't mind. He turned her face towards him. Her eyes were open, but they saw nothing. They had seen nothing for two days, ever since he placed a scarf around her soft throat and squeezed her life away. He lifted her out of the bath and walked with her to the bedroom. Laying her gently on the plastic sheeted bed he dried her body carefully with a lint-free cloth. He stood back to admire her.

'You know, Silver, you were the one I always wanted. Those other girls meant nothing. It was only you, only ever you. If only you could have stayed with me, but you put that crap in your veins and I cannot stand that. Why do you poison yourselves, all of you, why do you do it?' He gazed at her lying so peacefully. He sniffed and cleared his throat. 'Still, it's too late now.

'I haven't decided where we're going to put you yet. There's a nice spot down on the riverbank. You can sit in the reeds and watch the boats go by. Would you like that?' He looked at her. 'Yes, I thought you would. I'll need to check the tides. Don't want you floating off down river now, do we?' He smiled at her, but she still did not respond. 'I'll just clean your nails and I think we're done.'

He stood back to appreciate his handiwork. Satisfied with what he had done, he collected the girl's clothes into a black bin liner. He removed his paper suit and placed it in a separate bag. 'I have to go to work now. I'll drop these off while I'm out and then later we can go down to the river together. See you soon.'

He blew her a kiss and closed the door behind him.

'So, did you recognise any of it?' Tina Hoyes asked. She sipped her coffee and looked at her friend, waiting for a response.

'I dunno,' Shazza shook her head. 'Bits sort of looked familiar. Bits didn't.'

'Well that's 'cos you're always off your head, innit?'

'We ain't all as good as yam, Miss High and Mighty. When did you become my mother?' Shazza punched her friend lightly on the arm. 'It's so good to see you, Tina. You look fantastic. Well, you know that of course. I like your hair like that. You look great.'

Tina patted her hair. She too liked the new look; the

copper streaks made her usually mousy brown hair appear livelier. Reaching across the table, she touched her friend's face gently. 'Shazza, Shazza. Calm down. Slow down. How are you doing? Getting clean?'

'Doing me best.'

'Sure? Can you look me in the face and say that?'

'I'm doing me best, Teens. Honest. But it ain't easy. You know that.'

'Yeah, I know,' Tina nodded. 'I know just what it's like.' Her thoughts drifted to her first few days in prison. Unable to sleep or even lie still, her hot and cold sweats had soaked the sheets that first night; the muscle spasms and runny nose could have been flu, but she had heard enough of cold turkey to know exactly what was happening to her. Rather than go through another night of clucking, the following morning, she'd got help and started to put her past behind her.

'Sorry,' she said, 'I missed that. What were you saying?'

'I was saying, I go out the flat, wander about for a bit and go back in. I walk a different way home, so I don't go past Ned's flat. Yesterday I went for a walk, clear me head like, and I found myself right outside his door. Took all I had not to knock and ask for some Golden Brown.' Shazza chewed her thumb, peeping at Tina through a veil of hair hanging over her eyes.

'But you didn't?' Tina put her coffee down and ate some of the chocolate cake.

'No. I walked away, but I turned back and stood at his door three more times at least. I hope he wasn't watching. He would've thought I was a right nutter.'

'So what did you do?'

'Sat on that bench opposite. You know the one just inside the park.'

Tina nodded.

'I sat there and just watched all the losers coming and going,' Shazza said. 'In the end I decided that I was better than that and I went home.'

'I'm so proud of you!'

'Yeah well, I went past the offy and got a bottle of vodka instead so don't be that proud of me,' said Shazza. 'But I didn't score. This morning, I went and saw my key worker. She's got me 'scripted now so we'll see if that helps.'

Tina reached across the table again and squeezed her hand. 'Well done, you'll get there. I know you will,' she said. 'So, come on then, tell me about these photos. Do they reckon it's the same bloke?'

Shazza squeezed back, looking around the café. When she was satisfied no one was watching them, she pulled her phone out of her pocket and pushed it across the table. Tina scrolled through the pictures, whilst Shazza told her everything she knew.

'You've seen all this before, then?' Poole asked.

'Hum, yes, something like it. Back when I was a DC in Lytham. The bastard reckoned he was doing us all a favour by cleaning the streets.' Carlson twisted the cardboard cup around on the desk top before taking a swig of tea. 'He sent in videos. Letters too. Some of the letters proved to be fakes. Wannabe copycats. There are some weirdos out there.'

'But you got him in the end.'

'Yeah, more by luck than anything else though.' Carlson leaned back in his chair, exhaling slowly as the memories flooded back. 'He was speeding. Got stopped by a wooden top who recognised the woman in the car. She was a known prostitute and so more questions were asked. The driver was beginning to get a bit edgy and asked if he could go for a pee. The PC let him but while matey was behind some bins, the wooden top took a look in the boot. He hit the mother lode. Sheets of plastic and a strong whiff of disinfectant. Matey tried to make a run for it. His car had false plates on it, so he might have got away, but he had the tax disc in the window. That had the right reg on and it was in his real name. It was only a couple of days before we nabbed him. His family were disgusted. Wouldn't hide him. There'd been fourteen women killed by that point. Mostly prostitutes, but two were young mothers in the wrong place at the wrong time and a student making her way home late after a party.'

'At least we haven't got any innocent victims.'

'Innocent?! We don't judge them, Ben. We just catch the bastard who killed them. We don't make judgements about their lives.'

'But they're all junkies. Just toms and tarts,' Poole protested.

'So that means they don't have a right to an investigation?' Carlson asked, his knuckles whitening as he squeezed the cup. He lifted it to his lips but, finding it empty he threw it at the waste bin, smiling to himself when he noticed Poole jump at the noise. 'You think their families don't have a right to know what happened to them? They don't work the streets by choice. It's not as though that's the box they ticked at their careers interview. Chance, or lack of it, brought these girls to where they are. They're just trying to escape from the crap life has thrown at them.'

'Next you'll be saying it's not their fault they're on drugs, sir,' Poole said, stiffly.

'I'm not sure that it is their fault. I think it's just something they drift into. As I said, trying to escape from the crap of their lives. If Jade —' Carlson stopped himself. 'Well, I guess we'll never know about Jade. Look, just try and keep your mind on the investigation and catching this guy. Leave it to some other bugger to be judge and jury.'

'Yeah, okay. It's just that —'

'It's just that nothing, Ben. We got pilloried in Lytham for not taking it seriously at first. Of course, we had taken the murders seriously, but, until the student was killed, the public shared your opinion that it was "just prostitutes" and it was all part of their "occupational hazard". Once Jessie McFarlane was murdered the whole attitude changed overnight. All of a sudden, the police weren't doing enough. It was the end of my old Guv'nor. He was never the same after that. I think it was the video tapes that got to him the most. We'd none of us seen anything like it. Our man was one sick fuck.'

'Where is he now?' Poole asked.

'Stanmoor. He made some suicide attempts after he was sent down and so he got moved there. And now we have to go and see him.'

'How can he help?'

'I need to know if he was acting alone. There's stuff going on here that never made it to the papers. Things only he, or someone working on the case, would know. I need to ensure we locked up the right guy and that he's not been giving away his secrets.'

'I'll give them a call and set it up, Boss.'

'Thanks.' Carlson rose from his chair and started tidying his desk in readiness to leave for the day.

Poole hesitated for a moment before going to his own desk and said, 'By the way, that girl was back in.'

'Which girl?' Carlson asked, only half listening as he shrugged into his coat.

'The tom, what's her name? Shazza? Sharon?'

'Don't call her a tom, please Ben, she's trying to put all that behind her. Was she helpful?'

'I suppose. Bit of a chip if you ask me.'

'Well, I didn't,' Carlson sighed as he faced his sergeant. 'Look, I'm heading off now. Get the visit organised. Tomorrow if you can. I'll see you in the morning.'

With that, Carlson turned a one-eighty and left.

CHAPTER ELEVEN

'That you, love?'

'Hi Dad, yes, 'smee.' Tina called back, while she pulled her key out of the door of their mid-terraced council house. The phrase had been a pet one when she was a child and it had always made him laugh. It still did, and he was grinning when he came into the narrow hallway wiping his hands on a tea-towel.

'Hey, I've been worried. Where were you?' he asked. 'Stacey called. She said she couldn't get hold of you.'

'I'm fine, Dad,' Tina said, but was unable to meet his eye.

'I know that look,' he said. 'You're not fine. What's up? Where have you been?'

'Just with some friends.'

'What friends? Why won't you look at me? Tina? Tell me you've not been to Gippingford? Tell me you've not been hanging out with those druggies again.' He folded the towel and faced her, hands on his hips. It was a stance she remembered only too well.

'Dad, I went to see Shazza. You know, Sharon Raby?' Tina

knew it was a mistake as soon as she said the name. 'Shazza knew both the girls who've been killed. So did I for that matter. She's been helping the police.'

'Arrested, you mean?' He snorted and started walking back into the kitchen.

'No, Dad. Really helping them. They had some photos for her to look at. She told me all about it.' Tina followed him and sat down at the tiny table which was squeezed into a corner. 'And she's getting cleaned up. She's going to rehab; got herself a key worker. She's off the game and is doing really well.'

'I still don't like you going over there. I'm worried you'll get caught up in it all again,' he said. 'You've only just got out of nick. Do you want to go back inside?'

'Sometimes, Dad, just sometimes, it's easier to deal with things when you're locked up.' Tina fiddled with her keys as she spoke, still unable to look at him and explain.

'What's that supposed to mean?'

'Nothing,' she sighed. 'Leave it, will you? I'm going upstairs. Need to chill for a bit.'

Tina ran up the stairs and slammed her bedroom door behind her. She leant against it for a moment and then flung herself on the bed. She knew it. She was sure she knew that flat. Thinking back to the photos Shazza had shown her, she was sure she'd been there. Couldn't remember the punter though. Think! Think, can't you? Imagine his face. She rolled onto her back, drumming her fingers on her temples. She closed her eyes, but the image stayed away. It danced on the edge of her memory as if it were something she saw from the corner of her eye. Each time she turned to see it, the face vanished. All through the rest of the week and the weekend she chased the memory, but it eluded her.

With its high, narrow windows, painted iron bars and Victorian red-bricked façade, Stanmoor High Security Hospital looked every inch like a prison. The welcome sign from West London Mental Health NHS Trust, printed in a similar font and colour to those used by Her Majesty's Prison Service, did nothing to detract from this first impression. Once inside, it had the familiar cloying hospital smell — disinfectant, dirt and disease. Next to each heavy steel door were anti-bacterial hand wash gels, as if psychosis were some contagion. Carlson and Poole were escorted to The Paddock, the secure unit, where Patrick Wheeler, the Lytham Lyncher awaited them.

'Mr Carlson, how nice of you to drop in. Are you staying for tea?' The gentle, almost effeminate voice belonged to a haggard, grey-faced man who waved them into the plastic chairs opposite him. Despite the extreme warmth of the room, he appeared cool and unruffled. 'Now, to what do I owe this pleasure?'

'Hello Pat,' said Carlson, sitting down opposite the man who had terrorised the north of England for over five years. 'This isn't a social visit. We've got a few questions for you.'

'Ah, Mr Carlson, always straight to business. I can see you've not changed. And I see you have your own monkey now. Have you been promoted to organ grinder?'

Poole took a step forward and Carlson spread out the fingers on his right hand. Poole saw the signal and seized a breath.

'Oh, no offence, dear boy. Times have changed since I was first incarcerated here, courtesy of your nice Mr Carlson. I didn't mean to suggest that you were a simian, merely that it appears Mr Carlson has risen in the ranks.'

Poole glowered, but said nothing as he took notebook and pen from his breast pocket and sat at an adjacent table.

'Someone's been stealing your thunder, Pat,' Carlson said. 'Up to your old tricks. Did you have a trainee when you were on the other side of these bars?'

Patrick Wheeler did not reply, but the intake of breath flared his nostrils.

'Yes Pat, your old modus operandi, even down to the film footage. So, have you been passing on tips? Running a master class? Or did you have an accomplice all those years ago?' Externally, Carlson was calm with steady rhythmic breathing. Internally, he remembered the terror Patrick Wheeler had wrought all those years ago. Before driving down here, he'd replayed the early interviews of Wheeler and the young Detective Constable Carlson, and he knew he had been scared by this man. Sitting opposite him now, he knew he still was.

'I have not the pleasure of understanding you, Mr Carlson,' Wheeler replied. He looked at Carlson with a slight sneer and lowered his attention to inspecting his fingernails.

'Don't give me that BS,' Carlson said, roughly. 'And speak normally, can't you? You never spoke like this when you were on the outside. Why are you trying to sound like Noël Coward?'

Wheeler laughed. His voice reverted to the guttural, coarse sounds that Carlson remembered so well, and he suppressed a shiver.

'And what fun we had, Mr Carlson,' he said. 'How many times was I questioned? Four? Five? And always released without charge. No, I worked on my own, as well you know. I don't get many visitors and all my mail is checked. Incoming and outgoing —'

'And are they all sickos?'

'You'd be surprised. Some women think I can be redeemed. I don't let them visit. But, coming back to your question, no, I don't give away my secrets, never have done and never will.' Wheeler stabbed the table top with his forefinger to emphasise his point. 'If you've got someone copying me then you've got a leak somewhere. If someone is using my MO, they didn't get it from me.'

'They're getting it from somewhere. Okay, some stuff came up in the trial but there was always information kept back. It never made the papers about your two cameras. One set of footage for us and one for yourself. Come on Pat, you were the celebrated Lytham Lyncher, can you honestly tell me no one has wanted to hear your story? Sod it man, even the bloody sofa looks the same.'

'Then you really do have a problem, don't you, Mr C? That old sofa must have been destroyed.' Wheeler put his hands together, interlinking all his digits except the forefingers. These he rested against his lips and stared at Carlson for a few seconds. 'Seriously, Mr Carlson,' he continued, 'that sofa was hideous. Dated even when I had it. Seventies decor at its worst. Do you want to tell me what's been going on?'

'No, Pat, I don't think I do. I simply needed to see if you'd been sharing the secrets of your little games. Since you haven't, there's no point wasting my time with you.'

Forgetting it was bolted to the floor, Carlson tried to push back the plastic chair. He slid out from behind the table, stood up and nodded to the warden. 'We're getting nowhere here,' he said to Poole.

'Leaving already, Mr Carlson? What a shame. Don't leave it so long next time. I quite feel you'd forgotten all about me.' Wheeler waved in a parody of a small child.

Carlson strode from the secure unit back to reception,

and Poole jogged to keep up with him. They retrieved their phones and walked back to the car park at a more leisurely pace. Carlson switched his mobile on as soon as they were back in the fresh air and it rang immediately.

'Carlson!' he snapped. 'Hello Doctor. Yes. Good. Okay. Thanks. How soon can you get that over to me? Yeah, that's fine. And thank you. Again.'

Carlson's finger pressed the small icon on the phone with difficulty. He looked at the screen and realised he had accidently opened several apps. Frowning, he placed the mobile in the pocket of his padded coat, pulled the collar up and marched to the car.

He stopped short of getting in and leant on the roof, looking over it to Poole. 'We have news from the good doctor. He's confirmed that both women were strangled with a ligature. From behind. The second girl has been washed too. No trace evidence. Not a hair. Not a fibre. Nails had been cleaned. He's left us absolutely nothing to go on. We haven't got a clue who he is. We've not even had a sighting of him picking the girls up. I take it those cameras are working now?'

Poole nodded. 'Yes, Guv. For the time being at least. The dealers don't like them, so they pay the kids to take them out of action.'

'It's all intertwined isn't it? The drugs, the girls, the whole bloody lot. And some creep is taking advantage of that.' Carlson nodded at the car, Poole clicked the remote and they both got out of the cold.

'We'll get him, sir,' said Poole. 'So, Dr Kilburn agrees that both murders are connected? Are we going public with that?'

'Yeah, the doc is sure that we're looking for the same person. I just want to get him soon. I can see it all happening again. Not catching the bastard until he slips up. And how many more girls are going to pay with their lives before he makes that mistake?' Carlson put his seat belt on. 'Did we get anywhere with that film footage?' he asked. 'We'll need to compare it thoroughly with the original footage now. Have you arranged for it all to be transported from Lytham?' Carlson asked.

'Yes, Guv. It's all on its way. Do you think they're connected other than this current guy being a copycat?'

'No. I don't think Wheeler had an accomplice at the time. Not sure about this new one though. The doctor said there were no drag marks on the bodies, so either he wrapped them up well and took the wrappings away with him or he's strong enough to carry them there. Or,' Carlson said slowly, 'he has help.'

'Neither girl weighed very much though —'

'True, so he could be acting alone,' said Carlson. 'I don't know. I wish we had more to go on. I don't suppose Vice have decided to contribute at all?'

'Not as far as I am aware, Guv. I'll have a chat with Tim and see if he got anywhere. Then there's a couple of guys I was friendly with when I was in the Norfolk Constabulary, before we got combined. They might know who's best to talk to, if Superintendent Tasker is too busy to get back to us.'

Carlson gave Poole a sharp look, but the sergeant's face was all innocence.

'Okay,' Carlson said, 'we really could do with some suggestions as to which punters might suddenly decide to kill or if there are any new faces amongst the kerb crawlers.' Carlson sighed and wondered how long Jim Tasker would continue bearing the grudge.

'Back to the station then, Guv?' Poole's question broke through Carlson's reverie.

'I reckon so. Let's see what the team have got.'

April 1982

The voices got louder and louder. Screaming. High pitched. Words no longer distinguishable. A glass shattering against the wall. More screaming. The boy hid under his bed, squeezing his eyes closed and pulling a pillow around his ears to block out the sounds, without success, as the booms of slamming cupboard doors broke through his defences. The adults continued screaming at each other.

'Shut up. Shut up. Shut up,' he whispered.

He heard a thud. A scream. Then another thud. And another. Silence. He waited, poised for the next wave of violence. Footsteps sounded in the hallway. The main door slammed. The house was finally tranquil.

He lay on the floor for a while waiting for his mother to come upstairs, but all he heard was a rhythmic knocking of wood on wood. He crept to his bedroom door, gently opened it and squeezed his nose through the crack.

'Mum?' No answer. No noise at all save for the door. Slammed shut so hard it had bounced open and now thudded gently each time it hit the door frame. He came to the top of the stairs. The lights were still on below, but there was no sign of his mother. He stole downstairs, stopping on every step to listen for a noise. Everywhere was still, apart from the door. At the last step he sat hugging his knees and shivering. Eventually the cold drove him to shut the front door. He dragged a chair across the hall and wrestled with the top bolt. Finally, it slid into place. The boy wedged the chair under the handle as he'd seen on TV and went to the kitchen to find his mother. She looked more peaceful than he'd ever known her. Her arm looked funny and there was a big puddle of red by her head. But she was quiet. He went upstairs for a pillow and blanket. He went back to the kitchen, covered her with the blanket and cuddled up beside her on the floor.

CHAPTER TWELVE

Gasping, Carlson leaned against the doorbell trying not to breathe in the stench from the black bags outside the neighbouring flat.

'Alright, I'm coming. Where's the bloody fire?' Shazza wrenched open the battered door and a flurry of peeling paint floated into the corridor. 'You okay?' she said. 'Been running?'

He was surprised at the contrast from their first two meetings. She remained skeletal, that was true, but her face was free of make-up, old and new. Her clothes were still threadbare, but they were clean, and she had lifted her hair onto her head in a softer style than the harsh ponytail. Lighter hair was beginning to show through at the roots. She leaned against the door, blocking the entrance.

'Lift's out of order,' he panted.

'It's never been in order. Least, not since I've been here. Jeez, it stinks out here; s'pose yow'd better come in. What did you want anyway?' She stood aside to let him pass.

'Just to say thanks for coming in and looking at the

photos,' he said wiping his feet on the carpet. He noticed there was no doormat. 'My sergeant said you'd come by.'

'Did he now? And did he say what a pig he was?'

Carlson turned, frowning at the term, although he'd been called worse in his career. He stood back so she could walk past him in the narrow corridor.

'Nah, I can see that he didn't. Wanna cuppa tea? I was just making one.'

He nodded and followed her through to the tiny kitchen.

'Sorry, the tea's in the cupboard behind you,' she said stepping close to him.

He moved to let her near the cupboard and became rammed against the sink. She reached across him to pick up mugs. Carlson could smell her hair. Tangs of summer rain and fresh flowers. A sharp contrast to the bleakness of the day outside. Soft fuzz coated her ear lobes and crept towards the hairline. Golden. Just like Jade's. That was where the similarities ended though. For all that she had been through, this young woman was tough. With one of his own daughters, Carlson would have pulled them into his arms for a daddy bear hug and assured them everything was going to be alright. He found his hands raised to do the same to Shazza and stopped himself in time. Not that he felt able to assure anyone that anything would ever improve. Not now. Bewildered and aghast at his almost faux pas, he barged past her into the dingy hallway and stood there while she made the tea. She looked at him, surprised for a moment, then picked up a mug from the draining board, rinsed it under the tap and polished it with kitchen towel.

'Don't get many visitors,' she said, in way of explanation. 'Milk, sugar?'

'Just milk.'

She made the teas, passed him the freshly washed cup, and led him into the main room.

Carlson trod carefully across the ragged carpet and sat in the sagging chair opposite the sofa. He sipped the hot liquid. 'I'm sorry,' he said.

'What for? Your sergeant? He made it clear he didn't like my sort from the very beginning. No way he's gonna change his mind.'

'I guess you're right. It's just that...' Carlson hesitated. 'I wonder if you could give me more background on Josie and Natasha.'

'Natasha? Is that what she was called? I wasn't sure if it was that or Natalie. I only really knew her to say hello to. We weren't really mates. She was just one of the girls. I knew Josie better. She was a nice girl. Came from a nice family. Or so it seemed at first. Later, when I got to know her better, I found out a bit more about the family.'

'Which was?' Carlson looked over at her as he put down his tea and retrieved his notepad.

'Oh, you know the sort of thing,' Shazza said, sipping her tea. 'All very nice on the surface, but skellingtons in the cupboard. Dad could be a nasty bit of work. He smacked her Mum around. So Mum drank. Neglected the kids. All covered up though. All hidden from the neighbours. Josie got into the drugs scene just to escape from it. That's how I got into it too. We was the same. Birds of a feather. Used to like that when I was a kid. Always wanted a sister. Josie became like a sister to me.' Shazza sniffed and pulled a ratty tissue from her sleeve. She wiped her nose and eyes. 'We looked out for each other. But she'd had enough. She mentioned going home. See her sister and the new babby. When she disappeared that's where I thought she'd gone. Back home.'

'Except she didn't.' Carlson sat, pen poised, waiting.

'Nah, silly cow. I just don't get why she went out. She had the fare to get home. We'd even been to the project together. Trying to get clean.'

'The project?'

Yeah, the Mysia Project. Rehab programme. We'd talked about it often enough, so we went together. Got through the worst of it. You know, the clucking, cold turkey,' she said in response to seeing Carlson's sight frown. 'Then she ups and says she wants to see her sister and the new kiddie. So off she goes. Or so I thought. I'll never understand what made her go out again.'

'And that was the last you saw of her?' Carlson leaned back and sighed. He shot forward again as a chair spring nipped his back.

Shazza giggled. 'Like I said, I don't get many visitors.'

'Now you know why!' he laughed, rubbing his lower back.

Shazza continued grinning at him and the smiles transformed her face. The harsh streetwise look was replaced by someone much younger, more innocent, and more fragile. There was so much about her that reminded him of Jade. Carlson scrabbled to his feet. He found he could not tell her that Josie, far from giving up heroin, was still a regular user. 'I have to go,' he said, hiding behind formality. 'Thanks for coming in. Sorry about Poole being such a prat. Let me know if you can remember anything more about the photos.'

He rushed into the hallway, wrestled with the front door and fled the scene.

Back at the station his first thought was of Kirsty Russell. He strode down the stairs to the labs and offices in the basement, running a finger between his waistband and stomach as he did so. He was determined not to buy new trousers. He poked his head around the door. Kirsty was head down at her desk, leaning forward over scribbled notes. Her auburn curls, long enough to caress the surface, cascaded around her shoulders as she sat up to type onto the laptop.

'Gotcha!' he said, slapping his hand on her shoulder.

'Shit, Ronnie,' she hissed. The creamy skin of her cheeks flushed, and a hint of colour appeared on her neck. 'You made me jump. What are you doing down here? You usually summon us poor techies up to your lair.'

'Yeah, I need a favour,' he said, hiding one hand behind his back.

What's he up to? wondered Kirsty, thinking that at least he'd had the grace to look sheepish for scaring her.

'Go on then. What do you want?' she said, leaning back in her chair and cupping her chin in her hand.

'You know I've got two bodies now?'

She nodded. 'I can count. In fact, I'm known for it,' she said, arching her right eyebrow.

'I need you working with me. I want you to be all over this case.'

'I can't, Ronnie. You know that. I can't work on two potentially connected investigations. I'm a crime scene investigator. You need different investigators at each scene, otherwise the defence barrister would scream cross-contamination before I was sworn in and sat down in the witness box.'

'Yes, I know,' he said.

'And you've only got two cases. Are you expecting more?' Kirsty looked at his grey face and tired eyes.

'Yep,' he sighed. 'You know as well as I do, bastards like this carry on until they get caught. I need someone I trust to take care of the evidence for me. Keep the team straight, keep them focused on the facts and keep us in budget. If you took on the coordination role you'd be helping a lot.'

Kirsty sat back in her chair, placing her small feet on the desk. She knew only too well the pressures of modern policing. Catch all the bad guys, Mr Plod, but don't spend any money. Bloody austerity measures.

'I'll be an overhead,' she reminded him. 'Are you sure you won't be better off with a couple more junior officers?'

'Good,' he said, clearly ignoring the premise of her suggestion and rising to leave. 'I knew you'd say yes.' He slipped a box of dark Lindt chocolates onto her desk. 'Briefing in fifteen mins?'

Kirsty looked at his retreating back. I'm pretty sure I didn't actually say yes, she thought.

CHAPTER THIRTEEN

DS Poole stood at the white board in front of the team. 'Okay,' he said, 'this is what we have so far. Two female victims, both strangled from behind with a similar style of ligature, both body dumps hidden and not regular places for walkers. Does that mean he has local knowledge? Both washed with no forensics to go on. Kirsty Russell has now joined the team and will be working across both cases with us as Crime Scene Coordinator. Kirsty?'

'Thanks, Ben,' Kirsty took Poole's spot by the board. 'As already outlined, there's very little for us to go on forensically. Not only were the victims washed thoroughly before they were disposed of, their nails were cleaned too. They appear to have had rough sex, but Dr Kilburn has been unable to find a trace of semen on either body, therefore he's likely to have used a condom. Sometimes on other cases we've found bite marks on victims and have been able to trace the perpetrator through dentistry. Not so here.

Whoever this person is, he's hyper aware of trace evidence and forensics. However,' she paused, ensuring she had their full attention, 'I do not think that makes him ex-job or anything like that before you ask, although it makes sense not to rule it out entirely. With the TV programmes that are available these days, anyone and everyone knows enough about DNA and crime scene techniques to be at least partially competent. On the plus side, we have names for our victims and we've been given their phone numbers. Neither phone had GPS sadly, but you never know, we might get lucky with pings off masts. That means we can start mapping their movements through cell sites.'

Kirsty secured a map of the red-light district, overlaid with the masts in the area, to the white board. There was a sudden change of energy and mutterings of excitement echoed around the room. Kirsty sat down, and Poole took over.

'One thing that I want to point out to you all,' he said, 'is that he has a hidey hole, somewhere he feels safe enough to kill. Somewhere he won't be disturbed, where he can wash the victims and he can transport them from there to the dump site. That's somewhere we need to find.

'Fortunately, he was generous enough to send some footage of his time with the first girl and we're now passing out stills. Use these in the door to doors, see if anyone recognises this place. Right, you've all got your assigned tasks. Let's catch this bastard, people.'

Poole waited as the room cleared, then he wandered to where Kirsty and Carlson were in deep in conversation.

. . .

'Thanks, both of you,' said Carlson. 'Sod all to go on, but at least we have enthusiasm. I think the phone tracking will help us enormously.'

Carlson turned as DC Lacey was hovering at his elbow. 'Yes, Jane?'

'Sir, there's another one,' she said. 'Another girl has gone missing. Not been seen for a couple of days. Tanith Wilson. Tani to her friends. She's not answering her phone. She was supposed to go and see her family at the weekend and didn't turn up. Her name is known to us. She's been done for soliciting a few times. She works the Eastfield and Hanbury Road areas. Calls herself Silver, on account of the hair, like. Family are coming in with photos. Do you want them circulated?'

Carlson raised his eyes to the ceiling. 'Jane, I want to see the family as soon as they come in. Poole, we need to start talking to the press. Get on to media and organise a press conference, will you?'

Jane remained standing, waiting for Carlson to notice her again. 'Sir,' she said, holding a package towards him, 'this parcel was hand delivered for you at the front desk.'

Carlson snatched the package from her. He knew that with the number of hands it had been through there would be little chance of fingerprints on the outside. The parcel was identical to the earlier package, even down to the label and font. It was another message from the killer.

Squeezed into the small laboratory, the team crowded around, peering at the plain envelope which had been in the package with the DVD. It was clean and unmarked. Kirsty Russell slipped on a pair of blue nitrile gloves and the team watched as she laid the envelope carefully on the steel bench and began to slice it open with a scalpel.

Carlson passed her a pair of tweezers and she prised the envelope open. She held the opening ajar with the scalpel and carefully pinched the letter with the tweezers. Using the blade now to hold the envelope in place she pulled the letter free. Slipping the bottom half of the paper into an evidence bag the rest unfolded as it slid down inside the plastic.

Kirsty placed the envelope into another bag, sealed both, smoothed out the printed letter and handed it to Carlson.

Dear Mr Carlson, he said aloud.

I hope you enjoyed the video footage I sent you recently. Enclosed is more — me with the latest two girls. In time, I hope to provide you with as full a collection as my predecessor did. I think I will have time to play my little game for quite a while before you catch me. If ever you do. I think you will not.

I have not quite finished with the third girl. You can have her back soon. She is, I should say was, so much prettier than the other girls, that I wanted to keep her a little longer. She did not struggle like the others either. It was as if she was waiting for death and welcomed it. I was happy to help her. She is at peace now, but she is such nice company I cannot let her go — well, not just yet.

Enjoy the film, fare thee well.

(I did wonder what to sign myself, but decided to stick with the classics)

Yours

Jack

Carlson stood up straight. He rolled his head back and, looking at the ceiling, let out a long breath.

'Shit,' he said. 'So, we have another body to find. Not what we wanted. Not what we wanted at all.'

He was motionless, but only for a moment, suddenly he was all action. 'Right, Kirsty, copies and analysis please. I don't suppose there will be prints, but dust anyway. And I want someone to read it through and see if there are any of those… what are they called?'

'Socio-linguistic patterns?' said Kirsty, helpfully.

'Yes, those things. Come on people, we've got work to do.'

CHAPTER FOURTEEN

DCI Carlson, flanked by Poole and Russell, blinked at the bright lights and flashes as he took his seat and faced the audience. He looked down at his notes and waited for the coloured swirls to fade. Vision restored, he raised his head and faced the cameras.

'We are appealing for witnesses in connection with the discovery of the bodies of two young women, Josephine Paul, known as Scarlett, and Natasha Collins, whose street name was Amber. Both girls were addicted to Class-A drugs and worked in the red-light district of Gippingford.' Carlson checked his notes once more before relating the exact dates that the girls had vanished and taking the reporters systematically through the subsequent discoveries of their bodies. He briefly described their injuries but, as agreed with the Assistant Chief Constable, no details of the film footage were released. He ended his statement with a standard call for questions.

'What about the other girl, Chief Inspector?' Sarah Jenkins raised her hand. Carlson looked at her intense eyes;

they were the colour of wet slate but bright with the passion of self-righteous zeal.

'I can confirm that a third girl, Tanith Wilson, often referred to as Silver, has been reported missing. We are naturally concerned for her safety in the light of recent events.' Carlson kept his face impassive as he stared back at the reporter. He wanted to be sure that the letter writer was kosher before panic spread in the town.

'Do you think she'll be the next victim?' Sarah asked.

'As I said, we are concerned for her safety and would like her to contact the police, or a friend if she prefers, to let us know that she is okay.'

'But you do think the two deaths so far are connected?' Sarah persisted, sitting with pencil poised over the shorthand pad.

'There are distinct similarities between the two incidents, yes.'

'So, Chief Inspector, when you find the body of this third girl, we'll have a serial killer on our hands?'

Carlson felt his throat tightening. He tidied the knot in his tie and straightened his collar. 'So far, Tanith Wilson is missing,' he repeated, as he stared over the sea of faces. 'We hope that she is alive and well but would like her to confirm this. I have no wish to start speculation about connections between the two deaths which have occurred. Nor do I wish to scaremonger with the idea of a serial killer. Thank you all for your time. Good day.' He stood abruptly and turned from the cameras, nodding for Russell and Poole to move with him into a "back-turned" huddle of quiet discussion.

'You know the drill, look like we are talking and wait for that lot to leave,' he said quietly.

Carlson listened to the journalists scurrying from the room. Rats heading back to the gutter, he thought. When peace had descended, he glanced around and realised not all of them had left. The hard-eyed reporter was rising from her seat. Motioning for Russell and Poole to go back to work, he collected up his notes and waited.

'Sarah Jenkins, Chief Inspector,' she said as she approached the dais. 'You may recall I found the first body. I'd like to do a more in-depth piece with you.' She stopped a short distance away from him with her hand held out.

'I remember the name, but no, not a chance,' Carlson said, ignoring the outstretched hand. 'I'm in the middle of two murder investigations. I've got nothing to say to you separately from what I've given your colleagues.'

'But I need to know if he's started sending you the films again,' she insisted.

'Films?' Carlson queried, biting the inside of his cheek to keep his face impassive.

'You know what I mean, Mr Carlson. You worked a very similar case in Lytham. Patrick Wheeler, the Lytham Lyncher. I've been doing my homework.' She smiled but continued to consider him with gimlet eyes. 'I've been checking up on you.'

'Then you've been wasting your time, Ms Jenkins. Please do not waste any more of mine. Good day to you.' Carlson turned around and, before Sarah could ask another question, he signalled a female uniformed PC to escort her from the room.

As Sarah left by the revolving door she noticed a young, scruffy woman with dyed black hair entering the station by the same means. She whirled around in time to see the girl and Chief Inspector Carlson shake hands. Strange, she thought. Very strange. Too young to be a police officer. So, who was she?

As the revolving door brought her back to the atrium again, the constable blocked her way.

'The press conference is over now, Ms Jenkins,' she said in a low voice.

'Who's that girl talking to DCI Carlson?' Sarah asked.

The police officer didn't bother to turn around and look before she said, 'I have no idea. Good day, ma'am.'

Sarah craned her neck as she was ushered back through the revolving door. Carlson and the girl walked away deep in conversation together and, whilst Sarah's curiosity was piqued, she decided to wait.

The landscape was bleak and grey. A shimmering ball of light hovered above the surface then raced eastwards. He saw his corpse lying in the distance and sped towards it.

Do you want to resurrect now? [*Yes*] [*No*]

Poole clicked on [*Yes*] and Da'anarth sprang into life. The orc warrior halted, sensing movement behind him. He spun around and came towards Da'anarth once more, snarling and with cleaver raised above his head. Da'anarth readied himself and swung into battle. Suddenly a second figure appeared and joined Da'anarth. The orc grasped a sword from his belt and fought both warriors, one on either hand. The clash of metal on metal burst from the speakers alongside grunts from the combatants. Blow after blow was rained on the orc and slowly its lifeline dropped, fading from bright green to a pale amber. Finally, it lay on the ground before them.

'Looked like you needed some help.' The words flashed up on the screen.

'*My thanks, good sir. I've been battling the creature for many an age. My life has been forfeit on numerous occasions. Pray allow me to offer you the prize,*' Poole typed.

'No, you're okay,' came the reply. 'Happy to help. Do you want to join me on a quest?'

Poole looked at the time and shook his head. '*I can't,*' he typed, thinking there was no need to stay in role if the other player wasn't bothering. '*I really must get some sleep. Got a heavy day tomorrow.*'

'Okay. Save me on your friends list and we can catch up another time.'

'*Will do.*' Poole clicked on the friend's list option and saved Treallis's avatar. It was the only name there.

Turning off the computer he padded barefoot to the bathroom. As he cleaned his teeth he scrunched his toes, relishing the luxuriousness of the thick matting. He rubbed a hand over his chin. Shave? Maybe in the morning. Not too bad tonight. He switched off the lights and slid beneath the black sheets, spreading himself across the width of the bed. He pulled a freshly washed silk-covered pillow into his neck and slept.

Poole woke late and by the time he arrived, the incident room was already buzzing with activity. Carlson was facing the white board, arms folded regarding the photos of the three girls.

'We'll find her, Boss,' Poole said, passing Carlson a carton of coffee.

'Thanks for this; you didn't have to,' Carlson said, as he raised the cup to his lips. 'Anyhow, the call just came in. She's already been found. Or at least I guess it's her — the description matches. Car's waiting.' He handed the keys to Poole and pointed towards the door with his coffee cup.

Poole felt a stab of excitement. Three victims now made

this his first serial killer case. He'd studied them of course, but this time it was for real. Thinking about his earlier reprimand, he immediately suppressed the feeling. Real lives had been taken. It was no longer text books, case notes and supposition. He scampered after Carlson's impatient strides.

'Where?' he said.

'River side. Not far from Faverstone Marina. She was spotted by a passing yachtswoman. She —' Carlson lapsed into silence and stared out the window as the town was left behind, transitioning to fields and meadows.

At the perimeter line they donned over-suits and booties and followed the trail left by the crime scene technicians to the site where a girl sat. A gentle breeze rustled the reeds around her. The sound was musical, reminiscent of wind chimes. The sun dappled light on the open water near her body. She leaned against a tree trunk. Her hands rested in her lap, but she played no heed to sights or sounds. Her eyes were open and gazing out to the river beyond, but they saw nothing and never would again.

'What do you think, Ben?' Carlson's voice was soft, muted.

The use of his first name was still uncharacteristic enough to surprise Poole, and it was a moment before he replied. 'He's making fun of us, sir. He's taken time to pose her. Look at her legs. Ankles crossed, hands resting. She looks as if she's just sat down for a moment. This has taken thought and planning. Were there any footprints?'

'I think you might mean footwear impressions, DS Poole.' Kirsty Russell appeared behind them and grinned at Poole. Carlson noticed that not only was the grin returned, but Poole ran a finger around his collar and adjusted his tie.

'There would have been marks, yes,' she continued. 'However, it would seem he can read a tide table. These footwear marks you can see here' — she pointed — 'belong to the first officer on the scene. Our killer's impressions are likely to have been taken away by the tide. He lined her up carefully with the high-water mark so that when the tide came in, and subsequently left, it took any of his footwear marks with it. We've not managed to pick up any traces on this gravel path at all.'

Carlson cursed under his breath. 'He is definitely playing with us. Has she been washed like the others, Jervis?' he asked, tilting his head towards the medic kneeling beside the girl.

Dr Kilburn looked up from his crouched position. 'Yep, cleaned thoroughly from what I can see so far, nails have been cleaned too, and these appear to be the same sort of ligature marks. I can't give you much more than that at the moment, Ronnie.'

'Time of death?' he asked hopefully.

'How long has she been missing? Five days?'

'Over a week now,' Carlson replied.

'I think she's been dead for much of that time, Ronnie. Are we okay to move her now?'

Carlson nodded his agreement, said thanks, and returned to the perimeter line. He looked at Poole.

'Thoughts?'

'Well Guv, one, he's clearly a planner,' Poole replied and counted his points out on his outstretched fingers. 'Thinks things through. Two, he's organised. None of this is done in a rush. But three, does he pick the girls at random? Or is all that planned out too? Four, how does he get rid of their clothes, their phones? And five, is he local? He must have good knowledge of the area.'

'I can see that profiling course wasn't a complete waste of

time.' Carlson smiled, grimly. He rubbed his eyes with one hand and pinched the bridge of his nose. Shoving his hands deep into his pockets he wandered back to the car.

Poole trailed behind him, thinking of the fragile figure left behind and that he would have to change MISSING to DECEASED under her photograph.

CHAPTER FIFTEEN

'What's up with you, missy?' said the old lady, looking at Tina Hoyes in the mirror. 'You're usually much chattier. Hardly had a peep out of you today.'

Tina stood behind the old woman, removing the curlers and smoothing her grey hair into soft curls. She returned the stare in the hairdressers' mirror. 'I'm really sorry,' she said. 'Something I've been trying to remember. You know how something is right there in your mind, but you can't quite… well, pick it up almost.'

The old woman smiled knowingly. 'Yes love, but don't chase it. Go home tonight, lie quietly, think about something else, some music maybe, and it'll just come to you. Memories are like men: the more you chase them, the more elusive they are.' She chuckled. Tina wasn't sure if it was because of an old memory or a man, or both, but she laughed too.

When she went home that evening, she did exactly as the customer had said. Instead of racking her brains, she laid on her bed, eyes closed, listening to some music. She mentally scrolled through the photos of the flat that Shazza had shown to her and was just drifting off when her eyes popped open. Yes! That's who it was. Now she remembered. *Now* she remembered.

She knew exactly what she needed to do.

Seven o'clock she was told to be there. A little late, Shazza pushed open the door. Her nose wrinkled as several aromas hit it. Sweat — both stale and fresh, a hint of urine from the open toilet door, a cloying musty smell of clothes long damp and a sharp tang of something she later discovered was Tiger Balm. Even here in reception the air was warm and humid. In the hall she could see the windows running with water.

'Yes, love?' A slim, shaven-headed man spoke to her. He smiled as he looked her up and down. At first she was angry, but realised in time that it was an assessment of her musculature and fitness, and not lascivious as a punter's gaze would have been.

'Yeah, I called earlier. You said you could teach me to kickbox? My name's Shazza Raby.'

'I reckon we can do that. What sort of experience have you got?' he asked.

'Of fighting?' she said. 'Scrapping in the playground, mostly.'

He laughed, deepening the lines around his eyes. 'Yeah, that's where most of us started. I'm Bo. Put your trainers in the rack over there. No shoes on the dojo. We start in about five minutes. There'll be a warm-up and some basic exercises, some group work and then we finish off with some fitness work and stretches. Reckon you can manage that?'

'I can only give it a go.'

'Good. First class is free as I said on the phone. If you like it, you can join up and we'll sort you out some kit and a timetable for classes.'

The next ninety minutes passed in a flash. Shazza learnt the difference between a hook and a straight punch. She was taught to front kick and to side kick. Paired up later with a woman on the punch bag, Shazza finally let all her anger and frustration fall away. By the end of the class, when all students placed their hands by their sides and bowed to the instructor, she was hooked.

'Your first class?' Shazza turned. It was the woman she'd paired with on the bag work.

'Yeah, but I will be back. I've not felt so relaxed since —' she hesitated.

'Since?' the woman asked, but Shazza shrugged and shook her head. The woman continued, 'Listen, a few of us go and have a drink in the Swan over the road. Come and join us.'

'I can't. Not tonight. Maybe next time?'

'Okay. Next time it is then. I'll hold you to that. I'm Sarah, by the way.'

'Shazza.'

'See you next week then, Shazza.'

Sarah Jenkins sat on the bench, slipping her shoes on as she watched the girl walked away. Smallest town on the planet, she thought. I'm so glad I decided to find a club and get fit again. Now, by good fortune she had met Shazza, and Sarah was even more curious as to what she and DCI Carlson had been discussing. Still, she now had a name and even if Shazza never showed again, Sarah was sure she could get more information from Bo. And if not from Bo, well, she had other means at her disposal.

As Shazza reached her flat, she switched her mobile back on and it beeped immediately. A text from Tina. Cool, she thought. What's she been up to? Shazza pressed a button and read the message.

I no who he is! T xx

For a long time Shazza looked at the message wondering what to make of it. She sat down and texted back,

Don't do anyfink stoopid. S xx

She placed the phone on the table in front of her and leaned back in the chair. Actually, she thought, that copper was right — it is a bit uncomfortable. She moved to the sofa and switched on the TV.

CHAPTER SIXTEEN

It was after ten when Poole arrived home to his exquisite riverside apartment. He cooked himself stir-fried chicken and Chinese vegetables. Preferring to wash up by hand rather than use the machine — it wasn't as effective as he was — he collected up his plate and utensils. Once he'd cleaned the black granite countertops and the ceramic hob such that everything was pristine again, he poured a light beer and switched on his computer. The solid-state hard drive had been expensive but worth the extra cost. It was silent, no whirring fans. No overheating. He fired up Dragon Quest, his favourite online game and immediately he logged on, his new friend Treallis appeared.

'Good evening Da'anarth,' appeared on the screen.

'*Good evening Treallis,*' he typed back.

'Quest?'

'*Of course.*'

The two companions battled orcs, dragons, evil sorcerers, goblins and gnomes. As soon as one quest was won, Treallis begged him to complete another. Before long Da'anarth's saddle bags were overflowing and his horse was struggling under the weight of the booty.

'*I must away good Knight,*' he typed.

'Not one more quest?' Treallis came back.

'*I fear I cannot. I have other quests to battle IRL, good sir.*'

'Quests IRL? Sounds serious,' Treallis replied. 'What quests?'

It was close to two am and Poole could not maintain character any longer. '*I must sleep. My quest is to catch a killer. A murderer of women,*' he typed.

'In Real Life? Yeah right? What are you, a copper?'

'*I prefer Police Officer,*' he typed, '*but yes, I'm a detective.*'

'Cool. In that case, I wish you good fortune in your hunting. Fare thee well. Until next time. Good night.'

The other player disappeared, and Poole looked at the screen for a moment. He could see other battles in the distance and an orc lumbered towards him. Before it could kill him and take his treasure, Poole logged off. He pulled the glass towards him, but the beer was flat and warm. Rubbing the back of his neck, he decided against another, poured the remnants down the sink, rinsed the glass and refilled it with water from the dispenser on his American-style fridge.

Shazza woke later with the TV channel now demonstrating the prowess of a combined juicer and food processor. She stretched, easing out achy muscles, unused to so much exercise. Picking up the phone, she saw it was two am but Tina had still not replied to any of her voice messages or texts. She texted again but decided to wait until morning for a response. It wasn't unlike Teens to disappear for a bit, as she knew. Or at least it had been like her — she was much more responsible now what with getting clean and all. I'll wait for the morning, she thought. I'll make a decision then. Reckon it'll all be okay.

Shazza made her way to the tiny bathroom, cleaned her teeth and looked at herself in the mirror. The death's head mask was slowly mutating into clearer skin, filling out and with a glow she'd not had before. Her hair still hung limply but was beginning to feel softer. She'd enjoyed the class, the muscle burn making her feel more energised than she had in a very long time. Satisfied, she wandered to the bedroom and after staring at the ceiling for a while she finally put out the light and slept.

As the low winter sun made its way through the tattered curtains, Shazza drifted into consciousness. She was still coming to terms with waking without a hangover or the yearning for a fix. Someone had once told her that if you didn't do booze or drugs then, when you woke up, that was as good as you'd feel all day. With booze or a fix, you always had something to look forward to. She remembered how bad she'd felt the day after going in to talk to the cops. Jesus, now that was a hangover! She'd been sick for two days. Funny how you got out of the habit. Then it hit her. Teens! Had she replied? She groped for the phone, finally finding it under the bed where it had fallen during the night. Nothing. No reply. Where the hell was she? She called the number again, knowing Teens would be pissed at her, but it went straight to voicemail. The phone was never switched off — must be out of battery. She'd try again later.

Tina didn't go into work the following morning, deciding to call in sick instead. Ignoring the calls and texts from Shazza and waiting until her father left the house, she spent her whole day in preparation. Satisfied, she posed in front of her mirror, pulling her hair back into a high ponytail and shook it, watching it waft from side to side. Gone was the natural mousy brown with the red highlights. The suicide blonde was back. She put on skin-tight jeans and a low-cut top. She grabbed her old leather jacket from the back of the wardrobe and opened the bedroom door.

'Tina! For God's sake what have you done to yourself?'

Shit! She'd not heard the front door go. Tina faced her father defiantly.

'Something I gotta do, Dad.' She pushed passed him and down the stairs. He grabbed at her arm, but she slid away.

'Tina, no! Come on, after all you went through getting off the game, the drugs, don't go back to it! Please. Tina. Why?'

'It's not like that, Dad, it's just... a girl's gotta do what a girl's gotta do.' She'd heard that somewhere. Before he could grab her again, she skipped lightly downstairs and ran out the door towards the railway station.

When she arrived in Gippingford an hour later it was just beginning to get dark. Even though it was still a little early for trade, as the office workers and commuters who were usually the early clients hadn't started to travel home, Tina made her way to her old stomping ground. She decided to have a couple of drinks before she got to work and headed for The Bell. Gary looked surprised as she approached the bar.

'What the fuck, Saffron? I thought you'd given all this up,' he said. 'Usual?'

Tina nodded and pushed some cash across the bar. She smiled at Gary, trying to remember how long it was since she'd been Saffron. Picking up the change and her glass, she pushed past a couple of regulars and found a seat in the corner. She slid along the bench, sitting behind the table and facing the room. Glancing at her phone, Tina re-read the messages from Shazza. She'd reply soon. Now that she was here, she wasn't sure what the best plan would be. Wait here to see if he turned up, or talk to some of the girls? She thought for a moment and decided to wait in the warm for her quarry.

CHAPTER SEVENTEEN

April 1982

'Go on. In you go. No one's going to bite you.'

The boy found himself propelled through the door into a large airy hallway. Coats, shoes and bags littered the area. Lots of coats, shoes and bags. The social worker pushed the child further down the hall.

'Denise! Denise, I've got the new one for you.'

A woman appeared from a room which the boy discovered later was called a kitchen-diner.

'Oh, hello you. What's your name, sweetheart?'

The boy said nothing. Denise raised a single eyebrow at the social worker, who replied.

'He's called Bernard.'

'Bernard? Oh Fliss, what kind of a name is that to saddle a child with?'

'Bernie,' the boy whispered.

'Excuse me?' Both women were now looking at him.

'Bernie. My mum calls me Bernie. Where is she? I'd like to go home now.'

Denise knelt down in front of him and took his hand in hers. Bernie noticed they were red and cracked. Not like his Mum's. She had nice hands. Or she used to, before Bill moved in. Bill told her it was all a fuss and nonsense and she didn't need to bother now. Sometimes she still put the cream on her hands. She'd stroke Bernie's hair afterwards and he'd go to bed with the smell on his hair and it would rub off on his pillow. Although there had been times she had not remembered to put him to bed at all. She'd sit asleep on the settee snoring. Or she'd just be staring at the ceiling. Bernie didn't like those days. There would be no food in the house and he'd be hungry all day. Sometimes the next day as well. Mrs Jensen, his teacher, was nice though; she'd let him have her sandwiches if it was a hungry day. He suddenly wondered if he'd still see Mrs Jensen.

'When am I going home? I have school tomorrow and Mrs Jensen will worry if I'm not there. She sometimes comes and gets me. She gives me her sandwiches too,' he said. 'I like Mrs Jensen.'

'Who's Mrs Jensen, sweetie?' The woman called Denise had her face really close to his. Bernie could see the red lines around her nose and her breath wasn't very nice.

'She's my teacher,' he said.

'Well, you won't be seeing her anymore,' said Fliss briskly from behind him. 'You'll be going to a new school and you'll have a new teacher. You won't need to eat her sandwiches because Denise will feed you and give you a lunch to take in with you.'

'And my mummy?' Neither woman replied, but Bernie saw the looks they gave each other over his head.

'Fliss, why don't you get off now and I'll get Bernie settled in,' said Denise. 'The others are just having tea, so he can meet them all.'

Bernie saw three children peeping around the door frame and he hung back, but Denise pushed him in the room and he heard the front door bang. He put his hands over his ears as all the children started shouting at once.

'Who is he?'

'Why is he here?'

'What's he done?'

'Right you lot, sit down,' Denise yelled. 'You,' she pointed at Bernie. 'You can go at the end there. Crystal, get him a plate and a mug.'

Obediently, the children all sat down. There were nine in total. Bernie made it ten. The table was only just big enough to seat them all. There was not much in the way of elbow room, but he didn't need much. Two slices of burnt toast were shoved on the plate and baked beans dolloped on top. They were dried up from having sat on the hob too long, and Bernie felt his mouth dry out as he took the first bite. He shoved the plate away but the girl next to him put it back in front of him. He looked at the congealed mess and moistened it with his tears.

'Why the bloody hell didn't you say this before?' Carlson shouted at her. He was red-faced and with fists clenched.

Shazza hugged her knees and withdrew deeper into the armchair.

'I'm sorry. I'm sorry,' he said, realising the impact he was having. Taking a deep breath, he tried again. 'Start from the beginning and tell me all that you can remember.'

Shazza glared at him in insolent silence.

'I'm sorry,' he repeated. 'I won't shout again. I promise.

Take your time and tell me everything, but I mean everything!'

'Okay,' Shazza said, 'so like I told your mate —'

'DS Poole?'

Shazza glared at him again and Carlson raised his hands in mock surrender.

'Yeah, your mate. So, like I told him, when yow go to a punter's place you ain't taking in the sights. You get the job done and get out of there. But them photos, there was sumfink familiar about that place. So, I met up wiv me mate Teens and told her everything. She thought she'd been there too, but we couldn't remember where it was. We had a good think too. Then yesterday evening when I came back from me kickboxing class' — Carlson suppressed the surprise and amusement he felt at that statement — 'I had a text from Teens and she reckoned that she knew who he was, this bloke yam after. I texted her back but ain't heard nuffink from her. She can be a mardy bitch. So, I left it, but I tried to call her this morning and she ain't answering. Now the phone's going to voicemail. No ring at all. It's bin like that all day. I was starting to get a bit worried. Then, I called you.'

'What did Teens — Tina — say about the flat?'

'Nuffink. I described it to 'er and then I got the text. Like I told yow.'

'You must be very good at descriptions,' Carlson muttered, almost to himself. 'Where does she live?' He took a notepad and pen from his pocket to scribble down the details.

'Out Barton way — wiv her Dad. Ever since she got outta nick.'

'And her surname?'

'Not sure.'

'Do you know where she was in nick — prison?'

'Yeah, Gallowtree. She mugged someone, he didn't hand his wallet over straightaway, so she thumped him one.' Shazza's face lit up at the memory. 'She got sent down for eighteen months 'cos of the assault. She reckoned it was a good thing. She got clean and started a hairdressing course. She was looking great.'

'Right.' Carlson made notes while she spoke.

'Are you gonna find her?'

Carlson looked Shazza in the eye.

'I don't know, love. I really don't know.'

CHAPTER EIGHTEEN

Marguerite Carlson sat in front of her elegant dressing table and looked at herself in the mirror. She twisted her head to the left, to the right and ran her fingers though her short wavy hair. She parted sections and looked at the roots. Slivers of silver glimmered under the bedroom light. Yes, probably time for a touch-up, she thought. Perhaps her hairdresser could fit her in before she went back to work next week. She sat up straighter in the chair and sniffed as tears started to prick her eyes. She pulled a tissue from her sleeve. She always had tissues about her these days. Once there was a time when she would have worried about an uncomplimentary silhouette to her outfit. Not anymore. She dried her eyes, pushed the tissue into a pocket and picked up her comb to tidy where she had pulled the coiffure apart. None of that now, she told herself. If everyone else can move on, you can too. But she couldn't. She slumped, elbows on the dresser and head in her hands. Work was going to be a struggle. That much she knew. She was lucky she still had a job. They had been generous. Understanding. Kind, even. Of course, they'd put her on half pay after a while. But even that was okay. She didn't work because she needed the money. She did it purely for her own sanity. She envied Ronnie. Jealous that he'd been able to put it all behind him. Gone back to work. He was fine. Coping. So typical of a man, she thought. Marguerite could feel the tines sticking in her hand. She unclenched her hand as she stood, and the comb fell to the floor. She pushed the stool back and scrabbled under the dresser to find it.

'Mum?'

Marguerite jumped at the sound and hit her head on the underside of the furniture. She remained on the floor, embarrassed at the lack of dignity and rubbing her head.

'Mum, you okay?'

'Yes, yes, I'm fine, you just made me jump. That's all.'

'I was thinking…' Aspen began.

'Yes?'

'I was thinking that we could sort out Jade's room. A little tidy up. Dust, hoover and straighten up. Maybe take her clothes —'

'NO!' Marguerite hauled herself to a standing position, screeching the single word; it reverberated around the room. Instantly ashamed, she hid her face in her hands and collapsed back onto the stool.

Aspen jumped at the sound and began reversing into the hallway.

'I'm sorry,' she whispered, 'I didn't say it to upset you.' She hovered near the door.

Marguerite looked up. 'Yes, me too. I'm sorry. I didn't mean to shout. I'm just not ready yet.'

'But Mum, please, it's been over six months,' Aspen said, clutching the door frame.

'I know how long it's been, Aspen! I told you, I'm not ready.'

'Do you want me to —?'

'No! Leave it,' Marguerite replied. 'I don't want you to do anything. Just leave it. Leave it all alone. Leave me alone!'

Marguerite turned her back and watched in the mirror as Aspen returned to her own room. She heard the door shut and the creak as her surviving daughter flung herself on her bed. Within moments Marguerite heard the faint sounds of sobbing and, stepping away from the mirror and thoughts of work and hairdressers, she curled herself up on her own bed and wept too.

When Carlson arrived at the station, Poole was gazing at the images and reports on the incident board and sipping coffee from a cardboard beaker. It smelt good, Carlson thought, regretting telling the DS that it wasn't necessary to get him one every day.

Instead he said, 'You've taken my spot.'

'Huh?' Poole blinked, looking confused until Carlson nodded at the board.

'Don't worry,' he said. 'What have we got?'

'Nothing. Nothing new at any rate,' Poole chewed a corner of his thumb. 'He's leaving no clues. We've got no forensics yet. He takes their clothing —'

'Nothing from the landfills?'

'It's... well, the searches are underway, but a town this size?' Poole left the thought hanging. 'We've got a call out to all charity shops, but those charity bag collections come direct from houses. No idea if they'll comply or not. Some of them are scams, but we'll see. He could have dumped the clothes anywhere. Even driven out of town. To the next town.'

'So that's a clue right there, isn't it?'

'It is?' Poole looked doubtful.

'Yes, of course it is, Poole! Come on, think about it. If he's got access to dump out of our region. To be away from home. Perhaps for days with no one worrying about him or maybe not even noticing he's gone.'

'But Guv, anyone could do that. Needle? Haystack?'

'No, you're wrong,' Carlson replied. 'My thoughts were more along the lines of occupations of the kerb crawlers already interviewed. Any sales reps? Any lorry drivers amongst them? Anyone who can absent themselves and not be noticed. For it not to be unusual.'

'Damn, yep, I see where you're coming from. Sorry sir, bit slow this morning. I'll get Tim to start collating. Shouldn't take long to pull the info from the Police National Computer.'

'Good. That's better, Ben. Wake up and never say never.'

Carlson turned as DC Jane Lacey approached. 'Everything you asked for from Lytham is in the conference room, sir.'

'What conference room?' Carlson frowned. He'd been at Gippingford over ten years and had never noticed a conference room before. Even the press conference had been held in the sports' hall.

'That's what the Super wants to call it, sir. To be honest, it's a couple of the old offices we'd used for storage and a partition's been taken down. Tables all pushed together in the middle. So now it's a conference room. First floor, room 51. All the evidence from that old case you wanted? It's in there.'

Carlson palmed his face.

'Of course it is, Jane. Of course it's a conference room. And we've got everything, have we?'

'Yes, sir. As far as I can tell, sir. There had been a fire at the warehouse facility, so some of the files are a bit water damaged —'

'Great,' muttered Carlson. 'Come on Poole. Let me show you how we had to do it in the old days.'

'Guv?' but Poole trotted after him.

As both men walked into the room, Poole shuddered. He fought his need to flee. Tables had been rammed together to form one large surface. Dust motes hung in the air and grey webs, spiders long departed, drooped from the ceiling, the light fittings, even from the blinds. Worse still was the smell from the boxes. Many were crinkled from the damp. Some still had labels, and these had mould spores covering their surfaces. A slight aroma of burnt paper still lingered. Poole shivered. He pulled out a chair and wiped it with his handkerchief but even then, he could not bring himself to sit down. He glared at the handkerchief, unable to replace it in his pocket. Seeing a box of nitrile gloves, which Jane had thoughtfully brought to the room, he placed them on the table. Carlson, not bothering with gloves, pulled the nearest box to him and opened it up. He picked out a file and began to read. Poole donned gloves and retrieved another box. Lifting the lid, he sifted through some of the files and evidence bags. He turned the box on its side, pulled everything out onto the table and pushed the items into separate piles. He looked inside the lid for the inventory, detailing the items in the box. It was missing. He opened a couple more boxes. Same thing.

'Guv, I don't suppose the contents would have been stored on computer, would they?'

Carlson looked up at him with a smile. 'Nah then son,' he said, attempting and failing to imitate a Northern accent,

'What dost thou want with one of them there new-fangled computah things?'

'I'll take that as a no, shall I?' Poole said, grimacing. 'That's a pain. Looks like several of the contents lists are missing.'

'Bugger,' was Carlson's response. 'This is going to be slower than I thought'.

By late afternoon and with only a handful of boxes sorted, the two called it a day.

'Get Jane and Tim on this tomorrow, Ben,' Carlson said, heading for the door.

CHAPTER NINETEEN

Tyres squealing against the smooth warehouse floor, Bernie Latimer manoeuvred the forklift and eased the pallets off the pile. He reversed and guided the vehicle towards the curtain sider in the loading bay. The load scarcely made the trailer move. Bernie had been fascinated by trucks ever since he was a child. He'd loved the big freight lorries and even now would go to the local docks and watch the sea containers being loaded onto the ships. He never stopped marvelling at how the forty-foot corrugated steel boxes looked so large on the road and so small on the ships. One day he'd get a job on the cranes. He'd failed interviews twice so far, but that was just because the managers he'd met were so stupid, he thought. Too dim to see his potential. The last one had even told him he could do with passing some exams. How stupid was that? What qualifications did you need to drive a crane? Jolted from his contemplations, he saw that he was being beckoned by Dave Bradwell, the lorry's driver.

'I dun it for yer.'

'Done what?' replied Bernie.

'What you asked. I dumped the bag in a bin in Whitby.' Dave pulled a packet of cigarettes from his pocket, offered one to Bernie and then lit up.

'Where?'

'Truck stop. In the roll-top wheelies out back.'

'Anyone see you?'

'No.' Dave pursed his lips and casually blew the smoke into the air yet making sure he avoided Bernie's face.

'Cameras?'

'Oh, come on Bernie. It's the back of the caff. Just the bins. Nothing to steal. Nothing to see. No cameras. I dun wot you asked.'

'Good.'

'So that's this week's payment sorted then?' Dave asked, as he watched Bernie run the calculations.

'Yes, this week's.'

'Thanks mate.'

Bernie nodded and spun away in the forklift.

Dave leaned against the back of the truck and lit a second cigarette from the glowing tip of the first. What's he up to then? Dave wondered. Been fleecing me for months. With his income from driving for the Gainsborough Boys' drugs cartel, Dave could easily afford the money. True, he could have told Justin Gainsborough all about his little problem and Bernie would be gone, just like that. Unfortunately, one of the many problems with Justin was that you never knew how he would react. If he discovered that Bernie had found out about the other reasons for the runs up north, not only would Justin have Bernie dealt with, it could be Dave's turn too. Nah, truth be told, fifty quid a week and the flat rent wasn't that much, but why has he let me off the bullseye this week? Just for dumping a bag of women's clothes. Odd, thought Dave, very odd. Bleeding good job I hung onto 'em. Might get the bastard off me back once and for all.

CHAPTER TWENTY

'Aspen says you won't let her tidy up Jade's room.' Carlson poured himself a whisky, then raised the bottle questioningly at his wife. She shook her head and leaned back in the pale green armchair. She plucked at an imaginary thread. Carlson added a splash of water from a small jug as she replied, 'I don't want it touched.'

'But isn't it about time, love?'

'No, not for me it isn't.' Marguerite thumped the chair's arm. 'I can't bear to close the door, either. I hate this house without her. It's deathly. Too quiet.'

'I miss her too, Mags,' Carlson murmured. 'I miss her desperately, but we do have another daughter. Aspen needs us too. She's given up a whole year of university to be with us. Don't you think she deserves some attention as well?'

'Do you think I don't know all that?'

'So why are you pushing her away? You two have always been so close.'

Marguerite shrugged. She shook her head, winced and rubbed her temples. He knelt beside her chair.

'Come on, love, talk to me. What's going on?'

'I don't know, Ronnie. I can't cope anymore! I wake each day and for a moment I've forgotten. Then it all comes back. I can't take it anymore. I can't take all the blame on my own. Ronnie? Ronnie, listen to me!' She clutched his forearm, digging her fingers in and preventing him from moving away.

He looked at her hand and then returned his gaze to the glass. Watching the water meld into the single malt. Swirling patterns where the two liquids had not yet meshed. He raised it to his lips and sipped. The liquid was cool at first then warming as it slid down past his chest to his stomach. She released the fervent grip and her hand slipped away as he stood up and walked to the fireplace. He placed the whisky on the mantelpiece and breathed in before he turned to face her. 'Blame?' he whispered. 'Who blames you? All this time I thought you blamed me. What kind of man can't protect his own child? His own family?' Carlson saw his wife flinch as his voice rose to a shout. He flexed his aching hands; he'd not realised he'd been clenching his fists.

He turned back to the mantelshelf and picked up the tumbler again. Looking closely at the glass, he saw the knuckles surrounding it were paler than the rest of his hand. He watched as the glass sailed across the room, hitting the wall and smashing into minute pieces. The sound made them both jump. Pale rust rivulets ran down the eau de nil wallpaper, pooling on the hardwood floor and encapsulating the crushed crystal.

'Oh, well done, Ronnie,' said Marguerite wearily. 'Once again you've made it all about you. And you can clear that up.' She pointed at the debris. 'I've taken about as much from you as I can manage. I'm going to bed. You! You can sleep in the spare room.'

The door closed quietly behind her. Seeing the wasted

Macallan on the floor, he thought of the wasted lives he'd seen in his career. He thought finally of Jade. Of her life, her pathetically short wasted life, and he slid down the wall to the floor, put his head in his hands and wept.

Upstairs in her room, Aspen listened to the argument. She heard her mother come upstairs and fumble with her bedroom door. The door didn't slam but clicked shut with a softness that seemed at odds with the brittleness of those in the house. In the silence that followed, Aspen cried too.

The man on the doorstep was dishevelled and slightly out of breath. Despite the short distance from car to house, his dark curls were coated in fine droplets from the drizzle. A gentle steam rose from his suit jacket. She beckoned him to stand in the hallway.

'You must be Aspen,' he said, running his hands through his damp hair.

She nodded.

'I'm Tim Jessop, I work for your Dad. DS Poole sent me to get him. Is he ready?'

'No, he's not quite.' Aspen looked him up and down. She noticed the cute brown eyes which had begun to pucker slightly at the corners, the girlish curls, and yet there was something more about him. An air of intelligence tempered with humour.

He was sizing her up too. She was a little distant, he thought. Not aloof, but as if she'd been lost somewhere far away and was struggling to find her way home. Still, after what she'd been through it was no wonder she was lost, he told himself.

'Okay, could you tell him I'm here? I'll go and wait in the car.' She nodded, and a tiny tendril of pale gold hair fluttered across one eye. Tim had to resist the temptation to tuck it behind her ear.

He turned to go, hesitated, and looked back at her.

'This is my card,' he said. 'If you need someone to talk to. No funny business, just a chat and a drink. Anytime, phone's always on.'

He pressed the card in her hand and turned to leave.

'Call me,' he said, and pulled the door shut behind him.

Aspen looked at the closed door for a moment and then trotted upstairs and knocked on the last bedroom door.

'Dad? Dad, you awake?'

She edged the door open and poked her head through the gap. Carlson was sprawled face down across the bed.

'Dad?' Aspen called. She wondered how long she would need to stay at home and referee her parents' marriage. Already she had missed the autumn term at university. There was no point going back now, and she suspected that all the friends she had made would have moved on without her.

Carlson raised his head and lumbered from his prone position so that he could face her. Punching the pillow, he finally settled for a foetal position on his side. He rubbed his face and, as his hand lowered to his chest, he loosened the tie a little more. He smiled at her, and unable to stop herself, she smiled too.

'Coffee, Dad?'

'Please,' he croaked.

'I'll bring you some up. One of your baby detectives is waiting outside in his car. Your sergeant sent him.'

Carlson rolled over on his back. He swallowed. Unsuccessfully.

'Tell him I'll be down in ten,' he croaked.

'I'll tell him fifteen, Dad,' Aspen looked at her father, mimicking his single raised eyebrow habit. 'You might need a long shower.'

Aspen pulled the door shut, crushing the edges of the card into her palm as she did so. She opened her fist. The card was crumpled, and she flattened it out. She knew she would call him. She really would. Maybe not this week. Maybe not this month. But she would make that call. One day.

She surprised herself by just how soon she did call.

CHAPTER TWENTY-ONE

'I am so glad you could spare the time in your busy schedule.'

'Sorry, I got asked to go and fetch the Guv from home,' Tim said, looking down into the shining, dark eyes of Jane Lacey. A flash of different eyes, different hair came to mind, and he grinned.

'Ha,' she said. 'I've got just the thing to wipe that smile off your face. We've got the lovely task of going through the old case notes, cataloguing and documenting them. The DS and the Guv made a start yesterday, but there's nothing that stood out, so we have some nice warm indoor work on a cold day.'

'Jeez,' Tim groaned. 'Let me get an old t-shirt on before we start. I've got one in my locker. I don't want all that soot and shite on my suit.'

'Good idea,' said Jane. 'Ten mins?'

Tim nodded and went to grab the t-shirt and change. Within the agreed ten minutes he was back. His hands full, he elbowed the handle and pushed the conference room door open with his hips, carefully manoeuvring into the room. He saw Jane's face change from puzzlement to a beaming smile.

'Coffee? You are a superstar,' said Jane. 'I take it all back.'

'Well, if you like that, you'll love this,' said Tim, turning and pushing his bottom at her.

'What?' she spluttered.

'Biscuits,' he said. 'Back pocket. What did you think I meant?'

Jane covered her face in her hands and sniggered.

'Sorry, misunderstanding,' she smirked at him. 'Total misunderstanding.'

There was silence for a while as they worked through the last two boxes opened the day before but not fully catalogued. Once done, Tim put them at the end of the conference table and brought another one from the side console, plonking it in front of Jane. He fetched another over for himself.

'Tim?'

'Yep?' he said, not looking up.

'Have you been through this box already?'

He strolled over to where she was sitting and rifled through the contents. 'Nope,' he said. 'Not me. Why?'

'Look. Some of the bags have been opened.'

'The one I was working through is fine,' said Tim. 'What about the others?'

Jane was already at the side table, pushing boxes around. Of the twenty-three boxes not already reviewed, nine contained bags with clear signs of the tamper tape being ruptured. The two young detectives looked at each other and Jane muttered an expletive.

'Better call Poole,' she said.

Carlson and Poole looked from Tim and Jane to the upturned boxes with dismay.

'Right,' said Carlson. 'It's too late to find out when this happened. I'm pretty sure it couldn't have been while the boxes were here. It must have been earlier. In transit or at the depot. Best thing to do is sort them into two piles. You two can go through all the ones containing bags that have been tampered with, and I want details of exactly the sort of information that's in those bags. Make sure everything tallies with the list inside the lid — if that's been completed or is even still there. Most of the ones we did yesterday had no inventories, so there's a chance we're not just looking at tampering, but missing evidence. Compile a new list per box. And let me know when you find the video tapes.' He began patting his chest to locate the vibration. 'Yes?' he said, putting his mobile to his ear.

'Front desk, Guv. I've got a bloke here reporting his daughter missing,' said Sergeant Dobbs. 'She sounds like she might be the type of young lady that your chap might be interested in.'

'Ah, yes,' sighed Carlson. 'I'd asked him to come in. Can you get him a cup of tea and put him in an interview room? Tell him that Poole and I will be there in a moment.

'Ben,' he said. 'That potential misper I told you about, her Dad's come in.' He turned to the two constables. 'Right, you two, you know what you've got to do?'

'Yes, sir,' they chorused.

'Good. Ben, with me.'

Carlson took a deep breath as he placed his hand on the interview room door handle.

'Mr Hoyes?' he said. 'Thanks for coming in.'

'Yes, that's me, but call me Jeff,' he said, rising to his feet and proffering a hand. 'Thanks for calling. You're right. Me daughter has gone missing. I've not seen her for a couple of days.'

'Tell me about her. You weren't worried about her?'

'Yes, I was. But she's not a child. She has her own life and well… look… okay, so there's no easy way to say this, so I'm just gonna come out with it. It's just been me and Tina since she was about eleven. Her mum died then. Cancer. We were doing okay and then she got to about seventeen and just went off the rails. I'd thought we'd be fine. We'd got through the teenage bit, so I thought I was home dry. What a bloody fool I was.

'She met a boy. He got her into all sorts of shit. Then he dumped her, but not before leaving her hooked on bloody smack. She came back for a while and stole everything we had to sell, so she could pump more of that crap in her veins. I gave up on her. I kicked her out.

'She went and stayed with a mate from school who's also addicted to that shit. Sharon—'

'Sharon Raby?' asked Carlson.

'Yeah that's her. Well, she got my girl on the game. Easier than thieving, she told her. Anyway, I did manage to find her eventually. She got sent down, but it was the best thing that happened to her. She got clean, my Tina did, even started a hairdressing course. She was getting her life back together. Then last week she met up with that bitch Sharon again. Obviously, I was worried about that, but she comes home and for a few days everything seemed back to normal. Then I got home from work on Wednesday and she'd bleached her hair again. She was dressed up like a tart and off she went. "A girl's gotta do what a girl's gotta do," she told me. I ain't seen her since. She's not picking up. Phone's switched off. I don't know what to do. I've seen what's been on the news so I was going to come in and report her missing, but then you called me.'

'Thanks, Mr Hoyes,' said Carlson. 'Miss Raby is known to us —'

'I bet she is.'

'She's known to us because she's been helping with our enquiries. She also reported her concerns about Tina to me, which is why I got in touch with you.'

'Tina said that to me, but I didn't believe her.'

'No?' Carlson asked.

'No. I just thought it was something Sharon had made up. She was always telling lies. Always in trouble, ever since she was a teenager and her mum moved into the street. Tina said she was clean now, but I don't believe that either,' said Jeff.

'Let's get back to Tina. When did you last see her?' Carlson asked.

'Wednesday evening. Like I said, she tarted herself up again and went out. She looked like she was on a mission. She had that stubborn look her mum used to have.'

'Mission. What mission?' Poole interjected.

'Is she the type of girl who would challenge someone? Take them on?' asked Carlson.

'Too bloody right, she would. Tell her not to do sumfing and she'd do it. Nothing could beat her. I remember once —'

'Could you take me through the last time you saw her again?' Carlson interrupted. 'Oh, and did you bring a photo?'

Jeff reached inside his jacket and pulled out a creased photo. He smoothed it out on the table. 'You will let me have it back, won't you?'

'Yes, I'll make sure you have it back as soon as we've taken copies.' Carlson gazed at the bright eyes and defiant expression of a schoolgirl. 'Do you have anything more recent?'

'No, she didn't like her photo being taken much. It was hard enough to get her to have the school photo done. But you'll have mug shots of her, won't you? From when she was arrested. She looks better now, but even so.'

'Yes, we'll have those on file. Right, Mr Hoyes, step me through the events leading up to the last time you saw Tina again.'

CHAPTER TWENTY-TWO

Tim Jessop stood as she walked into the coffee bar. He pulled her chair out, wrestling with it as the leg became entangled under the table.

'I've ordered coffee. Do you like coffee? Sorry, I should have thought. How about tea? I can order some tea? Do you like tea?'

Aspen smiled at him as she loosened her scarf and took off her coat.

'Coffee is fine. Thanks.'

As he sat, he jolted the leg again, spilling the coffee onto the table. Aspen caught the barista's eye and he ambled over with a cloth, wiped the surface and returned with fresh coffee. Order was restored but Aspen couldn't help but wonder if he was the right person to help her. As she began to tell the tale, Tim jotted notes as he listened. When she had finished, the questions he asked and the comments he made were probing, but caring and insightful, and Aspen knew that she'd found the right ally.

'Okay, let me get this right,' he said. 'You don't think Jade was being blackmailed?'

'No, I don't believe so. I think she was being bullied but I don't think they were after anything more than making sure her life was a misery.'

'And what's on her computer?' Tim looked up from his notes and held her eyes a fraction too long. Aspen blushed.

'I don't know,' she replied. 'Mum won't let anyone go in there. I've tried to sneak in for a look, but Mum hardly leaves the house these days. Jade's phone was smashed up. She stamped on it over and over again. Dad was able to get some of the text messages back, but a lot came from pay-as-you-go phones. No contracts. So not traceable. Dad seemed to think that some of the texts didn't show a mobile number at all. Is that even possible?'

Tim nodded and then asked, 'Can you get the laptop to me?'

'I can try. Mum's going back to work next week. I can try then.'

'Would you know her password?'

'Probably not. Is that a problem?'

'Less than you might think,' grinned Tim. 'I have friends in low places who will be more than happy to help.'

'Thanks Tim. I really appreciate this. I have to know why. I know that Dad does too, but as you know, he wasn't allowed to work on the case. Then mum had a breakdown and he took time off to take care of her.' Aspen looked up at him, her blue eyes bright with tears, like sunlight on an azure sea.

Tim missed her next remark, but Aspen was still talking.

'Mum seems dead set against knowing,' she said. 'I think she thinks if she finds out what it was all about, it'll destroy her image of Jade. Her memories of her. I guess' — Aspen faltered — 'I guess she's right in a way. I may not want to know who or why in the end, but somehow the not knowing is worse. Does that make sense?'

'Don't worry. It makes perfect sense. The not knowing why would kill me.' Tim winced as he realised his poor choice of words. 'Sorry, that wasn't quite how I meant to put it. I was thinking "idiot" even as the words came out, but you know what I mean. I would need to know why. I'd *have* to know why. I wouldn't be able to stop until I'd found out the truth.'

'Thanks, Tim.' Aspen shook his hand. 'I hoped you'd understand. So, you're happy to help me?'

'Oh, yes,' he said. 'I'd be happy to help you.'

June 1987

Bernie allowed himself to be boosted up to the small window by Terry Hanslope. He slipped the Swiss Army knife he'd been given between the frames and opened the latch. People were so stupid, he thought. Even with double glazing, with a bit of effort on wooden frames, the latch could still be opened from outside. And Bernie was small enough to squeeze through any gap.

He stuck his hand through the window, reached in and passed the vase of plastic flowers to Terry who was behind him. He heard the tinkle of glass as the vase was thrown disdainfully onto the driveway.

'Shush,' he said. 'Keep the noise down. S'okay for you, you can run. I'm the one stuck inside here.'

'Get a bloody move on then,' replied Terry.

Bernie wriggled into the downstairs toilet, glad to find that the seat was down. He couldn't remember how many houses ago it was, but he'd stepped right into the loo and nearly lost his shoe around the S-bend. He'd had to go home with a wet foot. No fun.

He eased open the cloakroom door and tiptoed to the front door. He slipped back the locks; Terry and three larger boys walked into the house. They were well organised. Each had their own job to do. Each went to their assigned rooms. Bernie liked the kitchens, as he usually found snacks and crisps in the cupboards alongside things in drawers. He was always surprised with the number of people who left cash in a canister in the kitchen. Didn't they know banks were safer? He rifled the kitchen drawers and found a nice silver-looking cake knife. He'd never heard of a cake knife before he'd become part of this gang. He'd learnt so much being with them. Fancy having a special knife just to cut cake! Bernie had not had much cake in his life, even for his birthdays. He sneaked it into the rucksack he'd been handed at the front door and carried on searching.

He heard a strange moaning noise from the darkened conservatory. Curious, he wandered towards the sound and cupped a hand round his eyes to peer into the darkness. A couple were entwined on the floor, her legs wrapped around his torso. They writhed together, and the moaning continued. Bernie was entranced. The woman turned her head towards where he was, but her eyes were closed. Then they weren't closed, and she was screaming. The man jumped up and wrenched the door open. He grabbed Bernie by the shoulder as the woman covered herself. She was still screaming. Alerted by her cries, the other boys ran from the house and off into the darkness. By the time the police arrived the couple had dressed, and only Bernie had been captured.

CHAPTER TWENTY-THREE

'You were giving it some this evening, weren't you?'

'What?' said Shazza. 'What yow mean?' She finished wriggling her foot into the laced trainer. The woman who'd been her bag partner again was smiling down at her.

'You nearly knocked me over with some of those kicks. I was glad I was on the other side of the bag. Come on, you owe me a drink.' Sarah said

'Nah, I'm a bit skint still.'

'Then I'll buy you one. You look like you need one.' Sarah held out a hand and pulled Shazza to her feet.

'Yeah, go on then,' said Shazza. 'It's been a pretty shit week so far, and it's not even hump day.'

The two women crossed the road and shook the rain from their hair and loosened scarves as they entered the pub. Shazza asked for a soft drink.

'You sure?' Sarah asked.

'Yeah, I'm trying to cut down.'

Shazza found a free table and Sarah brought the drinks over.

'Come on, then. What's up?' Sarah asked.

'Me mate has gone missing. Her dad called round this afternoon and was shouting all sorts of stuff at me. Accusing me of...' Shazza hesitated and watched Sarah for a moment. 'Well, some stuff. None of it very nice. I told him I done none of the sort, but he just kept gobbing off at me. I had to kick him out in the end.'

'So where's your friend?'

'Dunno. She's disappeared though,' Shazza wiped the condensation off the exterior of her glass as she spoke.

'You told the police?'

'Yeah, they know,' Shazza bit her lip, unable to look Sarah in the eyes.

Do you think she's been taken by this bloke?' Sarah asked, and immediately regretted making the link so quickly. There was no way she could have Shazza remotely attached to the murders if she hadn't seen her at the station. She was figuring out a way to backtrack when Shazza spoke.

'Maybe,' Shazza's knee bounced and she jiggled the table.

'Shit! You really think so? Oh, Shazza. I'm so sorry. Do you want to keep talking about it?'

'Yes. No. Fuck it. I don't know.' Shazza rubbed her face with her hands and shook her head. 'That's what Tina's dad was shouting about. He thought I was encouraging her to take drugs again.'

Sarah watched her for a moment, scarcely able to contain her excitement. Yes! She had been right all along. This girl did know something. Her mouth had gone dry and her pulse quickened. Unable to decide whether to go just for the surface story or the full inside track, she hesitated. Just a small pause but it was enough for her to realise that she had to be truthful. It might mean Shazza would walk away, but she had to get the girl to trust her. There was one certain way to test that.

Sarah sighed and said, 'Look, Shazza, I should tell you that I'm a reporter. More than that, I found the first girl's body.'

'Josie! Her name was Josie,' Shazza snapped. 'Is that why you've been trying to get to know me. So you can get a story? The low down? Is that all you're after?' Shazza held her chin high, glaring at Sarah, but rather than storming out, which is what Sarah had feared, the young woman sat still. Her eyes full of a strange mixture of defiance and defeat.

Sarah decided not to risk the whole truth.

'No, honestly, I had no idea. Last week when we met, I just thought you were an interesting person and looked like you needed a friend. We all need friends, don't we?' Sarah said.

'But now you're connected to the killings, I thought I should tell you straight away what I do. I don't want you talking to me and not knowing I'm a journalist. That's all.'

Shazza's defiance seemed to leave her.

Sarah played the conversation through in her head. She didn't need to tell Shazza more. She didn't need to admit she'd recognised her from the off. 'Look, I'm sorry about Josie, though. Was she a very close friend?'

'You asking as a reporter or as a friend?'

'Friend,' Sarah said. She placed her hand on Shazza's forearm. Shazza didn't flinch or make to move it. 'I promise.'

'I'm not sure I believes yah, but yeah I knew her. I knew Nat and I knew Tani a little bit too. She and I scored off the same dealer. I guess you being a smart journalist you've already figured out that if I knew them then I was on the game too?'

'I suppose,' said Sarah.

'Cock for rock. That was Tani's phrase. What kept her going, I s'pose.' Shazza leaned back in the chair and let out a big sigh.

'But you're clean now? Off the game? Is that why you've stopped drinking?'

'Yeah, I'm trying to put the old life behind me and keep off the H. I've been scripted for methadone, and therapy sessions too, but if I want to keep clean then I must stay off the booze too. It just weakens your, your —'

'Resistance?'

'Yep.'

'Perhaps you could give me some hints and tips?' Sarah said after a moment's silence.

'Why do you need my help? You seem pretty together,' said Shazza. 'You know, I've been reading them stories in the paper. The ones about Josie and Nat. Are they all by you then? Are yam all doin' the writing?'

Sarah nodded.

Shazza held her gaze on Sarah, as if trying to decide to trust her or not. Finally, she said, 'I like the way you do it. You don't forget that they had families and friends. So, come on tell me, what's your problem?'

Sarah gave a low whistle, leaned forward and rested her forearms on the table. It was a move she instantly regretted, and she pulled her arms off the sticky table.

'I've just come back to live here,' she began, realising that if she wanted Shazza's story she would have to give up her own. 'I had a great job in London. Nice bloke, nice flat, everything was great. Then one day I picked up the phone and it was my brother, Phil, in New Zealand. We'd not spoken in ages and I was so excited to hear from him — that is, until he told me why he was calling.' Sarah swigged her drink and sat looking at the empty glass.

Sarah felt the noise in the bar ebb away as she remembered that conversation. She made to continue, but instead went to the bar and ordered herself another drink.

When she returned and sat down, she said, 'He was calling to tell me about our parents. They'd just retired and were on a cruise. All around the South China Sea. Mum had talked of nothing else for weeks. They flew into Singapore and boarded the cruise ship there. Thailand, Vietnam, Malaysia, the Philippines, the lot, then they were due to fly to Christchurch and stay with Phil for a couple of months.' Sarah took a swig of her gin and a deep breath before she carried on speaking. 'Except they didn't get there. I don't know the full story, I'm not sure Phil does either, but the coach they were on in Vietnam crashed on a mountain pass. It came off the road, rolled, and no one survived,' Sarah's eyes misted, and she took another gulp, almost emptying the glass.

'I agreed with my brother they could be buried near him in New Zealand, so I flew out there, and I don't think I stopped drinking the whole flight. Afterwards I came back and did the same on the return flight. Jason, my bloke, was disgusted when he picked me up. I could hardly stand, he said,' Sarah twisted her glass around in the puddle of condensation; it was her whole focus for almost a minute before she continued. 'Anyway, when I got back, I couldn't stop drinking. Then I lost my job and after a while, when I couldn't pay my way, Jason kicked me out. He changed his mind after I got my inheritance from Mum and Dad, the bastard, but I'd lost all faith in him by then. Being evicted by my own boyfriend did sober me up for a while and I'm not drinking as much as I was, but every so often, I go and hide at the bottom of a bottle. I went to see a therapist briefly but that didn't seem to help all that much, so I decided to come back to kickboxing. I did it three times a week in London and got quite good.' she sipped at the nearly empty glass, blew her nose and looked at Shazza. 'So that's my sorry tale. What about you? Why's your friend's dad so annoyed with you?'

For a moment Shazza was silent.

'He thought I encouraged Teens to go back on the game,' she began. 'Twat! He hardly knew her at all. Thing is, I hadn't, but I think I might have done worse.'

Sarah waited, but Shazza was not forthcoming.

'I'm here to listen if you want, Shazza,' she prompted.

'I think Teens might have decided to go after the bloke who's doin' the killings.'

Sarah battled not to gasp. She could feel the gin coursing through her and bit her tongue to stay quiet.

'Once Tina made up her mind to do something there was no stopping her. I told her not to do owt stupid and she just went ahead and dun exactly what she wanted to do. Her dad said she bleached her hair and looked like she was back on the game. Said she was dressed up like a tart again. He reckons it's all my fault. I couldn't tell him I thought it was worse than that. I couldn't tell him I think she got it into her head to go after this bloke. But I didn't ask her to do anything more than think about the photos.'

'Photos? What photos?' Sarah asked.

'The cops called me in to look at some photos of a flat. I don't know how they got hold of them, but I talked it over with Tina, then she texts me to say she knows who he is, then she ups and disapp —' Shazza stopped abruptly.

Sarah held her breath and waited.

'Shit. I shouldn't have told you that. I don't want this

appearing in your rag! I mean it, Sarah, forget I said anything. I should go. I'm sorry about your parents, I really am, but I've gotta go. Thanks for the drink.' Shazza stood up and her chair clattered to the floor. Several people turned around to look.

'Shazza! Talk to me. Please!' Sarah begged.

But Shazza was already at the door and off into the night.

CHAPTER TWENTY-FOUR

Tina pushed open the door of the public bar at the Bell. Gary, in his usual spot behind the bar, tilted his head to one side, frowning slightly before he nodded to her.

'Back again, love? I wasn't expecting to see you again so soon,' he said. 'Usual?'

She smiled at him and slid onto a bar stool, her feet barely touching the toe rail. Gary poured a vodka and slimline tonic water for her, two slices of lemon, no ice.

'Thanks,' she said.

'I really thought you'd moved on from this life,' he said.

'Yeah, I had, but something Shazza said made me want to come and have a look round again.'

'Has she caught up with you yet? She keeps calling me, asking if I've seen you,' he placed both hands on the bar.

Tina shook her head. 'Yeah, we keep missing each other,' she lied, as she slid a tenner across to him.

'Okay, you take it easy girl.'

'I will,' she replied, taking her change.

Gary stepped away as another customer had come to the bar. Tina slid off the stool and moved to a table where she had a good view of the rest of the room. She drummed a beat as she waited tap, tap with her foot and a slap with the hand on her knee, all the time the fingers of her left hand drumming a different beat. She wondered what life would have been like if she'd carried on with the drumming and not taken that first hit. No use worrying about what might have beens, she thought. Tina decided to make this her last night searching for him. She'd call Shazza, get the name of the copper and let him know everything she'd found out from the other street girls. She'd only been looking for the punter for a couple of days with no sign, but she was fed up with sleeping on floors and the constant temptation of the brown was getting too much. It would be all too easy to slip into that life again. She had begun to wonder if she'd made a mistake and perhaps he'd moved away. Someone walked past her table and she looked up at the passing man. Shit, it's him! Tina put her hand out for the vodka. Looking at the man and not the glass, she hit it and knocked it over. She scrabbled to rescue it, but the cool liquid slid across the table and onto the floor. Gary whistled, and she deftly caught the tea towel that he threw at her.

'Can I get you another?' the man in front of her said.

'Yeah, sure,' she replied. 'Vodka slimline, lemon but no ice. Gary knows how I like it.'

'I bet he does,' he said.

When he came back with her drink, he placed his beer on the table and sat without asking if that was okay.

Tina wasn't surprised. She knew how she was dressed, and most men did not feel they had to be polite to a working girl. Some did, but they were the exception.

'Not getting any warmer, is it?' he said.

Tina nodded, staring at his pale eyes, unable to start a conversation.

Her companion had no such qualms. From the weather he moved onto sport, tried films, books. Tina just nodded, unable to take her eyes off him but unable to speak either.

'Are you waiting for someone?' he finally asked.

'No,' she said. 'No one in particular.'

'I was looking for business,' he said. 'You interested?'

'Nah, I'm waiting for a friend,' she said.

'You just said you weren't waiting for anyone. So, what is it? Business, or you wasting my time?' he asked.

'I've gotta go,' she said. She held up her phone as if it were a defence. 'Mate just texted and asked me round. See yah later.'

'Okay,' he said, and ignoring her he turned back to his drink.

Tina tried to catch Gary's eye, but he was deep in conversation with one of his regulars. He did not see her leave.

Once she was outside the pub, Tina leant against its walls, breathing deeply. The pub door opened, a shaft of light shining on the damp pavements, and the man was there staring into the dark. Tina was sure he was trying to see where she'd gone, and she pressed herself against the wall behind the hanging plants. The man headed off around the corner and Tina decided to follow him. She crept behind him, trying to keep herself hidden and type a text to Shazza. When she raised her head, he was nowhere to be seen. She looked up and down the street and, following her gut instinct over logic, she headed south east. Bursford Road was very still when she turned into it. None of the shop fronts here had the beautifully lit displays of the high street; instead, their shutters were down, gaudy with graffiti and the Gainsborough Boys' tags. She winced as her heels echoed in the calm night, wishing she'd worn soft soles. She had had some in her early teens and she grinned, remembering her Dad calling them brothel creepers — if only he'd known! But this was no laughing situation, and she clattered down the road before stopping outside a door wedged between two barricaded shop windows. This was it, she was certain. She took a shot with her camera phone and turned to leave. She was no longer alone. The man from the pub had grabbed her elbow and was squeezing it hard. Tina whimpered with the pain.

'Hello.' He leaned in closely and Tina could smell his sour breath. 'You again. What are you after?'

'Nothing,' she replied, breathing heavily, 'Just checking the address. I think I got lost.'

'Don't worry, I'll take care of you. And you won't be needing this for a while,' he said. He took the phone from her, dropped it on the pavement, ground it under his heel and kicked it into the gutter. Opening the door behind him, he propelled Tina up the stairs and through a battered green door. He shoved her down the dark hallway and into the main room where he switched on the light.

Tina saw the battered sofa and the dirty rug. Well, she thought, I was right. However, she'd never intended to go in the flat, just find out where it was, and she had no idea how she was going to get out again. For the first time, it occurred to her that she may not escape from the seedy room.

'Drink?' he said, opening a door on the sideboard. Tina gasped at his calmness. He was acting as if she was there as a guest.

'No, I'm fine,' she said, rubbing her elbow. 'In fact, I'd like to go. I was supposed to be meeting someone. I told you I was just lost, and you fucking pushed me in here.'

Tina started backing into the hallway and towards the door. She turned and made it to the front door, but he'd double locked it when he came in. She was trapped. She pulled at the lock, but his hand closed over hers.

'Where do you think you're going?' his smooth voice whispered in her ear. 'You're here now and we are going to have some fun. That's what you were looking for, wasn't it?'

'No,' Tina hissed. 'No. Let me out. Let me go! I know. I know.' As the words left her lips, Tina rolled her head back, closing her eyes as she realised her mistake.

'Know what?' he asked. 'What do you know? Are you the one who's been asking all the questions about me?'

She stared at him, mute but defiant.

'What do you know?' he asked. He slapped the heel of his hand against her ear. 'What. Do. You. Know?' With each word he slapped her head until it was ringing.

'Nothing,' she said. 'I don't know nothing. I want to go now. My friend's waiting for me.'

'You are going nowhere,' he snapped. 'Your phone? Who were you calling?'

He swore softly, and Tina realised he was remembering what he'd done to the phone. Now he would not be able to see who she'd contacted at all.

'Who were you calling?' he repeated.

He wrenched her wrist, twisting it around until she thought it would break. Tina shrieked, but continued to struggle. He hit her again, smashing her head against the wall behind her making it spin.

He pressed his face to her and whispered, 'I told you girlie,' he said, pulling her down the hallway by her hair. 'You're staying with me.'

CHAPTER TWENTY-FIVE

Dave Bradwell would not have called himself a curious man, although he was very interested in what Bernie Latimer had been up to. Why was Bernie asking him to dump women's clothing, he wondered? It wasn't just the odd pair of stray knickers that his wife, Rose, may have found in the car. It seemed to be entire outfits. That first lot looked pretty new. It would be good to put paid to Bernie's blackmail — not for the money, though that rankled a little, but it was a question of principle. Dave knew people who could sort Bernie out permanently, but that would come to the attention of the management. It had taken Dave a long time to rise in the ranks; from direct supply as a youngster, to Elder, running a gang of Youngers, and now he had moved to wholesale supply. He was making much more money as a drug supplier than he was as a lorry driver, but he needed the cover to be up and down the motorway without raising suspicion. There were spies everywhere — automatic number plate recognition or ANPR as the boys in blue liked to call it was, in Dave's opinion, the worst invention of all.

Still, he'd have to find out what Bernie's game was, and

perhaps once he'd done that, he could sublet the flat and get some actual cash for it rather than letting that weasel Bernie have it for free. Dave knew that on Monday evenings Rose Latimer didn't work. Bernie stayed home with her and they had a curry and two beers each. Dave was aware of this because of the constant complaints about the two small bottled beers, not even a decent pint. It was the same every Monday, and Dave did not understand why Bernie put up with it; he'd never let himself be henpecked.

He made his way to the flat and put his key in the lock of the battered green door. He'd have to give it a lick of paint if he was going to get a decent rent, he decided. The door clicked behind him. The hall light was not working, and he felt his way down the hall to the living room. All was clean — well, cleanish — and tidy, and Dave could smell the faint chlorine scent of bleach. The kitchen was pretty spotless, and a search of the bedroom revealed nothing at all. What was he up to? Dave was convinced that Bernie needed the flat for something off the books. Something that he couldn't do at home and something that he didn't want the wife finding out about. What the hell was it? The news was full of the three working girls found dead, but that couldn't be Bernie. Or could it? He plonked himself on the sofa and leaned back with his left ankle crossed over the right knee. There was a tripod leant against the TV, and underneath, on the glass stand, he noticed an old VHS device perched on top of a DVD player. He walked across to them and switched the machines on to see what was in the drives, but neither one contained anything. He went to the sideboard. Opening the doors, he found a camcorder. Interesting, he thought. What's he want that for? He saw a metal box which he pulled out, but it was padlocked. It rattled when he shook it. Porn? Dave wondered. Perhaps that's all it was. Maybe Rose was the puritanical sort. He'd had to get rid of his own collection when he'd moved in with Julie. Dave was somewhat disappointed to find out it was probably something so unoriginal. Sod it, he thought. I was hoping to get something on the bastard. He picked up the keys and made to leave. Nah, he thought, I'll have a pee first.

Opening the bathroom door, he found that the smell of bleach was stronger. He lifted the lid and let go a long stream of urine which fizzed in the bowl. He flushed, washed his hands and moved the shower curtain to see where the towel was.

The girl was slumped in the empty bath. Eyes bulging, with her tongue protruding and her damp hair barely covering vicious-looking head wounds. Her skin was very pale and the red wheals on her neck stood out starkly.

Although he'd seen dead bodies before — one or two he'd even helped into that condition — Dave was shocked. He had a code. No women. He sat on the bathroom floor, leaning against the radiator while he tried to make sense of it. He couldn't. Rising onto his knees he slid closer to the bath.

Shit, Bernie, Dave muttered, as he lent over her, the sibilant exploding from his mouth, what the hell have you been up to? He knew the girl was dead but still felt the need to check. He felt for her pulse. He pressed harder, but still no beat. Yep, she was definitely dead. Flopping back onto the floor, he pushed himself away from the girl and the bath, propping himself against the radiator once more, and ran scenarios through his head.

One, he could go to the police, but he would have to explain why he was letting Bernie use the flat and why he'd come here to find out what Bernie was up to. There were no guarantees that Bernie would not dob him in once arrested.

Two, he could call the Gainsborough Boys and have

someone take the body away and clean the flat up, but again he would have to explain to the management why he'd let Bernie use the flat. Back to the reasons that he didn't have the Gainsborough Boys take Bernie out in the first place. Too risky to yours truly, he thought.

Three, he could get up, wash his hands and get the hell out of there. If Bernie had killed the girl — and, shit, had he killed the others too? — then he must have thought through how he was going to get rid of this girl. Three it was.

He found a cloth in the kitchen and wiped every surface he thought he had touched, put the cloth in his jacket pocket, washed his hands again and wiped them on his jeans. He closed the bathroom door firmly, switched off the lights and locked the front door behind him. Once in the street he gasped. He'd not realised he'd been holding his breath, but at least now he knew how to get that bastard Bernie Latimer off his back.

CHAPTER TWENTY-SIX

'Okay, okay. Hey! Settle down.' Poole held his hand up but, frustrated by the noise, he put his thumb and index finger together and placed them in his mouth. One very sharp whistle later, most of the team turned towards him with hands over their ears, crouching as if the noise were a hail of bullets, but the entire squad room was silent.

'Thank you,' said Poole. 'Now we'll go through the updates.

'These are photos of Tina Hoyes,' he said, slamming the pictures onto the white board. 'She won't look like this anymore, as one, she's grown up, and two, she's cleaned up her act and looks a darn sight healthier. However, when her father came in he did tell us that she'd died her hair blonde again and was dressed in the type of gear she used to wear when she was working the red-light district. We have no idea why she has come back here but we do know she was last seen in The Bell on Saturday night and she has not been seen since then. Witnesses are a bit confused; some say she was alone and some say she was talking to a man, but all of them say she did leave the pub on her own. Hopefully, she left of her own accord; however' — Poole laboured the intensity on the word — 'she has not answered any calls or texts since before the weekend. The good news is that her dad recently treated her to a smartphone, the bad news is that this has been off the grid since late Saturday. We are tracking her movements via that phone. Tina was at home on Wednesday, but her father has not heard from her at all since then. The last contact she had with her friend Shazza was when she texted that she knew who matey was. What concerns the Guv and me is that she may have tried to find out who he is on her own.'

Poole let his last comment sink in before he handed round copies of the photographs and organised areas for house-to-house enquiries.

Bernie Latimer put his tray on the floor having finished his Monday night curry. He picked up the small bottle of beer and swigged the last of it.

Rose looked at him, afraid that the usual argument would start any moment, but she liked their Monday evenings in front of the telly and, if he drank too much, he snored. Bernie's snoring was like a goods train on broken rails. She only had one night a week of sleeping at night-time without being disturbed. It would be good if she could give up the night work, but it paid so well and what with Bernie never being able to hold a job down for long, she knew she was stuck with it. She sighed.

'Oh, go on then,' she said, 'have another one.'

Bernie gave her a grin that made her heart melt, just as it had done when she'd first met him at the fair. She'd not been keen to go out that evening, but her friends had persisted until she'd finally agreed. Those were friends she didn't see any more. She'd met Bernie that night. He worked the dodgems and they'd looked down their noses at him.

'Rose, you can do so much better,' they'd said.

'But he's what I want,' she'd replied, and, one by one, they drifted away. They were right, of course. Rose realised that now, but she still found that she could not leave him. She loved him and, when he smiled at her, the world shone and was a different place.

She watched him as he flicked channels and decided that if she really wanted to stop working nights, it was now or never.

'Bernie, love...' she began.

'What?' he mumbled, focused on the remote, the television screen and his beer.

'I've been thinking.' Her voice sounded weedy and pathetic even to her own ears, but she carried on. 'I've been thinking that I'd like to get some qualifications, you know, an adult's education course, so I can get some GCSEs and get an office job. That way we can spend more time together. You'd like that, wouldn't you?'

Bernie looked across at her with the mouth of his beer bottle resting against his lips.

'When would you be doing this course?' he said.

'It's a day-time course. Three times a week.'

'In the day?' he asked. 'Who's going to cook my tea?'

'Well, I thought that you could cook on those days.'

'You did, did you?' He sneered, and Rose changed tack, conscious of the change in his mood.

'Or perhaps I could make you something in advance and you could heat it up when you got in,' she gabbled. It had all sounded so much better in her head.

'And how are you going to pay for this course?' he asked, looking at her and then back at the beer bottle.

'I do earn my own money, Bernie,' she retorted.

He stepped closer and she raised her hands to protect her face. He grabbed her hands in one of his and held the bottle up high, but he dropped it, letting the liquid spew over the carpet. He smirked at her as he twisted her wrists until she squealed.

'Your money?' he mocked, 'Since when has it been your money? I put a roof over your head, don't I?'

Rose decided that now might not be the time to mention that her money paid the rent, bought the food and settled the household bills. Bernie's income seemed to keep him in beer, cigarettes, a few clothes and very little else.

He let go of her hands and she rubbed her wrists.

'I'll think about it,' he said. 'Let me see the cost of the course and how much more you can earn with a day job and I'll decide whether it's worth it or not. Though how you think you can keep an office job if you can't keep track of your own things is beyond me. You'll have to maintain a diary, file papers and all that. I can't see how you'll manage — you're always losing stuff. And I let you have that weekend away with your sister, so I've still got the expense of that to cover. We'll have to see.'

'Thank you, honey,' she said, reflecting on the long weekend at her sister's house, and how she'd not lost her keys, her purse or her phone even once whilst she'd been away.

Bernie returned to flicking channels and finally settled on the news. The lead story was the same as it had been for days now.

'What makes someone do such dreadful things?' she asked, trying to appease him.

'I don't know love,' he lied.

Bernie always lied convincingly. He knew all too well why he did the things he did. He couldn't remember quite why he'd gone to the first prostitute. He'd never had any problem finding women for sex, but they always wanted something more. Security, income, and love, for fuck's sake. They all whined about love. It was more than he ever wanted to provide. Paying for sex was a pain too, but at least nothing more was expected of him and, if he cut up a bit rough, which he sometimes liked to do, then he just paid a tad more. If the bitch was still awake enough to remember. He thought back to Reigate. The fair had been in town for a whole week and he was bored of the nice girls. He went trawling for something more adventurous and he found it. She was somewhat older than the other girls, but that just made her more desperate for the money. Getting squeezed out by the competition, she complained. He thought she'd be more streetwise but when she took him back to her flat there was a kid asleep in a cot.

'S'okay,' she slurred. 'He won't wake. He never does.'

'You leave him alone? What kind of a mother are you?'

'He's fine. I give him a little something, so he doesn't scream the place down. I need to work. I could get a job in a shop but then all my wages would go on childcare.'

'But you can't leave him here alone!' Bernie found he was yelling.

'What the fuck has it got to do with you?' she said. 'I go out, do three or four Johns and then I come home again. I don't usually bring anyone back. You're an exception.'

'Just like my bloody mother,' he said.

'Your mother? She was a tom too?'

'Yeah, she was. Until she got killed by a punter. Do you let anyone touch him?'

'Sure, if the price is right,' she laughed.

The sound of the slap echoed around the small bedsit.

'Fuck's sake. What you do that for? I was fucking joking. Do you think I'd let anyone near my kid?' She wiped the blood from her lip. Her eyes were cold, face white with fury. She looked around and picked up the frying pan from the hob. It was full of greasy water which coated his new shirt as she swung it at him. He blocked her parry and knocked the pan from her hand. He slapped her again, knocking her to the ground and then helped her to her feet with his hands on her throat. He grasped tighter and tighter. Gurgling sounds came from her and the child woke, screaming. Bernie snapped to attention. He dropped his hands and ran from the flat. He rushed down the street and raced off into the night. When he felt safe, he stopped. He leaned against a wall and slid to the ground. His pants were soaked. He was still shaking with anger and fear at what he'd almost done. At first, his mind was numb. He was still quivering, feeling helpless, then everything became clear again. He scrabbled for the handkerchief he had put in his pocket earlier. He used it to wipe at his trousers but, feeling the stickiness on the inside, he stuffed the hanky into his pants. Bernie realised that, even though he'd already killed someone, the act of throttling the woman had turned him on like nothing had in his life before.

CHAPTER TWENTY-SEVEN

'Gypsy? Gypsy, where are you?' Gracie Evans called, looking frantically around. Low hanging mist hampered her vision but yapping from the centre of the copse in the hollow revealed the dog's location.

'You little sod. What are you doing there?' Gracie lumbered slowly down the slope to where the small dog was digging in the leaves. 'Come here! Now!' she commanded. Gypsy kept rummaging in the debris. Something pale and plastic appeared, but Gypsy kept scrabbling away. When the hand emerged, Gracie stood for a moment, unbelieving. Her jaw slackened but she jumped into action. She picked up the dog and made her way carefully back up the hill to the path. In her excitement she dropped her mobile, but it still worked well enough for her to call 999. Afterwards, Gracie stood on the path with her face buried in the fur on Gypsy's neck. She listened to the single bird chirping and the cascade of dew on leaves as a squirrel scampered up a tree. Sighing, she knew this was the last time she would ever enjoy the peaceful, natural sounds of the woods. It was the last moment she could ever enjoy this space alone.

. . .

Poole approached the old woman cautiously; he was not a fan of small snappy yappies, as he thought of them. Carlson was right about it always being the dog walkers. Poole wondered if he was also right about the possibility of crimes going unnoticed without them prowling the countryside. He hoped not.

The woman and her schnauzer looked the same. Grey facial hair, sour expression, matching frowns. She stood glaring at the crime scene technicians as if she thought they were doing it all wrong. Hearing the crunch of his footsteps on the stone path, she turned to face him.

'Mrs Evans?' he asked.

'Ms,' she replied. 'Not married. Never have been. But that's no one's business but my own. Now, who are you, young man, and what may I do for you?'

'DS Poole,' he replied, flashing his warrant card in front of her. 'I'd like to ask you a few questions.'

'Oh yes, of course,' she said.

Poole noticed that her eyes shone with excitement.

'I walk here every day with Gypsy. Early, so we have the woods to ourselves. I don't suppose I'll be doing that anymore,' she sighed. She related all the events and her actions to Poole. 'As soon as I realised it was a body, I picked Gypsy up and I walked backwards up the hill. I made sure I stepped in exactly the same place as I'd put my feet on the way down. I knew it was a crime scene and I didn't want to disturb it.'

Poole felt loathe to point out that by entering the area she'd already disturbed the scene, but he let her continue.

'I fell over, but only once, see. I don't think I dropped anything.' She put a hand in her pocket as she spoke, giving the dog a few small biscuits. 'Oh, maybe I dropped some of these. Will you want some for evidence? To exclude them from your enquiries?'

'You're very well up on forensics, if I may say so ma'am.' Poole forced his voice to remain neutral, trying hard to maintain his composure.

'Oh yes, my love. I've watched every episode of *Words of the Dead* that's been on. But I liked Sam, not this new one. What's she called? Gemma? Don't get me wrong, I love the actress, but the way she marches around in those high heels and tight clothes? Not my idea of a serious scientist at all.'

Poole let Ms Evans carry on talking; his experience told him that eventually she'd say something useful, something he could use. And there it was, the speck of gold. Ms Evans had seen a grey van in the lane. No, she'd not seen it before and she didn't see a driver. She couldn't remember the make and had not taken the plate number, but it did have a long scratch near the rear wheel arch on the passenger side. Would that help?

'It will indeed, Ms Evans,' said Poole. 'Do you need anyone to drive you home? I'll get someone to pop by later and take a more formal statement, but you've been very help-ful. Very helpful indeed.'

Poole was grinning as he returned to the outer cordon.

'What are you laughing about?' asked Kirsty Russell.

'The old lady,' he said. 'You would have loved her. Big fan of your favourite show.'

'Don't tell me,' Kirsty rolled her eyes. 'Witless Witness?'

'You guessed it,' Poole laughed. 'Oh, and I've got these for you.' He held up two evidence bags.

Kirsty frowned.

'She traced her steps back to the path, but as she was walking backwards, she tripped over. These are dog biscuits she may have dropped, and this' — he held up the second bag — 'is a sample of her hair in case any got caught in the branches.'

Kirsty smiled broadly. 'I might give her a job,' she said.

DS Poole drew the car to a halt just shy of the road bike in Jervis Kilburn's designated parking slot. It was something of a standing joke that Dr Kilburn retained the space even when he was training for a long-distance event and cycled everywhere that he reasonably could.

DCI Carlson sat for a moment, eyes closed and with his head against the rest.

'Sir?' said Poole.

'Yes, I'm coming,' he said. 'This is the fourth one now. I was just praying that we catch him before he kills anyone else. It's becoming like Lytham all over again.'

'We'll get him, Guv,' said Poole grimly.

Carlson didn't reply. He opened the door and heaved himself from the seat with a deep sigh. He was also wondering if he was getting too old for the job. Or perhaps the time off on compassionate leave had slowed him down. Or perhaps it was just this case. The age of the victims, or, more realistically, their lack of age. Everything before them, all that hope and opportunity. But then he realised he was thinking about Jade and not these girls at all. Need to focus on the job, Ronnie, he said to himself. When all this was over he would do some serious thinking about his future.

Dr Jervis Kilburn was waiting in his office for them. Kirsty Russell was there too.

'Ronnie,' he began.

'I know, don't tell me,' Carlson groaned. 'Same MO. Washed carefully. No trace evidence. Nothing to go on at all.'

'Actually no,' said Dr Kilburn. 'Different. Very different.'

He waved Carlson and Poole to the seats facing his desk, but it was Kirsty who spoke first.

'As you saw at the scene, Ronnie, this young lady had suffered a great deal more head trauma than our previous victims. Although, yes, she had been washed too, there was some leakage from a head wound while she was transported. We've found some small fibres. Possibly car carpet fibres —'

'Well, that's good news,' interjected Carlson.

'Ronnie, that's not the good news. Well, it is good news, but it gets better.' Kirsty leaned forward in her chair, her eyes shining with excitement. 'After she was washed it seems someone checked her pulse. We found an index finger impression on the radial pulse area. They pressed quite hard and they left a bruise.'

'Have we got him, then?' asked Poole.

'Are you telling me we can get prints off the bruise?' asked Carlson.

Jervis and Kirsty shook their heads.

'So, how's this good news? Does it help us or not?' Poole asked.

'Maybe, maybe not. If our guy had beaten her and asphyxiated her as he did and then washed her, I rather think he would know she was dead. Someone else may have come across her and tried the radial to see if she was alive. Why they didn't call it in is another question. But it's a bit of a break, and the first we've had, so certainly worth pursuing.'

'And are we absolutely certain that this killer was the same as the one who killed the other girls?'

Jervis and Kirsty looked at each other and then looked at the police officers. They nodded.

'Based on what?' asked Carlson.

'Based on the washing, the cleansing. It's the same product. Now, yes, I know it's pretty cheap and a popular brand,' said Kirsty, 'but the pattern is similar enough to the other three girls for us to be sure that, even with the deviation in method of dispatch, it's still the same person.

'But,' said Kirsty, 'we still haven't given you the best news. Now, given how careful our guy has been up until now, there's a likelihood that this is the second person, the one who checked her pulse, rather than the one we want, but when we ran the black light over her, we recovered some saliva from the cornea and her left cheek. Only a few specks, but it may be enough to get DNA.'

Carlson leaned back in the chair and rubbed his hands over his face. 'Good,' was all he said.

CHAPTER TWENTY-EIGHT

Carlson paced up the stairs to her flat. Each step was taken meticulously, trying to maintain space between him and the conversation he was about to have. When he reached her door, he stood for a moment, finger poised over the bell. No need.

She wrenched the door open and it clattered against the wall. Two small pieces of plaster dropped to the floor. Laying white in contrast to the dark carpet. Like shards of a broken heart.

'You've found her?' Shazza asked, even though she already knew the answer.

'Yes, love. I'm sorry. Can I come in?'

She flung the door into the wall again and marched down the corridor. When he reached the living room, she was hunched in her usual chair, folded in on herself.

'Was it him?'

'Yes, we're pretty sure it was,' he replied. He wanted to tell her of the team's convictions but, since it appeared Tina tried to track down the killer herself, he did not want to encourage Shazza down the same path.

'Pretty sure? Pretty? Yam don't know for definite?' Shazza's Black Country accent was stronger in her grief and anger. Her hazel eyes were flecked with specks of amber he'd not noticed before. 'Why ain't you schu-er?' The last word was spat out at him.

'There were differences,' he said. 'I can't go into too much detail, but how she died —'

'What? How she died, what?'

'She was strangled, like the other three,' Carlson said, 'but not with a scarf.'

'With what then?'

'Manual strangulation,' Carlson sought refuge in the formal words.

'What does that mean?'

'He used his hands, love. He used his hands,' he whispered. 'I am so sorry, Shazza, so very, very sorry.'

Shazza flung herself back in the chair. For a moment she sprawled, staring at the ceiling, then she drew her limbs close and, in this foetal position, she began to sob.

Carlson watched, helpless. After a moment he rose, took a pack of tissues from his pocket and placed them on the arm of the chair and went to the small kitchen. He was surprised how clean it all was, then reprimanded himself for those thoughts. He made tea and brought it into the main room.

Shazza was still curled in a ball but the sobs had subsided to sniffs.

'There are some biscuits in the cupboard,' she said.

'I'm on it.' When he came back in the room he laid the biscuit pack on the table and Shazza grabbed a couple.

'Thank you,' she muttered, dunking a Hobnob in her drink. 'For the tea and for coming to tell me. I know you didn't have to do that.'

'In a way I think I did,' said Carlson. 'I didn't want you to find out from the TV.' He watched her carefully, trying to judge how she had taken the news. Better than he had expected. He found himself wondering if she'd anticipated not seeing Tina again.

'Thanks,' she said after a while. She wiped her eyes again and took a deep breath. 'So, what now? You any closer to catching him?'

'We've got some leads.'

'What does that mean? No?'

Carlson took a deep breath and gazed at a damp spot on the ceiling. 'You should get your landlord to sort that.'

'I will,' she replied. 'I'm still sorting me at the moment.' Shazza looked at the damp patch and then at Carlson.

'Meaning?'

Shazza pulled back her sleeve. Her arm was scar upon scar. Slice after slice. Cigarette burns. Knife cuts. Others which would need a forensic anthropologist to tell of their origin.

Carlson gasped. 'I don't understand. Why do you do it?' Even Jade's self-harming had not been as vicious as this.

'I ain't done it all meself,' she said. 'But the rest of it, I dun it just to make meself feel.'

And that's what happens is it? That's what the smack does to you? You stop feeling?'

'Yeah,' she said. 'You become so out of it, the way back isn't easy to find.'

'You found it though,' he said.

'Eventually. And not without help. Josie, Tina, they were me route back to' — she put her mug on the table and took another biscuit — 'well, whatever the fuck it is we're making our way back to.'

'Normality?'

'A normal life. Jesus,' she rolled her eyes at the ceiling. 'That sounds so boring.'

'You won't know until you try it.'

'And is that what makes you happy?

'Probably not happy at the moment, but it stops me from jumping into the abyss,' Carlson said, although he wondered what did keep him going some days.

'The abyss! Wow, that sounds so cool. So final. The abyss. Nothing can ever touch you again?'

'And that's what stops me jumping, Sharon. I don't want to block out my feelings. I'm not ready to stop caring about the world, my family, about me. I'm just not ready to stop.'

'I don't understand why you'd want to stop. It's all okay for you.'

'Okay? Is that what you think? You think everything is okay in my perfect world?' Carlson laughed mirthlessly.

'Isn't it?' she said.

'No, love, it's all very far from okay.'

Carlson leaned back in the chair, blinking, trying to clear his eyes. When he opened them again, the room was still blurry. 'She was just coming up to her eighteenth birthday. My Jade. My baby girl,' he sniffed. 'The whole world before her and then it all ended. She —'

He took the pack of proffered tissues and wiped his face.

'She what?' Shazza asked.

Carlson stared over at her, wondering why he could talk to this girl, but that didn't matter. He could. That was what mattered. 'She killed herself.' He said it softly, like the saying of it made the reality of it come into focus. Brought it all back again and so had to be done gently. 'That's what. We came back one evening, the house was all quiet, which was unusual. And when Mags, my wife, went upstairs... it was the screams.

I can't get them out of my head. She just wouldn't stop screaming. I ran up. Pushed past her — the screaming just kept going. Then I realised it was me. Mags had stopped screaming, but I'd started. Inside I don't think I've stopped yet. Jade was hanging from the light fitting. A new belt that Mags had got her at the weekend. We cut her down immediately, of course. I tried to revive her, but the paramedics called it as soon as they arrived. She was already cold. Nothing we could have done. She must've' — he hesitated, unable to voice the act — 'done it shortly after we'd left the house. That bloody belt. Mags won't let me throw it away. It's still there on her bed. I think it's morbid, but Mags can't see that. My baby. My little baby.' Carlson wiped more tears from his face and blew his nose hard. 'So now you know. Nothing perfect in my world.'

For a moment Shazza looked at him, speechless and blinking away her own tears. 'I'm so sorry,' she whispered like a last breath. 'Why?'

'Hmmph,' he shrugged. 'Bloody internet. Some boy had taken photos of her. They were being passed around the school. Kept appearing on different sites. Been going on for months and she didn't say a word. I thought something was wrong, but she kept it all to herself.'

'What are your lot doing about it?'

'Of course, it's under investigation, but trails go cold. I'm not allowed to be part of it. Too close to be impartial about the case, but I do know false accounts get set up to do it apparently, and they've been closed. No idea who the bastards were. We're still not sure who took the original photos or how he persuaded her to pose for them. It was more than once though. Then they got posted with her name and other information. All sorts of creeps were getting in touch. You should see some of the filth that got put on the Facebook memorial page. Girls that had been her friends!

Little bitches, all of them!' He sighed, rubbing his face, wiping away the last of the tears. 'Anyway, so now you know.'

Shazza nodded as Carlson stood up.

'I'll see myself out,' he said.

Shazza lay back in her chair, listening to his footsteps recede down the walkway towards the stairs. Poor bugger, she thought. No wonder he can't catch this bastard.

CHAPTER TWENTY-NINE

August 1987

'All rise.'

Bernie felt himself being dragged to his feet by the large security guard. It wasn't his first time in court but now that he was over ten he could be charged and tried. It was, however, his first time in the dock. Denise had brought him along in the past, so he could see what happened to the others in his gang.

'I want you to understand what the future could hold for you,' she'd said. 'Stay away from them. They're trouble and only want you to do their dirty work 'cos as you're only nine they can't charge you. Once you're ten, your gang won't want to know you anymore.'

Denise had been wrong about that though. Bernie was small for his age and could slip through the smallest window. Even after his tenth birthday, when the Tridents usually replaced the youngsters, Bernie stayed. For the first time in his life he felt like he belonged. That he had a proper family. Now was payback time. He'd kept shtum. He'd not grassed and now he was going down. Bernie was excited and nervous about going to a young offenders' institution although his friend, Terry Hanslope, had never been the same after he came back from a six-month stint. Bernie came to his feet. He stared at the ceiling, not listening to what the magistrate was saying. His brief was glaring at him, trying to make him pay attention, and he could see Denise pointing furiously at the beak out of the corner of his eye.

Pah! he thought, a measly secure children's home. He could manage that, no bother.

He was wrong.

Bernie was pulled from the back of the van into the warmth of the summer night. Daylight had departed during the long journey and there were very few lights. The guard had hold of his jumper and shirt, but he was also pinching portions of Bernie's skin. He squealed and tried to wriggle free. The guard simply lifted him off his feet and dropped him to the ground.

'Stop messing me about,' he hissed in Bernie's ear. 'You are going in there and you are going to learn a lesson you ain't never gonna forget.'

Bernie looked around. He could see the low, rectangular building skulking in the landscape ahead of them; it was surrounded by a tall, chain link fence but the lofty, heavy gate stood wide open. Bernie was shoved through the gateway and on towards the main entrance.

As the front door opened, light flooded onto the walkway and grass. A short man with a glistening bald head stood sweating in the doorway. His shirt was yellowing at the armpits and there were several grease spots on the thin tie. He looked at Bernie over his half spectacles.

'Right, you, we'll find you a room and some pyjamas and then you can have a bath and get the filth off you.'

'I don't need a bath,' replied Bernie.

'You useless little shit. You'll have a bath whether you like it or not, sunshine. My house. My rules. You speak when you are spoken to and you do not speak without permission. Understood?'

Bernie wasn't sure if he had permission or not, so he nodded his head.

Mistake. The backhander took him off his feet. Bernie picked himself up off the ground and wiped the back of his hand across his nose. He smeared the blood on his jeans.

'Filth,' said the man. 'You can go,' he said to the guard, who seemed curiously speedy as he departed. Bernie stared at the man, keeping his face impassive. Still, he thought, if I don't like it I can make my way back to Denise.

Marguerite Carlson paused in the doorway, then, taking a deep breath, she walked into the open plan office. Faces looked at her briefly and looked away, not knowing what to say. She saw several emotions, but mostly sorrow and sympathy. Her eyes misted, and it took her a few moments before she found her own desk. There was a small vase of flowers and a note; 'Sorry' was all it said.

'Marguerite?' Her supervisor had approached softly. 'Do you have a moment?'

Marguerite smiled, dipping her head, and she followed Helen to one of the small one-to-one rooms. She noticed that the phone in the middle of the table was now accompanied by a box of tissues. She was not sure if this was a change in procedure since the latest round of redundancies or if they were for her. The tissues were not needed. Helen welcomed her back to work, outlined some changes in policy and gave her some duties for the day.

'Just ease yourself back in,' Helen said. 'You could have come back slowly, half days at first, so if you feel the need to leave early let me know? Oh, just one other thing,' she paused for a moment. 'You remember Sally Watts in marketing?'

Marguerite nodded. 'Vaguely,' she said.

'She lost her son last year. He was killed in Helmand. She said to come and find her if you needed to talk. She knows it's not quite the same, but...' Helen seemed unable to finish the sentence.

'It's not. It's not the same at all, but I do appreciate the offer,' Marguerite said. 'I'm fine. Honestly, I'm fine. I'd just like to put it behind me and move on. My husband seems to be doing that just fine.' She spat the words out and looked down, ashamed at her outburst. Her knuckles were white, and she opened and closed her hands to relax them. 'I'm sorry,' she said. 'I know I need to do the same.'

Marguerite stood, thanking Helen for her time. She wrestled with the frosted door and almost ran to her desk. She was grateful for the high partitions and she took a while to compose herself. Without really knowing how, she made it to lunchtime.

Marguerite sat in a corner of the canteen, pushing the limp salad she wished she'd not chosen around the plate.

'May I sit down?'

Marguerite looked up. The woman's face was grey, lined, very little make-up but her sad eyes seemed to engulf the rest of her features. This must be Sally Watts, she thought. She waved her hand to the vacant chair and Sally sat.

'How are you?' she said.

'It's funny how many people keep asking me that question,' Marguerite said. 'How do you think? I'm numb. You remember how needles got stuck in a groove on vinyl? I keep playing the same scene over and over again. I can't move past it.'

'Have you come back to work too soon?' Sally asked.

Marguerite thrust the salad away and sat back in her chair. She looked at the woman opposite her and wondered how to reply. At least it was a new question, she thought.

'No,' she replied eventually. 'I needed to get out of the house. I keep finding myself standing in the doorway to my daughter's room. Sometimes I don't even know how I got there. I read a book, watch television and then I'm back in that doorway. I've tried shutting the door, but that feels like I'm shutting her out. My other daughter is home from university and has been for a while, but she needs to go back. As it is, she's going to have to do this year all over again. And then I feel so angry with Jade for messing up Aspen's life. Then I feel guilty for being angry. It just goes on and on.' Marguerite slumped in the chair, exhausted. She'd not expected to reveal quite so much, but now that she had, it felt good.

Sally nodded. 'Yes,' she said, 'the guilt is the worst part. Logically you know you couldn't change anything, but it makes no difference.'

'But I could have done something. I could see how much pain she was in. I tried to get her to talk to me, but she wouldn't. She just wouldn't. So, yes, I do blame myself.'

Sally reached out and took Marguerite's hands in hers. 'I understand the guilt only too well,' she said.

She told Marguerite her own story. Jordan, her son, was in the 3rd Battalion of the Parachute Regiment. She had a little good luck mantra. She didn't change his sheets until she knew he was back in the country and safe. Except on that last trip. He'd been out drinking with old school friends and had vomited on the bedding. She had to wash it. He left for another tour and didn't come back.

'I was in a world of hell,' she said. 'I kept blaming myself. Kept reliving the moment I stripped the bed, over and over again.'

'But you got past it?'

'I did,' Sally said. 'Eventually, and not without help. That's what I wanted to mention to you. I went to see this lady.' She slid a business card across the table.

'She helped me through it,' Sally said. 'The guilt. The anger. The grief. She can help you too. Anyway, that's what I planned to share with you. Good luck, Marguerite.'

And with that, she got up and disappeared into the crowd of staff. Marguerite didn't see her leave the canteen. She looked at the card, thinking to leave it there, but as she rose to go back to her desk, her left hand reached out and slipped it into her trouser pocket.

CHAPTER THIRTY

Aspen Carlson read the text and slid the phone back in her pocket. Calling to her mother that she'd be back later, she left quickly before there could be any argument.

Aspen agreed to meet him in a pub this time, but wasn't convinced it was the best idea. The Old Feathers was so busy, she had difficulty hearing what Tim Jessop was telling her.

'Come on,' she said, 'there's a little bistro around the corner. My treat. It's cheap enough even for students to afford.'

Protesting that he should at least pay his own way, Tim followed her and, once they were ensconced in a quiet corner, he outlined why Jade had been so upset over the content and what else he'd found out so far.

'Okay,' he said. 'This has been with another team, and although your Dad has been pestering them to keep on with it, the trail does seem to have gone cold.'

'Oh,' Aspen said.

'No, don't worry, I do have some good news. So, I've been through everything that the Sierra team had got, and yes, they kept finding dead ends. But, and here's the good bit' —

he paused for dramatic effect — 'my mate Stuart has gone somewhat further. I can't guarantee that everything he's done is entirely legal and that might have an impact on future prosecution if that's the route you want to go down —'

'I'm not sure what I want at the moment,' interjected Aspen. 'At some point I'm going to have to take anything I do find to my Dad. Have you told him what you're doing?'

'No, not yet,' Tim replied. 'I guessed you wanted to find something out before bothering him, but I'm not happy going behind my boss's back. I wouldn't do it for anyone but you.' He smiled at her, holding her gaze.

'Thanks, that's good.' Aspen took a sip of her wine. 'So, what have you found out?'

'Okay, so a lot of it has been kids' stuff. Opening accounts, closing them, opening others, but what Stuart's been able to do is trace those accounts back to about half a dozen different IP addresses —'

'And those relate to specific computers?'

'Exactly.'

'So we've got them?'

'No, sadly not. Most of those IP addresses belong to computers in internet cafes. One here in Gippingford, one in Faverstone and a couple of others a bit further afield.'

'I didn't realise they still existed,' said Aspen.

'They are very few and far between these days,' said Tim. 'Some places still have poor broadband and some people don't have computers.'

'So, anyone at all could have used them,' mused Aspen.

'Yes,' he said.

'But hang on, you said most.'

'I did,' he grinned. 'One of the little twats used his own laptop to post the pictures in the first place. Him we have traced, and we can have a little chat with him.' Tim leaned back in his chair and laced his fingers behind his head.

'I can imagine the sort of little chat I want to have with him,' muttered Aspen tersely. 'I just can't get why he'd want to do it at all.'

'Sierra team have uncovered some pretty nasty texts between this boy and Jade,' Tim said. He leaned forward and put his hands on the table, spreading his fingers and then clenching his fists. Finally, he looked at her again. 'It appears that they'd dated for a while and Jade broke it off. He wanted her to sleep with him and she wasn't ready. He said that if she didn't, she'd regret it. It seems she blocked that number, but he got burner phones and they moved to apps which made the numbers anonymous. Sierra aren't sure if all the texts are from him or different people, but it could be a group of them,' Tim moved the linguine around on his plate, but pushed it away without eating.

'There were over a dozen phones being used at one point,' he said. It looks like as soon as she blocked a number, it all started again on a new phone. But the app they used — it's called Wik'd — well, there was no number to block. She must have been in a world of hell.'

'She was,' said Aspen, her voice shaking. 'I know she changed her number a couple of times last year. Mum said she had to stop doing it because of the cost. Mum wanted her to have contracts rather than pay as you go so that she'd never be out of credit. It was costing a fortune to change the number. If only we'd known.' She picked up her wine and twiddled with the glass before banging it down on the table. 'Why didn't she say anything?'

'I've no idea,' said Tim. 'Most companies will let you change for free if you tell them what's happening. I don't know why she didn't do that.'

'Because she'd have to tell Mum and Dad, that's why. Clearly she was too ashamed to do that. It's not easy being a copper's kid. Dad would have gone ballistic. He would have charged into the school and shoved a rocket up them. Jade would have been so embarrassed and not a jot better off.' Aspen looked down at her cold meal and then back at Tim. 'Do we know how he got the pictures?' she asked.

'This is the nasty chunk of information they uncovered, Aspen,' he said gently. 'It seems that many of them were taken in the showers at the local pool after swimming lessons.'

'But how would the boys have got in there?'

'Sierra suspect that it was girls or a girl in her class who took the photos for the boy. I don't get why they'd do that.'

'Jealousy,' said Aspen dourly. 'I bet the little bitch of a photographer wanted this boy for herself and Jade got there first. You've no idea how evil girls can be when there's a boy at the centre of it. No idea at all.'

Carlson looked up as a shadow fell across his desk. Poole filled the gap which formed a doorway to his double-sized cubicle. 'How was Mr Hoyes?' he asked.

'As you'd imagine. In bits.'

'Yes, it's never easy, even though he knew about her life-style, Ben.' Carlson pushed the keyboard to one side and pulled his tea closer.

'Yes, but since she'd got herself clean he hoped she'd put it all behind her, you know?'

'Oh yes, I know all about hope,' Carlson sighed.

'Boss?'

'No, nothing, another time maybe.'

Poole gave him a sidelong glance. It was the closest Carlson had ever come to opening up about his private life since Poole had arrived from the Norfolk force last year. What with Carlson's compassionate leave too, they'd not had a chance to get to know each other at all.

'Does it ever get easier?' Poole asked.

'Nope — well, not unless you lose your humanity. And that's easy enough to do in this job.'

'Hmm, you're not wrong.'

'Sit,' Carlson waved a hand at one of the vacant chairs. 'Come on. Thoughts? What sort of man does this?'

'You want the cop's answer or the profiler's answer, sir?' Poole hitched his trouser legs as he sat, revealing monogrammed silk socks.

'Both if I can get it,' replied Carlson, thinking of his own Marks and Sparks specials and wondering if Poole was independently wealthy.

'Okay, I think the degree of escalation is what's most interesting here. This guy has hit the ground running and is killing in quick succession. Most killers start, as you know, slowly and build up. The first killing gives him an enormous thrill and that persists for a while. Then, as that fades, he needs to do another to get the same kick.'

'Like drug addicts?' said Carlson. He raised his head and smiled. Poole twisted round to see who it was. Kirsty Russell clutched a thin folder and had a huge grin on her face.

'Hi, come in Kirsty.' Carlson half rose from his chair. 'Ben's just giving me the wisdom of his profiling course.'

Kirsty smiled warily and eased herself into the chair facing Poole. She placed the folder on her lap and gave him a wink of encouragement.

'No pressure,' she said. 'Continue.'

Poole rolled his eyes. Carlson reflected it was one of the few humorous things he'd seen the man do.

'I was just saying, it's exactly like that. Like an addict,' Poole said. 'Just like taking a narcotic, each killing gives a high but each time the ecstasy lasts for less time and he never ever quite achieves the thrill of the first kill. That's why we get escalation.'

'Always a he?' asked Kirsty.

'Not always, but yes, most serial killers are men, often white and usually between the ages of twenty and forty,' Poole replied, 'the theory being that testosterone levels are at their highest during this time in a man's life, and that's what leads to the flawed decision making and the additional levels of aggression.'

'I often wonder what starts them off. That's what I don't understand,' said Carlson, rubbing his chin. 'There must be some sort of trigger.'

'And I don't understand why he treated the girls differently,' said Kirsty. Both men looked at her. 'Well, think about it,' she said. 'He's quite rough with the first one, extremely rough with the most recent girl, but the other two? Almost reverential. Why did he pose Tanith? That's completely different from the others. Those girls were just dumped like garbage.'

'That's the part I can't answer. I don't understand his change in behaviour at all,' said Poole. 'What I have learnt is that many offenders keep the same modus operandi, which is the *how* they carry out their crime, but the MO can change as time goes on and they develop their skills, becoming more proficient, say. But the signature is the *why* they do what they do, and that doesn't change because that's the reason, that's their motivation. Unless...' Poole paused. 'Unless there was a special connection between him and the third girl. Was she the one he was after all the time? I just don't know.'

'He's also very forensically aware,' Kirsty said. 'I know that's not impossible these days, but usually first kills have a bit more panic about them. I'd expect a mistake. But he was very careful.'

'So, what you're saying is that *our* first girl may not have been his?' asked Carlson.

Both nodded in assent.

'Then we need to find out if there have been any other unsolved murders with similar MOs, don't we? Ben, can you get Tim and Jane on to that? Sorry, Kirsty, I didn't ask why you came here.'

'I have news,' she grinned. 'Familial match on the DNA.'

CHAPTER THIRTY-ONE

After dropping Rose at work, Bernie decided to go to the flat. He made tea but, since the milk was off, he poured it down the sink and mixed a vodka and tonic. He took his padlocked box from the sideboard and sat on the sofa with his feet resting on the arms, sipping his drink. Jeez, could nothing go right for him? The tonic water was flat and insipid. He forced himself to relax and thought of what he had got away with. He smiled. *Yeah, there were a few things that had gone right for him, after all.*

He pulled the box from the sideboard, unlocked it and began thumbing through his collection. He held the old VHS tapes up, pleased that he'd been able to copy the contents onto DVD. One he hugged to his chest. A particular favourite. The source of the idea, how it all started. He could not believe his luck when the boxes fell into his hands. Well, when he had taken them into his hands. He smiled again, remembering the fate that had befallen their previous owner.

Hour after hour he'd spent rifling through old case notes and delving into the minds of perps — he preferred the American word — and how they'd let themselves get caught.

It was just a shame he'd not been able to get hold of any others. He kept track of his own case in the papers and on the net. Staying one step ahead. Sending the letter was a risk but he'd been unable to resist the temptation. He'd giggled when he signed himself Jack. I'd love to have seen that copper's face when he read it, he thought.

He decided to watch the first one again and popped the DVD in the player. He enjoyed the first film that Patrick Wheeler had made and then the second version of the same film. Pat was a smart old bird, he thought; that's where he'd got the idea of two cameras from. Made the editing process so much easier. He had no worries that Rose would find anything on his PC at home. She was too stupid to crack his password, even if she knew how to turn on the computer. She could scarcely use her smartphone — well, that was when she hadn't lost it again. He chuckled. He was going to have to come up with some new hiding places though; she was beginning to check the regular ones before admitting to him that she'd lost something again. Still, it had taken her days to find her keys in the flour jar. Her own fault, he thought. She should do more home cooking. How she was going to find the time to do a day course, work at the call centre and look after him and the house was beyond him. Good as her word, she had let him have all the details and he hadn't decided yet whether he would let her do it or not. It would be a bore and a tie having to help her with the home-work, and he was sure there would be homework, all the time.

On the other hand, he wondered, as he selected one of his own films to watch, it might be good for her to realise just how stupid she was. He'd lost count of the number of times she started something, and he'd had to finish it off for her. It was about time she heard from someone else just how dim she really was. But, in all honesty, he liked her working nights. It gave him free time for his own activities. He settled back on the old sofa, raised his drink to his mouth, and the film of the second girl he met in Reigate began.

Having opened the wrapping on the CDs and placed them in the machine, Poole sat down at the table. It was close and intimate in the interview room. Poole looked at the wall behind Dave Bradwell where hundreds of heads had rubbed their denials as they pushed themselves back from the table. He knew Bradwell's head would be rubbing up against that wall in the next hour or so.

'Please state your full name, address, date of birth and national insurance number for the tape, please.'

Dave complied.

'Also present is Mr Bradwell's solicitor.'

'Harding Couchman.'

'And,' said Poole.

'Detective Chief Inspector Ronald Carlson.'

'And I am Detective Sergeant Benjamin Poole,' he said. 'I need to remind you, Mr Bradwell, that you are still under caution and that we wish to question you in respect of the kidnap and murder of Christina Elizabeth Hoyes.'

'I don't even know who that is,' said Dave. The solicitor placed a pudgy hand on Dave's forearm and gave a small shake of his head.

Dave sat hunched in the plastic chair darting looks at Couchman, a lawyer he hardly knew and hadn't requested. What he did know was that Couchman was a personal friend of Justin Gainsborough, but how the leader of the drug enterprise in Gippingford had found out about Dave's predicament was too complex to fathom. The day-to-day politics of survival in the gang were enough to give Dave a migraine. If Justin knew he had been arrested and was being interviewed, there would be no good news in Dave's future. There would be no client confidentiality with Couchman. Gainsborough would be told everything.

'All in good time,' said Poole. 'We'll come to your connection with the deceased.'

Poole read out the charges and then came to the crux of the matter.

'This is your DNA sample which we took at the time of your arrest,' Poole said, showing the report to them both, 'and this is a sample taken from the victim Miss Hoyes at her post-mortem. You will see that they match.'

'Excuse me, DS Poole,' interjected Couchman. 'How did you come by this match? Have you done a speculative trawl of the DNA database? That contravenes my client's rights under Article 8 of the 1998 Human Rights Act.'

'On the contrary,' retorted Poole. 'The initial search gave only a familial match. A simple search of the voting register and our own records gave us a list of family members who still reside in the area. Once Mr Bradwell was arrested, we took his DNA and were able to conduct a one-to-one search. All standard procedure, as you know only too well, Mr Couchman.'

'Hummph,' said the solicitor, and settled his bulk back into his seat, his ample buttocks breaching the sides of the chair.

'It don't make no difference,' said Dave. 'I still don't know who she is.'

Poole slid a photo of Tina across the table. A nerve under Dave's right eye twitched but he still insisted that he had never met her.

Poole was to be disappointed that day. Dave Bradwell did not back his chair away until he was against the wall. After over an hour of questioning, Jane Lacey knocked on the door and passed him two notes. Neither gave him the information he wanted. The first was a demand from Superintendent Tasker to halt the interview and report to his office at once. The other was confirmation that on the day Tina Hoyes had last been seen alive, Dave Bradwell's mobile phone and the tachograph from his lorry placed him 250 miles away in Leeds.

Treallis smiled to himself as he logged on to Dragon Quest, pleased to see that his new quest-mate, Da'anarth, was already playing.

Well met, good knight, he typed.

Good evening, kind sir, responded Da'anarth. *What is your quest?*

Gold, always gold, Treallis typed. I hear tell that there is a dragon with a treasure trove hidden in yonder mountains.

Then let us away, replied Da'anarth and they turned their horses and galloped towards the far away hills.

Distance was of no significance in the dragon world and soon the two knights were climbing the steep hill, stopping to dismount and walk their horses up the stony path.

At a stream they watered their horses and rested awhile.

How goes your quest IRL? asked Treallis. Have you found your man?

Who says it's a man? Da'anarth replied. *But no, he, or she, evades us still.*

Treallis leaned back in his office chair, smirking. He

wondered how far he could push the questions without giving himself away.

Have you no clues as to the identity of the varmint? asked Treallis.

Da'anarth laughed and strode to his horse. *Some,* he said. *We have some ideas. Come, night draws near, and the dragon's lair does not.*

Treallis decided not to question any further, although it was clear the copper had no inkling who he was, but there was no point in giving the whole game away. He was sure that the cops had nothing on him so far. He'd been careful, done his research, even down to finding out one of the local cops was a fantasy gamer. Dave's brother in law had done well there. Might even need to thank him properly.

CHAPTER THIRTY-TWO

Once he was released from police custody, Dave Bradwell wasted no time tracking down the cause of his latest problem. He strode into the staff canteen, where he saw Bernie eating his sandwiches — alone, for a change. Depending on his mood, and Dave knew he could be a moody bastard, Bernie could be surrounded by laughing colleagues as he told his wild stories or did his stand-up comic act. Sometimes, but not often, he would be completely isolated like today. Never any middle ground with Bernie, he thought, but he had no time for reverie today.

'What the fuck, Bernie! What the actual fuck!' Dave hauled Bernie out of his chair and shoved him against the partition wall. It reverberated, and a ceiling tile fell to the floor.

Bernie, squashed against the wall, raised his hands. His usual arrogant look replaced by one of confusion and consternation.

'Dave? Mate,' he said. 'I've not seen you for a few days. What's up?'

'Outside!' Dave pushed him out of the building to the

smoking shelter. A few stragglers puffed the last of their dregs and wandered slowly back to the main building. They lingered at the entrance to watch the change in dynamics.

Bernie pulled his uniform jacket straight and himself to his full height. His initial shock had passed, and he had regained his composure. His pale eyes fixed on Dave. 'I said what's up?' he whispered menacingly, pressing his nose to the other's.

'That's what I want to know, you shit,' Dave shot back at him. 'I've been in a police cell for the last few hours. They had a bloody warrant to search my house, my car, my lorry. Eventually they let me go, 'cos they weren't able to prove I was around when she disappeared.'

'When who disappeared?' Bernie asked, all wide-eyed innocence.

'Do. Not. Piss. Me. Around.' Dave prodded him hard in the chest with each word. 'I know what you've been up to.'

Bernie took a step backwards, realising he'd have to get the situation under control. He wasn't used to situations being out of his control. He decided to change tack and raised his hands in a deprecating manner.

'Okay Dave,' he said, 'You tell me what you think I've been up to.'

Dave related his trip to the flat and what he'd found there.

'But Dave,' Bernie cooed, 'we agreed you let me have the flat in return for me not letting the police in on your other activities. What made you break that agreement?'

'I wanted to know what you'd been up to!' Dave seethed. 'I had my suspicions, you sick git. I wanted to get you off my case. Now I know, but the filth are on my back and the people I work for aren't very happy about that.' He glared at Bernie, teeth clenched and breathing heavily.

'How's that my fault?' Bernie asked. 'How did the police get hold of you? What did you do, you bloody twat?'

'I saw the girl in the bath. They reckon I left saliva on her.'

'How the hell did you manage that?' Bernie sniggered as he considered the image. 'Were you licking her?'

'No!! For fuck's sake, no!' Dave covered his face with his hands, shaking his head from side to side. 'No, Bernie, strangely enough, I was a bit surprised to find a dead girl in my bath and swore out loud. The cops told me that I spat some saliva out when I did.'

'You prat,' Bernie said. 'What exactly do the police know?'

'The police? They're the least of your worries right now. I got hauled in. Like I said, the people I work for won't like that. I've not said anything to the filth, but the Gainsborough Boys? I'll be telling them everything I know. They're much more persuasive than the cops, if you know what I mean. They don't take "no comment" for an answer. And if they don't like what I have to tell them, then it'll be good night Vienna for me. Do you bloody well understand that?'

Bernie said nothing. Dave gave an exasperated sigh.

'I want me flat keys back Bernie. You ain't using it again. You understand? You can find somewhere else for your sick little games. Our deal is over. Yer getting no more cash from me either and I'll not be dumping no more clothes. I guess that's what you've had me doing, isn't it? You and me?' — Dave waggled his finger between himself and Bernie — 'We're through.'

Jane Lacey pushed her chair back from the desk with its debris of boxes and evidence bags. She started to rub her eyes but, looking at her hands, she thought better of it. She rubbed the knots in the back of her neck instead and groaned.

She still wasn't sure that enough information had been taken for the current killer to be a copycat. Yet, looking at the number of bags that had been tampered with, it seemed that whoever it was probably had the opportunity to look at the Lytham case evidence frequently. *Did they have enough though? Who knows? I can't even be sure how much is missing.* Jane had taken every single box of evidence and checked the contents against the list in the lid or on the front of the box where there was one. If there wasn't, she had created a list, but that hardly proved what had been there in the first place. It was a truly thankless task. That Tim Jessop was useless, she thought. After the first day of helping he'd disappeared and had his head stuck in a laptop or on the PNC. She wasn't sure what he was up to, but it was not related to this case, that much she did know.

Jane lifted her coffee cup and went to drink. Yuck! Cold! Again. That was the third cold cup she'd had today alone. She glowered at the cup and then glared at Tim as he burst through the door. Her glare changed to a grin when she realised he'd done it again. Proper coffee, piping hot, and a slice of carrot cake. Perhaps he wasn't so bad after all, she thought.

He set them down in front of her and gave her what she supposed he thought was a winning smile. 'I need your help,' he blurted. 'I need you to pretend that you're a teenage girl.'

'Bloody cheek,' she said. 'It's not that long ago I was one.'

'Okay, well that's even better. You'll remember what it was like.'

'What *what* was like?' she asked guardedly.

'So, you're a teenager and you like a boy, but he likes someone else. What do you do?'

'How old am I? Fourteen is different to nineteen.'

'Fifteen, sixteen at most,' Tim said.

'Me? I'd have waited. Seen how it went. Now my friend Sandra on the other hand, she took a different tack,' said Jane, opening the plastic lid to the cake. She ran her finger through the icing and licked it clean. Then, remembering how filthy her hands had been, she grimaced.

'What did your friend do?'

'Everything she could to make the other girl look stupid. Hid her clothes while she was showering. Accidentally tripped her over.' Jane mumbled through a mouthful of cake, holding a napkin in front of her mouth. 'Gave her the wrong homework notes. Loosened the salt cellar lid so her lunch was covered with the stuff. Loads of senseless stuff.'

'Did it work?'

'Oh, come on, what do you think? Sandra thought she was in an American romcom. Of course it didn't work. It was obvious it was her, so the little toad disliked Sandra even more. She was devastated. You know what it's like at that age. It's the end of the world.'

'That's not much help,' said Tim

'Does that mean I have to give you the cake back?' Jane had already eaten most of it, so it was something of a moot point.

'Nah, you're okay. I just wanted to know what girls were capable of.'

'Worse stuff than that, I can assure you,' said Jane. 'It wasn't a case I worked on, but my sister teaches in a high school. One of the girls brought a knife into school to stab another in a fight over a lad.'

'Jeez! You're kidding. What happened?' Tim asked, his coffee halfway to his lips.

'Fortunately, nothing. The fight was stopped before it

really got going. A bit of hair pulling but a teacher saw it kicking off, stopped it, and the knife was found later,' Jane sighed. 'It could have been a very different story.'

'Over a lad?' Tim was aghast. 'Blimey, when I was at school we just thumped the shit out of each other and then were best of pals. Although it was always best if the girl chose someone else completely different. Then we could take the piss out of them both.'

Jane nodded. 'I don't think we always appreciate how strongly young girls feel.'

'So, you'd not be surprised at one girl getting revenge on another to win some boy around?' he asked.

'Oh, good grief, no. That would be simples. Totally simples,' Jane said. 'Where have you been, Tim? Pluto? Of course, girls can be completely evil to each other.'

'You're a star,' said Tim. 'I'll be back to help with all this tomorrow. I promise.'

Before Jane could retort her disbelief, Tim raced out of the door. She was sure he was skipping his share of the tedious duty, but the coffee and cake softened her annoyance.

CHAPTER THIRTY-THREE

Carlson straightened his tie and smoothed his hair back in the mirror. He saw Assistant Chief Constable Paul Charlesworth's PA pretend not to notice as she waited to direct him into the office.

Carlson was surprised to see Superintendent Jim Tasker from the Serious and Organised Crime Investigation Team already seated opposite Charlesworth. His dark beady eyes glared out from underneath eyebrows that would have not looked out of place on an Aberdeen Angus. He had the alcoholic's morning sheen of sweat, and the smell of peppermints wafted across the room towards Carlson.

'You wanted to see me, sir?' Carlson looked at the ACC and then at Tasker, expecting that the latter would leave, but he remained entrenched in the small armchair.

'Yes, come in Ronnie. We wanted a chat.'

We? Carlson thought. He sat in the third chair and waited.

'What did you want with Dave Bradwell?' demanded Tasker. He sat forward in the chair, legs wide apart with his stomach hanging in the gap, threatening to tip the chair over.

'His DNA showed up on one of my murder victims. What

exactly is your interest in him? Why did you insist he was released?' Carlson asked in as temperate a voice as he could muster in the face of Tasker.

'He manages the logistics for the Gainsborough Boys.'

Carlson pursed his lips. The Gainsborough Boys were not a gang who took interference in their business interests lightly. Anyone who got in their way was usually out of the way quite soon. 'Logistics? Isn't that a tad grand for someone who does a bit of driving?' he said.

'Maybe,' said Tasker. 'But we know that he does rather more than driving. He got promoted early last year.'

'What's he doing now?' said Carlson.

'We've had him under surveillance for a while. It was looking like he was the main distributor for the North East.'

'All we did was question him, Jim, and then we let him go. He had an alibi for when our most recent victim was last seen alive. Although his DNA had got on her, we think that's more likely to have happened after she was dead. I wanted to know how that happened,' Carlson shrugged, 'but you insisted I release him. That we did, albeit very reluctantly.'

'Ronnie, he works for the Gainsborough Boys,' Tasker repeated. 'Just being picked up is going to be very hard for him to explain.'

'And why is that our concern?'

'Oh, why do you think, Ronnie?' interjected ACC Charlesworth.

Tasker shrugged, rolling his eyes at the ceiling. His palms raised uppermost. 'Don't be dim, Ronnie. He was our snout. We'd been working him for months. We were getting close to a major bust — the main players, not just the street dealers — and thanks to your interference, you've blown it for us.' He leaned closer and Carlson could smell Tasker's minty breath as he sprayed his words. 'Thanks for that, Ronnie, thanks a bloody bunch.'

'You should have made me aware,' Carlson said calmly. 'This is my patch too. If you don't share what's going on, how is anyone supposed to know? What happened to the "one team" idea? Are we not all on the same side any longer?'

Tasker shrugged again. 'Leaks,' he said.

'On your team, perhaps, not mine.' Carlson retorted. 'There's no one on the take in my team. You take a look at your own lot. Leave my guys out of it.' Carlson's short nails were digging into his palms. He shot a glance at ACC Charlesworth. 'If you'll excuse me, sir. I have a killer to catch.'

Charlesworth inclined his head in assent. 'Don't leave it too long, Ronnie,' he said. 'You know how nervous it makes the press.'

Carlson gave him a grim smile as he stood. He wasn't sure if Charlesworth's last remark had been a threat or not.

Carlson slammed back into the conference room and sat at the end of the table. Poole looked at him but said nothing. He continued talking softly with Jane Lacey about the contents of the boxes.

Carlson waited for his anger to subside, but sitting here staring at his DS and DC was only making them uncomfortable. He pushed himself out of his chair and returned to the main squad room and stared at the white board in the hope of an inspired thought. Apart from their job and drug habit there was nothing linking the girls. To the trained eye, even the causes of death had as many differences as they did similarities. Jervis Kilburn was convinced that despite this they were looking for one perpetrator. Carlson wasn't so sure.

Footage and a note had arrived after the first two girls but not the third or fourth. He was less worried about this as, with his previous case, no notes or film had been received until quite late on.

The methods of disposal were very different too, although he thought he could blame TV crime shows for that. Why think of different ways of getting rid of someone when a new method was being shown each week. He'd hoped for more out of the carpet Natasha had been found in. But forensics thought it likely that it had been taken from a skip and had little or no relationship to their killer. Then why so careful with the third girl and so violent with the last? He needed to think. Some fresh air and some thinking time.

Carlson made his way down the quiet side street and into the main thoroughfare. A freezing January had given way to an even colder February and now that they'd had their post-Christmas pay packet people were out on the streets again. It was quieter in the evenings though; he knew from reading the reports from the night shift. Nothing like a serial killer on the loose to keep even the criminal fraternity at home tucked up in the warm, he mused.

He ordered coffees for Poole and Lacey and a tea for himself. As he stood waiting, he looked around the cafe. Tucked away in a quiet corner were two heads he knew very well. The silken blonde of his daughter, Aspen, and the dark curls of a certain DC Timothy Jessop. Call yourself a detective, Ronnie? he thought. You didn't see that one coming. He watched them for a while, wondering what they were discussing so intently. He also wondered if he should saunter over and ask outright. He decided against embarrassing his daughter, thinking perhaps he'd done it once too often with Jade. *Oh well, they could both do a lot worse.* He considered texting Poole, asking him to call Tim back to the office. He picked up the cardboard tray and made his way back into the street. He ignored the rapid footsteps behind him until they had fallen into step with his own.

'Guv? Fancy seeing you here.' Tim Jessop was out of breath.

Not from having run, Carlson suspected. Much more likely to be guilt from having been caught in a tryst when he should have been in the office on the case.

'Coffee run, DC Jessop. I would have got one for you, but we didn't know where you were. There's been a bit too much of that recently, Tim. I need you on the team or off it. The choice is yours, but I need everyone's head in the game.'

'I... I, um...' Tim began, but stopped short of saying anything more.

Very wise, thought Carlson.

Tim held all the doors open for Carlson as they made their way back to the conference room. Both Poole and Jane stood as they walked in.

'We've got something, sir,' said Poole. 'Come on, Jane, you found it. Your story.'

Jane blushed and pushed her dark hair behind her ear.

'Well, Guv,' she said. 'I started off checking everything that was here should be here. That took long enough.' She looked at Tim as she spoke. 'Once I'd done all that, I found that there were two anomalies. The first we already know — some of the evidence bags had been tampered with — but I've also found that where I did have an original list there were some items missing.

'Yes, sir, I know,' she said, in response to Carlson's attempted interruption. 'This was in a secure storage locker inside a warehouse. Nothing should be missing at all. But here's the thing, sir, the fire in the warehouse? Everything that was salvaged was put into temporary storage. Outside contractors were used to transport and store the boxes. I've spoken to the civilian administration officers that were in charge and one of them admitted that because of budget cuts there weren't always enough staff to monitor every transport. He wouldn't say more but I also got the impression they used civvy contractors to look after the temporary storage location on occasions. We — I, that is, think that someone got access then. I've made a list of all the items that I think ought to be here which aren't.

'What I've not been able to find out, sir,' she continued, 'is if anything is missing where the original list has been lost, as I've not had anything to reconcile against. Some of the boxes were destroyed more by water than fire and they were just replaced with fresh ones, but their inventory lists weren't recovered. It was an oversight at best, sloppy at worst.'

She passed a list across the table to Carlson. As he ran his eye down it, many aspects of the case came back to him. It had been a strange one too. Patrick Wheeler had terrorised the people in the north for years before he was caught. He'd changed his method frequently, so at first they'd not been sure if they were dealing with one killer or many. Carlson had "leaked" a story to the press that the police suspected a group of copycats. It had the desired effect. As soon as he realised his work was possibly being put down to other killers, Wheeler wrote the first letter claiming credit for all the women. The letters were genuine. He mentioned things that had never been in the press, then he sent in a video of himself in action. Carlson ran his eye further down the list.

Damn it! The videos were missing. Not that first letter though. That was still in its bag, but the tape sealing it shut clearly showed that it had been tampered with. Carlson swore quietly under his breath. It was clear that they did have a copycat. Now the only questions were who, how and why, but if the damn evidence boxes had been looked after by rent-a-mover then the search could be even more difficult. On the upside, it might not be a cop, which is what Carlson had dreaded.

CHAPTER THIRTY-FOUR

Shazza peeped her head around the door of the reception area. Bo was behind the desk as usual. 'Hey, love. Missed you last week. How you doing?' he asked.

'I've been better. You know?'

'I do, love. Never a good idea to bring anger to your training, but it's a good place to leave it.'

Shazza frowned at him for a moment, then smiled, pretending that she'd understood his comment perfectly. She wandered to the shoe rack and removed her trainers. Popping her purse into one of them, she tucked it deep into the toe and her mobile phone into the other. It still seemed strange being able to leave something of value lying around and knowing it would be there when she got back. The call of heroin was so strong it overcame everything else. Family, friendships, everything. Shazza knew there had been times she would have sold her soul for a fix. Since there was no money in souls, unless you were one of the American evangelical preachers she'd seen on late night TV, she'd sold her body instead. She knew that if it had not been for the punter who had tried to kill her, the heroin would have done for her in the end. She could remember the first two, maybe three punches, and the pain as his fist caught her cheekbone, but after that there was nothing. It was waking up that she remembered most. She was clucking, but she had been washed and the sheets were clean. Crisp and pressed. Her hair was still filthy, though. Greasy, gritty with lumps of vomit and matted bloody clumps. The pillow case had taken on the same smell as her hair. She had been unable to sit up without help, but the nurse had let her take a shower and even provided some shampoo and conditioner left by another patient. She'd not felt so clean, so human for a very long time. It was not to last. The siren song of Golden Brown was irresistible. Within days she was back on the street, selling herself for a fix again. The only difference was keeping her hair clean. Even if it meant washing it in cold water. Shazza only realised on reflection that it had been the first step on her way back to the semblance of a real life.

She jumped as a hand clamped on her shoulder. 'You're back,' cried Sarah, sitting down and swamping her in a huge hug that was held longer than Shazza expected. She finally brought her hands up and reciprocated. She heard Sarah say quietly, 'I'm so sorry about your friend.'

Eventually Sarah sat back, hands on Shazza's shoulders, holding her at arm's length to get a good look at her. 'How are you coping?'

Shazza shrugged and bit her lip. She wasn't used to someone being concerned for her.

'I think it's time you and I exchanged phone numbers,' Sarah said.

Tears pricked Shazza's eyes. Tina's face swum before her. She reached up and squeezed a hand. 'I'm shite, thanks,' she said. 'It's been a shit couple of weeks and I feel the need to kick something. Very hard.'

'Come on then,' said Sarah, pulling Shazza to her feet. 'I'm your girl.'

Smiling for the first time in several days, Shazza allowed herself to be dragged to her feet and followed Sarah onto the dojo. They both bowed to the sensei with hands by their sides. The warm-up began, slowly at first, then with increasing intensity. By the third round of twenty seconds of running on the spot as fast as she could, Shazza's heart rate was pounding and the serotonin was pumping around her brain. Not the same high as heroin, Shazza knew that only too well. Nothing would ever beat that high, but this was cleaner, healthier, cheaper and above all guilt-free.

Dave gasped as the cold water splashed over him. He forced his eyes open; blurry figures appeared, and voices murmured in the background.

The voices became lounder as the figures approached, but his vision was still fuzzy. When he attempted to move, he found himself strapped to an old wooden carvery chair. His hands clenched the grips and he yelped in agony.

'I'd be careful there Dave, might be a bit sore for a day or two with no fingernails.'

There was raucous laughter as Justin Gainsborough spoke, his educated tone belying his true nature as his weasel features, wearing a vicious smile, finally swum into a hazy focus for Dave.

'You've got a couple of nasty shiners as well mate, but I wish you'd stop passing out on me. You're wasting water and that's precious.'

More laughter.

Dave pulled back in the chair, squinting as he tried to

focus properly. His left eye was closed, his right swollen and closing, but he could see all too clearly what Justin was holding. He was unable to avoid the baseball bat as it was swung at his left knee; the screams echoed around the otherwise deserted warehouse and the force of the blow toppled him and the chair to the floor. Unseen hands lifted him up and Gainsborough swung the bat at his right knee. Dave screamed again with sobs following as he crashed to the floor once more. Again, he was lifted upright and shoved back into position.

Justin squatted in front of him. 'Now come on Dave,' he cajoled, 'tell me what you told the filth, and all this will be over.'

'Nothing,' Dave tried to say, his jaws clenched in pain, making him scarcely able to form the words. The salt water of his tears stung his eyes and he wheezed, 'I told them nothing.'

Gainsborough looked at his crew. 'Did any of you get that?' he asked. Each one shook his head. 'No, me neither.'

He hefted the bat onto his shoulder and looked at Dave thoughtfully for a moment. He sighed and swung the bat at Dave's head, a glancing blow not with any real malice. Dave slumped in the chair and the bat came from the other side. Dave whispered 'nothing', but he was no longer sure if the words were only in his head.

He came to in the back of Gainsborough's Range Rover. He was gagged, trussed hand and foot and they had thrown him in the rear. He kept his right eye closed; it was easier and less painful that way. The left he had no choice over, he wondered if he'd ever open it again. Whilst having no idea where they were taking him, Dave was pretty sure it wasn't to the local hospital. From his prone position he could hear Justin and his men speaking in the front of the vehicle. He recognised three voices; the fourth member of the team was either absent or his Neanderthal brain was totally focused on driving.

'I've got a cousin who could take over the northern runs for a while, Boss.' Dave recognised the wheedling tones of Ryan Selkirk.

'I'll think about it, mate,' Gainsborough replied. 'I've got other things on my mind right now. You are right though. We can't afford to lose that income stream for long. I was thinking about handing it off to some of the homeless kids we use, but I'll get back to you.

'Tony,' he continued. 'What have you found out about our other problem?'

Dave lay listening to Tony Pincent talking to his boss about their various cafes, nail bars and massage parlours — cash-intensive businesses ideal for money laundering and staffed by cheap but transient Eastern European staff. Gains-borough was always happy to take advantage of desperate people needing a cash-in-hand job. Leaving the European Union and the freedom of movement it allowed could shut off that stream of workers. Gainsborough also had concerns over stronger border control and getting his product into the country. The men chatted quietly as they drove through the deserted streets, various options considered and rejected. They fell silent as the Range Rover turned into what, from the different road surface under him, Dave guessed was woodland. The powerful vehicle thrumming as the tyres rode over the slush of the last snows. Then Selkirk drew it to a halt and the hatch opened.

'Back with us again, Dave?' Gainsborough asked. 'All be over soon.'

Tony and Ryan pulled Dave from the boot and he saw his own car parked at the end of the lane. He scuffed his feet against the muddy path, but the huge men dragged him to the car. The driver's door opened, and the fourth man of the team stepped out. He lifted Dave's feet and they shoved him in his car. The gag and bindings were removed, and the door shut. Dave squinted at the rear-view mirror as Selkirk sprayed *GRASS* on the rear window of the saloon and they all laughed. He knew then he'd been sussed. Gainsborough had known all along. Couchman, the solicitor, must have told them that Dave was released by the police too easily and too quickly. The beating was just for kicks. Dave looked to his right and saw Gainsborough raising a shot gun to his shoulder.

It was the last thing he saw.

September 1989

Bernie was on stampdown again. At least that's what the other kids called it. It was his twenty-first day locked in a small room with only pyjamas to wear. He had been denied all privileges, When he was first told he would have his privileges taken away from him, he laughed out loud. Privileges? He'd not had much in the way of toys or comics or TV with his mum. Even with Denise, all those had to be shared by nine other screaming snot-nosed kids. By the time he got to get his hands on anything it wasn't worth having. However, what Bernie soon discovered was that at Trablos Grange, privileges were not books or games or TV or comics or even family visits. Not that he had anyone to visit him anymore, he thought; even Denise had stopped bothering. Loss of privileges at Trablos meant no clothes, no bedding, not seeing the other children, not being allowed to attend school, no reading materials, no writing paper. He was not permitted to speak to staff without knocking his locked door to ask to "impart information" — even a trip to the loo was a reward that had to be earned. He had a bucket but no toilet roll. He'd had to clean himself the best he could and then wash his hands with cold water. He was cold, shivering all the time. Meals were bread and water. Toast if he was lucky, but that was usually because the bread was already stale. He was allowed out to exercise for one hour per day, but that was in the freezing cold and only in his vest and pants. The humiliation and degradation were meant to break him, bring his behaviours under control, but so far it had not. He simply became more and more angry.

He was denied sleep. Every time he dozed off it seemed that someone banged on the door to wake him. The lights were switched on and off at random. All in an effort to control him. To make him obedient. To stop him running away. Bernie was no longer under the illusion now that a secure children's home was an easy option. Now he knew why Terry Hanslope had changed. It wasn't the solitary confinement that was the worst part though. The worst part of being alone was being vulnerable and available to Mr Dewsbury.

The beds at Trablos Grange were a solid divan style. When his mother had been alive, Bernie had been able to hide under the bed to get away from Bill. Bill never wanted the hassle of dragging him out from under the bed, especially if his mother was in the house. Too much noise. Mr Dewsbury didn't care about the noise and he didn't have to drag Bernie out from under the bed. Once Bernie was so scared, he messed the mattress. Leaving it covered in faeces, Mr

Dewsbury dragged him to the shower block, doused him in cold water and took him to the office. Bernie screamed, but no one heard. Afterwards, Mr Dewsbury threw him back into the room with the filthy mattress. Bernie had to earn privileges to be allowed to clean it.

Bernie's anger festered, growing every day that he was locked up, every day that he was abused. But not anger against the system or the abusers. He seethed at his mother for dying and leaving him alone. It was all her fault. She was to blame. If she'd not brought Bill back to their home, she would still be with him. He was fourteen now and he could have looked after her, but she'd let that scum Bill into their lives and he'd killed her. Bernie knew it was all down to his mother's weakness for smack. Her and all the women like her. One day, he promised himself, one day he'd get his own back on them all.

CHAPTER THIRTY-FIVE

Sarah Jenkins sat in the cold corridor clutching her briefcase to her breast. She was looking forward to the interview, knowing that it was the best way she could get a jump on the London papers. She was surprised that none of them had thought of speaking with Patrick Wheeler, but on the other hand, they did not have the inside information from the police through Sharon Raby that she did. Just as Sarah was about to ask the receptionist how much longer Dr Bertram would be, the woman herself opened her door and welcomed her with a warm smile.

Sarah shook the proffered hand and, squeezing past Dr Bertram's bulk to enter the room, she sat in the leather chair in front of the mahogany desk.

'What a beautiful room,' she said.

Dr Bertram smiled again. 'Not mine, I'm afraid.' She waved her hand at the rest of the room. 'All of this comes with the job, although I have come to love it as my own.'

She settled back in her own chair and fixed Sarah with her piercing blue eyes.

'Tell me,' she said, 'what do you hope to get from this interview?'

Sarah took her notepad and pencil from the briefcase and using it as a desk she thought about her response.

'I want to understand his motivations,' she began. 'What led him to commit so many murders, what started it all, to learn a little more about his childhood and background.'

Dr Bertram steepled her fingers, 'Not much at all then,' she said. 'What do you know about psychopathology?'

'Not a great deal,' admitted Sarah. 'Naturally, I've done some reading in preparation, both about Patrick himself and about his condition.' Sarah was confident that she was well prepared for the meeting, having studied everything she could find about the man and his crimes. She'd even spoken with a psychologist about psychopaths; she was convinced her homework would be enough to get her through one interview.

Dr Bertram pushed back her chair and rose. Sarah thought she was going to be asked to leave, but instead the doctor began to pace the office and speak as if giving a lecture to a hall of students.

'Patrick isn't redeemable,' she began. 'He is not someone who is going to get better.' She waggled her fingers as she said the last two words. 'Patrick is a psychopath, pure and simple. He scores highly on the psychopathology checklist. You've heard of that?'

Sarah nodded.

'Very good. He is a compulsive liar and will continue with the lie even when you've demonstrated to him quite clearly that it is a lie. He'll just brush it off.' Dr Bertram stopped her stroll briefly to ensure that Sarah was taking everything in.

'He'll try to convince you that he's changed,' Dr Bertram

continued, once satisfied that she had a rapt audience. 'He will never change. He cannot. He will tell you how guilty he feels about his crimes. This is a lie. He does not feel guilty because he does not understand the emotion, the concept of guilt. He understands various emotions such as fear and empathy as an intellectual exercise, but he does not experience them in the way that you and I do. However, he can fake them rather well.' Dr Bertram paused and looked at Sarah again. 'Don't let him suck you into his world,' she said.

Dr Bertram held out her hand again. Confused, Sarah was about to shake it, but Bertram shook her head. 'No, your list of questions. You were going to show them to me?'

Sarah retrieved the sheets of paper from her briefcase and handed them over.

'Very well,' said the doctor, after she had read through them. 'I'll get someone to take you down to him. There will be a nurse in the room at all times. You will not be alone with him. Please do not touch him, do not allow him to touch you, and do not give him any of your papers. He is still a very dangerous man.'

With that, Dr Bertram picked up the handset, spoke quietly into the phone and Sarah left to wait in the corridor for her escort.

As the first steel door clanged behind her, Sarah jumped. Her entire body was chilled and her heart pounding. All she carried with her were her questions, a notepad and a pencil. Everything else had been placed in a locker. At least Patrick Wheeler had agreed to see her. He could have declined her visit but, in the end, it had been remarkably simple to arrange. She had been eight when Wheeler, the Lytham Lyncher, was finally caught. In preparation for meeting him she had reviewed the old news reports and newspaper cuttings. Some she vaguely remembered from childhood, although her parents had been keen to keep her and her brother away from the horrors of Wheeler's crimes. What she considered appropriate research into psychopathology undertaken, Sarah felt well prepared to meet the man responsible for the demise of so many women.

Dean, the guard, or nurse as she supposed she should call him, was squeezed into white scrubs like conkers in a pillow case. Sarah smiled to herself, bemused to see patterns of the Superman 'S' on his t-shirt underneath the tight top. Three more steel doors and they had arrived.

'Ready?' he asked. Dean's voice was a higher pitch than she'd imagined it would be from his build, and she stifled the smile that threatened before inclining her head in the affirmative.

'I'll be in the room, but you won't know I'm there,' he assured her.

Sarah was not sure how that could be the case but whispered her thanks.

She sat on a plastic bench that was bolted to a steel table that in turn was bolted to the bare concrete floor. She shivered as she contacted the cold plastic, at least she hoped it was the plastic which was making her shiver in the relatively warm room. Then he was there, escorted in by another "nurse" and immediately sliding across the opposite bench. Patrick Wheeler, rapist and murderer. She had expected him to be shackled, hands and feet, like some US gangster but he wasn't even handcuffed. She instinctively put out her hand to shake his, but Dean shook his head and she snatched it back.

Wheeler smiled, lighting up his worn face, pale from lack of sunshine and fresh air. Sarah noticed the smile did not venture as far north as his eyes. His hands rested on the table, stained with nicotine, nails bitten to the quick. Sarah could not drag her eyes away from them and jumped when he said, 'Good afternoon.'

He laughed, a deep rasping sound, and the amusement did reach his eyes this time. Sarah saw the twinkle and understood why so many women could have been taken in by him.

She busied herself for a moment by getting her questions and notepad from the case.

'Hello, Patrick,' she began. 'Thank you for agreeing to see me. I wondered if I could start by asking some questions about your childhood and upbringing?'

Wheeler groaned. 'Tell me about your childhood. How banal. I'd hoped for more interesting questions. Haven't you done your research? There have, after all, been numerous articles and even some books about me. One or two of the more academic articles aren't too bad. But first, tell me, what's in all this for me?'

'As I said in my letter,' Sarah replied, holding his gaze, 'I am writing about the series of murders taking place in Gippingford. Slayings which have a striking similarity to your own, shall we say, method of dispatch. I wondered how you felt about that, but first I wanted to get some background, and when my piece gets picked up by the nationals then you'll be front page news all over again.' Sarah gave him what she hoped was a winning smile. Good grief, woman, you sound desperate, she thought.

'Okay,' he said. His eyes roved over her, settling on her breasts and soft white throat. Dean, the nurse, snapped his fingers and Wheeler laughed and looked away.

'Sit comfortably,' he said, 'and I'll begin. I had rather a boring childhood. My parents were Catholic, fairly strict but not hugely. I was quite a lonely child. I didn't make friends easily and preferred my own company.'

Sarah scratched shorthand on her notepad, as he began to talk about some of the, what he called, games he'd played on his own as a boy. She stopped writing altogether when he described breaking into a neighbour's loft of racing pigeons and trying to burn the birds' wings with a lighter. The neighbour had caught him, and his father belted him. A few weeks later he went back to the loft with petrol. He didn't bother to break in.

'What was going through your mind at that time?' she asked.

'Nothing,' he said, tilting his head to one side. 'I suppose I just wanted revenge for the hiding. He didn't have to tell my dad. He got what he deserved. The pigeons he had were never any good. He never won anything with them. Anyway, he made a mint on the insurance. I did him a favour. They had the money to move to a new house later that year.' Wheeler shrugged; the episode was scarcely worth mentioning for him.

'Talk me through the incidents leading up to the first woman you killed. I'd like to understand how you came to that decision,' she said. 'What triggered the attack?'

'Jeez, girl, now you're taking me back.' Wheeler leaned back in his chair, resting his head in his laced hands. A smile spread over his face as the memories returned.

'Oh yes.' He leaned towards her, clasping his hands together and pressing an index finger under his lip. 'Now I remember. The blues had lost at home. It had been a shitty season, to tell you the truth. I was working in a factory, so I was out with the lads, we'd all have a few pints to drown our sorrows. I was walking home, well, staggering really' — he chuckled at the memory — 'and there she was in front of me. Even though it was dark, I could see she was a tart, like, but she was a looker. I asked her how much, and you know what the cheeky cow said? Told me she wasn't interested. To me? I couldn't believe the bloody cheek of her. So, I gave her a slap or two and she ran off. I chased her and then when we got alongside this alley I found meself pushing her down it. I hadn't planned to do anything more than give her another slapping, but she had this bag, see, with a very long strap, and putting it round her neck seemed like a really good idea. So, I did. I squeezed. She was scared. I liked it.'

He sat back again, his eyes glazing over as he relished the recollection; Sarah swallowed hard to quell the bile rising in her throat. She'd made a mistake wanting to come and look at this man. What on earth was she going to learn from him other than he was as evil as everyone had told her? She wondered how quickly she could leave without it being reported as odd by her escorting guard.

'No, I guess you never really forget your first.' Wheeler leered at her, taking in a deep breath and releasing it in a long sigh. 'Thanks for bringing the memory back for me.'

Sarah was unable to hold his gaze. She heard him snigger as she looked away. It caused a flare of anger in her and she thrust her chin out, forcing herself to look at him once more.

'And what about the films?' she asked. 'What made you start filming your, er, your…'

'Crimes?' he said. 'Isn't that what you want to say?'

Sarah nodded.

'It just seemed like a good idea at the time. I had a mate who was selling video cameras at the pub. Fell off the back of a lorry. Still not cheap mind, but I had a place to take women by that time. I think I slowed down a bit that year, I was getting a bit bored, truth be told. I had the film to watch. I thought it would be a giggle to send it to the cops.'

Sarah looked up from her notebook and pulled her prepared questions from underneath the pad.

'You killed fourteen women in total. How do you feel about that now?' she read the question from her sheet. She had skipped a few and thought she would be skipping a lot more.

'Well obviously, since I've been in here and talked with Dr Bertram and her many, many predecessors I know that what I did was wrong. I'm mortified at what I did, but I have found God now and he has forgiven me.' He sniffed and wiped a tear from his eye, although Sarah saw that his hand was dry. He bowed his head and then looked up at her almost shyly. 'I pray every day for the souls of those poor dead women. I wrote to the families asking for their forgiveness too. I didn't get any replies. But that doesn't matter, I get lots of other letters. People are still captivated with me and what I did. One woman writes to me every week. Always wants to know how I am, and she likes me to tell her all about what I did. The more graphic the detail the more she seems to like it.'

'That sounds really fascinating,' Sarah said, looking at all the unasked questions on her list. They didn't matter. There was no great insight to be had. Patrick Wheeler was evil. He killed for the pleasure of it. That was all she needed to know. All she had succeeded in doing was scaring herself by coming face-to-face with a real-life bogeyman. 'You know, I think I've got enough to be going on with for now. I'll let you have a copy of the article before it goes to print.'

'Wait, you can't go just yet.'

Sarah was already rising from the bench. 'Why not?' she asked.

Wheeler reached into the small breast pocket of his prison shirt and withdrew a photograph.

Sarah hesitated.

'I haven't shown you her picture.'

Sarah frowned. It looked to her like one of those stock images sold with a photo frame. Wheeler was beaming at the image.

'The woman who writes to me. She's wonderful. We're going to meet up when I get parole. She's called Bernadette.'

CHAPTER THIRTY-SIX

'What did you make of him?' Dean said, as he escorted Sarah back to the reception area.

'I don't think I got anything I didn't know already, but just being in his presence confirms an awful lot that I couldn't get by reading about him. Was he really allowed to write to the families of his victims?' She watched Dean's face carefully while he answered.

'Yes, he wrote to every single one of them,' he said. 'None of the letters were posted though. He isn't allowed to seal his post. They're checked before they are sent. None of them got out. They were not exactly as remorseful as he said they were.'

'But what about this woman he's been writing to, sending her all those details?'

'*That* is something that we are going to have to look into,' said Dean, holding the large steel door open for her. 'He shouldn't be able to send anything like that to anyone. He can send letters to his solicitor and those are private. He might have managed some other way. As I said, it needs investigating and it will be without delay.'

They reached the exit and Dean was about to depart when he said, 'Don't believe everything he told you in there. He's no more turned to God than I have, and he's not getting parole any time soon. There isn't a parole board in the country that would let that man back on the streets. Thing is, he knows it too. Good luck with the article.'

Sarah watched Dean stride towards Dr Bertram's office, where he knocked on the door and walked straight in without waiting to be asked. I wish I could hear that conversation, she thought.

Sniggering to himself, Bernie laid his copy of the Gippingford Post on the canteen table. Dave Bradwell's face smiled up at him from the front cover. Beside it, a photo of Dave's car with the damage to the window on the passenger side clearly visible. Front page news, Dave, he thought. Famous at last, hey mate?

Although maybe not the fame Dave had sought. And a nasty shock for some poor sod. Gunshot wounds were so messy. All that blood. It was one reason Bernie preferred his own method. But, at least it had been contained in his car. Well, most of it. He turned to page three where the rest of the article was printed. He read how the twelve-bore had taken off Dave's lower jaw and the speed of the blast had forced it through the passenger window. Dave's other injuries didn't rate much mention, although Bernie gleaned the basic facts. Still, he thought, at least I can continue using the flat for a little while longer. Whistling, he left the paper on the table and wandered back to work.

Poole put the phone down and stuck his head around the edge of the partition to Carlson's apology for an office.

'Boss?' he said.

Carlson looked up and yawned. Poole resisted the temptation to do the same.

'What is it?' Carlson asked, pointing at the chair. 'Any news from Lytham?'

Poole nodded and sat down opposite his DCI.

'Yes, so much I almost don't know where to start.' He took a deep breath. 'Right, so as you know, Lytham got a new police station, but it was decided rather than take up expensive new office space to store old case notes, they'd hire secure storage. Everything was sent to a warehouse, night security guard properly vetted and all that. Anyways, after a while that decision was reversed, the bean counters said it was too expensive and a cheaper option would be secure units — you know, like people use for household stuff?'

Carlson nodded.

'Well, before that could happen there was the fire at the warehouse. What Jane told us was right. Some records were lost completely and others were water damaged,' Poole continued. He leaned his elbows on his knees, reading notes from the pad he held in front of him. 'It was before it was all computerised and a lot of the records of what should have been in the evidence boxes were also in the warehouse. Consequently, they were destroyed too. The sergeant I spoke to said we were lucky to get as much from the Lyncher case as we did. He reckoned if there were appeals on some old cases they'd not have anything to take to court. The only good thing he figured was that some of the cases were so old that the criminal in question would be dead already.'

'Okay, so how did supposedly secure material get nicked?'

'The salvaged records were moved to temporary storage

and the sergeant I spoke to confirmed what the civilian administrator told Jane — some of the records were moved unescorted. He also reckoned the new night guards at the temporary place didn't have proper vetting as the budget wouldn't stretch to it. Basically, from the night of the fire until all the records were eventually returned into the new secure units, which was two and a half months, there was ample opportunity to tamper with them.'

'So who are our suspects?' Carlson mused. 'Security guards? Firemen? But they'd be lucky to get what they wanted first try. Or maybe one of the van drivers moving the records around? But the same applies to them as the fire brigade. We've no real idea if it happened before the evidence was moved to the warehouse or after.'

'Well I do have something that's quite interesting,' Poole said, looking back at his notebook. 'The night security guards used at the temporary facility. There was still a record of their names, but when all the material was moved to secure holding, one of those guards disappeared. William Travis, as was. He still has a driving licence issued, but no passport, no P60s, no tax returns, no records of any kind since back in 2006.' Poole smiled, teeth white against his dark skin. 'Now don't you find that just a little suspicious?'

Tim Jessop dashed into the café to find Aspen already seated and coffee ordered.

'I can't be long,' he said. 'I got a bollocking from your Dad for not being on the ball and my thoughts being elsewhere.'

Aspen looked up at him with her wispy hair covering her eyes. 'I'm sorry,' she said. 'I won't keep you long. It's just that you're the only one I can talk to. I've searched Jade's room now, and I can't find her diary. I know she kept one. I bought her a notebook last Christmas. Leather-bound, handmade paper,' Aspen twisted her hands together as she spoke. 'She told me she loved the book and she wrote in it every day that I was home for the holidays. Now it's nowhere in her room. I suppose she could have destroyed it before she...' Aspen fell silent.

Tim reached out and squeezed her hand. For a moment she looked down at their hands together and then she squeezed back.

'Are you sure that your Dad hasn't got it?' Tim asked. 'I'm told he was pretty pissed off with Superintendent Tasker as they weren't making headway on the case. It was easier before; they were both the same level. Now that Tasker is the Super, your Dad must pay him the respect due to his rank, even if we do all think he's a twat. Tasker I mean, not your Dad,' he added hurriedly.

'I hadn't thought of that,' Aspen replied. 'He was so angry at the time, I didn't like to ask him. Now he's just so sad.' She pulled a tissue out of her bag and wiped her eyes. 'Mum's being an absolute bitch to him and he won't discuss it with me.'

'You need to talk to him,' Tim said. 'He did everything he could to find out who was behind it. He and Tasker had a stand-up row in the canteen, that was just before he went off on compassionate leave. Most people think it was stress —'

'It was,' said Aspen, 'but thank you for telling me. He keeps it all to himself. Doesn't let anyone in. At least I know for certain that he was doing all he could. I thought he would.'

'He's a great bloke, your Dad.' Tim squeezed her hand once more. 'I'm sorry, I really do have to go. We've got a briefing in half an hour and if I'm late he won't be quite so great to me,' he grinned at her. 'Meet again later? I'll text you when I'm leaving the office.'

'Yeah, sure,' said Aspen, and watched him leave. She held her own hand where he had held it.

Tim just made it back in time for the team briefing. One of the crime analysts, a geek with greasy hair and bad skin, was seated near the white board. Poole beckoned the guy and he stood up to address the team.

'Hi,' he began, in a voice stronger and more confident than his appearance suggested. 'I've spent several days following the movements of Tina Hoyes via her smartphone. As you all know, the phones ping from cells masts, but we can also trace someone's movements by what we call secondary data. If you don't switch off the Wi-Fi on your phone, it connects with places that have Wi-Fi. So, we'll get a trace if you've walked past Starbucks or Costa, even Maccy Dees. These,' he said, placing a map on the white board, 'are the last whereabouts of Ms Hoyes. As you can see, she was spending a lot of time around the London Road area. I don't think she was working because you never see the phone move at speed. What you do see is her in pubs and coffee bars — pinging the Wi-Fi there. She's not moving fast, so she is most likely to have been on foot.'

'But what was she doing?' Tim asked.

'I know, or at least can make a good guess,' said Jane. 'She's chatting to the girls and punters. Her Dad's interview script says she looked like she was on a mission. The info from your confidential informant says the same, Boss. You don't think she was trying to find out who this bloke was, do you?'

Carlson released a huge sigh. 'I think you might be right,

Jane. I know that she'd been told about the photos and the last text my CI got was that she knew who he was. Oh, silly, silly girl. Why didn't she come straight to us?'

Carlson thumped the table, making several of the team jump. 'Well if you thought that's bad, we have even worse news,' he said. 'Ben?'

Poole nodded and took up the spot at the front of the room. 'Right,' he said. 'Thanks to the effort Jane has put in, we are now confident that we have a copycat. We don't know exactly how he got hold of the old case notes or even how much he has got, but we have a fair idea. We do know that the information we were sent is not complete. We have a possible suspect in a night security guard, details in your folders.' He indicated the manila files on each desk, 'But we don't know his whereabouts. Jane is going to lead on that aspect of the investigation with a couple of people from uniform to help her out. He needs to be traced to see if he knows anything.'

'Tim,' Carlson continued, 'I need you to trace Tina's movements using the Wi-Fi map. See who she was talking to and what they were talking about. Talk to the working girls. They no doubt know something and, now that four girls have been killed, they might change the habit of a lifetime and actually talk to us. Ben, you and I have another autopsy to attend. As if we haven't got enough to do, the Super wants us to have a look into this gangland killing of Bradwell, the guy we had in for interview. Though why his team can't take it on is beyond me. It was his bloody snout after all.'

CHAPTER THIRTY-SEVEN

Sarah came back to the table with fresh drinks. 'I've had an idea,' she said, 'about catching this guy.'

'Don't you think we should leave it to the police, Sarah?'

'But you just told me that his mind's not on the job?'

'I told you that for your ears only. Not to spread it around. Don't you go putting it in your bloody rag.'

'In confidence, yes, I know, but all the same.' Sarah wasn't sure whether to be offended about the reference to her paper or not. Inwardly she smiled, as it was not that long ago she'd been calling it the same thing, and she needed Shazza's help to complete her story. She looked at the glass and twisted it round in the condensation puddle which was forming at its base on the table. 'Don't you think we can find out who he is?'

'No! That's what Tina was trying and look what happened. Don't be daft,' replied Shazza. 'Don't take no risks. He's dangerous. He's killed four times now. Four of my friends. Don't yow get that? I don't want to be next.'

'You wouldn't be. I won't put anyone else in that position,' said Sarah, sipping her slimline tonic.

'Oh, you think you could do it? Bloody hell woman, you'd actually place yourself as a target? Apart from you being mad, completely and utterly effing mad, how's it going to work? You tell me that.'

Sarah leaned across the table to her new friend. Quietly and slowly, she laid out her plan to Shazza with guffaws of disbelief from the other.

'So I'm gonna dress you up as a tom?'

Sarah nodded.

'No, I'm sorry, I won't do it.' Shazza pushed back from the table. 'I can't help you, Sarah, I'm sorry. I'd be happy to take you down there to meet and talk with some of the girls, let you get a feel for what it's like. See how they are feeling. I know some girls have given up the game. Lots more are working from parlours and clubs. Not as much money in it, but it's safer.'

'Okay,' Sarah said, beckoning Shazza to sit down again. 'I have to say that I was kinda going off the idea after I met that Wheeler guy. I know there were guards in the room, but Wheeler was terrifying. His eyes seemed to drink me up, yet there was no life in them. Just nothing. But,' she said, 'will you still help me pick out some appropriate clothing?'

'Nah, don't be daft, you'll be fine as you are. If you're with me, I'm sure some of the girls will still talk to you. You don't have to dress like a tom to talk to one.'

'Well,' Sarah twisted her glass around again. 'It was more that I was thinking... I was thinking it would be more authentic if I was dressed the part. Get my own impression. Experience the cold. The vulnerability. You know the sort of thing.'

Shazza sighed. 'Yeah I know,' she said. 'Being for sale. Yeah, go on, if that's what you want to do I'll give yah a hand. But Sarah, you know I believes in yow, please don't do anything stupid. I believed in Teens, you know. But what she did was dangerous and stupid. I don't want you putting yourself in danger just for a story!'

'But it wouldn't be just for the story. It would be for you, for the other girls, for justice.'

'Oh, justice my arse! You want a scoop.'

Sarah laughed at the old-fashioned phrase. 'Well, okay, maybe I do, but justice would be part of the story. Wouldn't it?'

'If you say so.' Shazza glared at her but caught the infectious smile.

'So you'll help me?'

'Yes, I'll help you. But not to go after the guy. I'll help you get a feel for the streets. But that's it. Agreed?'

Sarah nodded.

'Okay then. You got a name yet?'

'A name?' Sarah looked puzzled.

'Yes, working girls have street names. I used to be Pepper, 'cos I was a bit feisty like.'

Sarah thought for a moment. 'I could be Danni,' she said, 'after my dog, Danvers, but I guess that's too Game of Thrones. Oh, I've got it. He's a black and tan Doberman. I can call myself Ebony.'

Shazza laughed and shook her head. 'We might need to colour your hair a bit darker,' she said.

Sarah tottered into Westerfield Road, swaying slightly. The shoes she wore were far higher than anything she'd ever tried before. Shazza had picked them out from a rack in the shop and held them aloft as if they were some glittering prize. Sarah guessed she'd be giving them to Shazza afterwards. She was glad she had given up on the original idea of hunting down the killer. Now that she was on the street though, with the wind whistling up the short skirt, goose bumps on her arms, legs and chest, she realised just how stupid this immersive experience was too. Even her stomach was cold.

'How did you do this night after night?' she hissed at Shazza, who stood in the shadows.

'I needed me fix. That's how.' Shazza hissed back. 'I told you, that's all you think of. Nothing else matters. No one. Not. One. Thing. All that matters is the smack.' She turned to chat to some other women who were now lounging on the edge of the road too. They gathered, talking away as if they were at the office water cooler rather than a street corner. Sarah stood on the fringe. None of them, it seemed, wanted to talk to her at length. Occasionally one would look at her. Run an eye up and down and laugh before turning back to their conversation.

A car turned into the road and they dispersed. Lining up on the pavement edge, a short distance apart from each other. Giving the kerb crawler enough time to survey the goods. It was a market after all. The car stopped, and one girl placed her hand on the roof of the car, bending down, talking to him through the open window. The driver stretched across and opened the door. She got in. As it drove away, Sarah heard a few phones clicking. Some of the girls were holding theirs up, taking a photograph of the number plate.

'Safety measures,' the one called Kandis said, slipping the phone into a tiny bag. 'We have to take care of each other.'

'Why do you do it? Aren't you scared?' Sarah asked, taking in the woman's too-high heels which made it impossible for her to stand up straight. Kandis's shoulders were pushed forward and her rear backwards, so she could maintain her balance. Her calves, wiry and muscular in otherwise skeletal legs, were beginning to show the first hint of varicose veins.

Scared?' she spat the word at Sarah. 'What good would it be if I was scared? Yer just gotta get on with it.'

'Is getting a fix that important?'

'A fix? A fix?' said Kandis. 'I ain't no smack head. I've got kids. I can't bring 'em up on what the government gives me. They want the same as all the other kids at school and I've gotta provide it. I can't get a nice little office job like you. I've got no choice. Stupid bitch. Now piss off home. Show's over.'

Sarah stepped backwards from the pavement edge. She looked at Shazza. 'You know, I'm terrified just standing here,' she said. 'I think I've had enough. No one wants to talk to me anyway.'

'Thank fuck for that,' Shazza retorted. 'Come on, time I bought you a drink. Let me introduce you to Gary and The Bell.'

They made their way to the pub, not noticing the car sat at the end of the road. Lights off, engine off, the driver still and watching.

CHAPTER THIRTY-EIGHT

It didn't take long for Sarah to decide that The Bell was not the type of pub she would ever feel comfortable in. She was confident that this would be her only visit there. Street girls came in to get warm and use the loo for a quick clean up between customers. Men came in to meet street girls. Trade was brisk, but Sarah found the mood predatory and threatening. Each man who looked at her assessed her skills, assumed her likely price and whether she'd be worth it. Beverages, drugs, food and girls; everything was a commodity with prices negotiable. Sarah stood leaning on the bar taking in the atmosphere. Despite the warmth, she shivered and wiped her clammy hands on her miniskirt. A man approached her and cupped her breast with his hand, giving it a small squeeze.

'How much, love?' he whispered in her ear.

Sarah pushed him away in disgust, and he laughed at her.

'I can't stay here,' she hissed in Shazza's ear. 'This whole idea was a mistake. I'm sorry, but thanks for helping me out today. I appreciate it. I'll see you Tuesday night, yeah?'

'You sure will,' said Shazza. 'You gonna be okay getting home in those heels?'

'I'll get a cab.'

'Yeah, well just get yourself up onto the main drag. Getting in a taxi round here might not be quite what you're expecting.' Shazza grinned at her and raised her drink in salutation and farewell.

Sarah smiled back and wandered out into the night. She ducked down the side street which led to the centre of town. She'd be able to get a taxi from the rank there. She tottered along, using the wall to keep her upright. When she stopped, the soft, light footsteps behind her stopped too. She looked behind. Nothing. Imagination, she thought. She carried on walking but slightly faster. The steps following her kept pace with hers. She could hear the rapid breathing as he got closer. Sarah could see the bright lights of Charnwood Road ahead and she started to run. At least she tried to. A hand sneaked around her mouth. Sweaty. Salty. Stale. She raked the heel of the stiletto down his leg and he laughed. She stamped again on his toes, but he chuckled again, all the time squeezing her nose and mouth. Sarah gasped for breath and registered the sweet-smelling solvent before she slid to the ground.

She was lying on a dirty sofa. It smelt of rancid fat, stale cigarette smoke and, if she wasn't mistaken, a hint of damp newspaper hung in the room. Fresh air had long been a stranger. She pushed herself into a sitting position.

'Where am I?' she said groggily, peering around the room while it swum into focus. A face appeared in front of her. 'Who are you?' she asked it. 'What am I doing here? How the hell did you get me here?'

'You ask a lot of questions.' The man in front of her sat on his haunches. 'Where were you off to? One minute you were waiting for business and then you left. You're new. I was interested in trying you out. Then you just pissed off. I didn't like that.'

'Yeah, you're right, I'm new. I just changed me mind,' Sarah tried to mimic the voice of the woman Kandis. 'First time. Bit scared, see.' Sarah scrabbled around on the sofa, trying to cover her legs.

The man moved closer. He ran his hands up her legs, his thumbs brushing the inside of her thighs.

'I can help you with that,' he murmured. The smell of cheap aftershave was overpowering. 'Help you overcome your nerves. Break you in like.' He continued whispering and pawing at her.

Sarah pushed herself as deep into the sofa as she could. She managed to get her hand in her pocket and wrapped it around her mobile phone. She moved her fingers as slowly and unobtrusively as possible. It failed.

He pulled her hand from the pocket and she squealed as he twisted her wrist. The mobile fell to the floor. He picked it up and studied it.

'Nice model for a druggie,' he said. 'Who were you texting?' He leaned over her. Sarah tried to move away but she was trapped in the corner of the sofa. 'Who are you?' he whispered.

'Nobody, I'm no one,' Sarah babbled, trying to stay in character. 'I was just texting my mate to let her know I was okay and where I was. You know we're all doing it now; trying to keep safe with this nutter about.'

He stood up and took a pace back. Without warning, he stepped forwards and stung her across the face with a backhander. 'I don't buy that. You're not like the other girls. Who are you really?'

'I told you, no one.' Sarah raised a hand to her jawbone. The lip was already swelling. She tasted the salty-coppery tang of blood filling her mouth.

He grabbed her handbag and tipped the contents on the grimy table. Notepad, tissues, pencils, lipstick, purse, a digital recorder. 'Jesus! What are you? An effing copper? Shit, shit, shit!'

Bernie raised his hands to his face; they continued rising until he was clenching his insipid hair. He sighed deeply and looked at her again. 'So, what are you? Vice? Murder?' Opening the purse, he found a few notes and coins. No cards, no ID.

'Yes, I'm a police officer,' she said. 'Any moment now, a dozen coppers are going to raid this place looking for me. My phone has GPS, so they know exactly where I am.'

He looked at her and laughed out loud. 'Don't worry love, I have a way of dealing with phone signals,' he said. 'Where's your ID though? Even if you're undercover you'd need to prove you're a copper. So, come on, tell me. Who are you really?' He slapped her again. She wanted to cry but she wouldn't give him the pleasure. She felt a rage building in her.

'Okay, I'm a reporter,' Sarah glared at him. Her head was pounding but her dark eyes shone with defiance.

'A reporter, hey? And what does a reporter want with me?' he said, as he flicked through her notebook. He frowned at the shorthand and placed it back in the handbag.

'Some background on the killings. I wanted to find out about the type of men who pick up prostitutes, you know, that sort of thing.'

'I was watching you, you know. You were with another

girl. You both let half a dozen punters by. Why was that? You could have spoken to any of them. What were you up to?'

Sarah opened her mouth, then closed it, unable to speak for the blood welling inside. Bernie passed her a tissue. It seemed to her such an incongruous thing to do. She spat into it.

'Were you waiting for someone?'

'I — we weren't.'

'Bollocks! You were waiting for the killer, weren't you?' He laughed, 'Wasn't that rather stupid? Did you think he'd let you get your story and allow you to walk away?'

Sarah shrugged. 'I changed my mind,' she said.

'Well that was probably sensible,' he said, 'apart from one thing. You got your story. It's me they're after.'

Sarah's eyes widened and, although in the back of her mind she had known it already, she still let out a gasp. She looked quickly around the room. The tiny table was clear, but she saw a corkscrew lying on the drinks' cabinet.

He caught her gaze, shook his head sadly and sniffed. 'Not going to happen,' he said. 'I'm gonna have to kill you now. You know that, don't you?'

Sarah nodded, her defiance disappeared and tears ran down her face, but she kept the corkscrew in her peripheral vision.

'Shame,' he said, fondling her legs once more. 'I was looking forward to some fun with you.'

CHAPTER THIRTY-NINE

As Marguerite left the warm office with its colourful cush-
ions, warm blankets, cheerful paintings and plentiful tissues
she was beginning to feel better. Not yet happy, but happier
than she had been in a long time. She had seen the therapist
recommended by her colleague six times in the last two
weeks. So far it was going better than expected. Although,
deep down she knew that it was going to take some time to
come to terms with what Jade had done and, more importantly, to forgive her, Marguerite felt that she had at least
started the journey. However, there was one aspect which
had come out of the therapy that she had not anticipated.
Not quite sure what it was going to entail, she had assumed it
would be comfortable, almost cosy, chats about the impact
the suicide had had on her. Marguerite had not envisaged
that the therapist would put across Jade's point of view. Far
from allowing Marguerite to wallow in her own misery, she
had taken the step of discussing cyber-bullying with her in
detail. Making her think about the impact it had on the
victims. How isolated and powerless they believe themselves
to be. How under siege and helpless Jade would have felt. At

first it did nothing to make Marguerite any better; in fact, she thought she was regressing rather than improving, and she hated the therapist for putting her through the anguish again. She felt guilty for not having spotted it and was convinced she was a poor mother for not seeing Jade's pain, but that wasn't the route they were going down either. The therapist assured her that there would have been nothing she could have done; not once Jade had made up her mind. Marguerite needed, she said, not just to forgive her daughter but to forgive herself.

However, before she did anything else Marguerite knew she needed to talk to Aspen to apologise, and together they would both spring-clean Jade's room. Jade hated her room being cleaned, and the two of them would laugh about that and they would become friends again. As she drove home Marguerite had it all mapped out in her head; perhaps they would start on Saturday. It would be a healing process and they would start to forgive each other again. It would be perfect. She would make sure that it was.

Shazza rolled out of bed and wandered to the kitchen. She put the kettle on, popped a tea bag in a nearly clean mug and checked her pockets for her mobile. Nothing from Sarah. Shazza swore softly. *Bitch, you were supposed to let me know you got home okay.* She wondered if it was too early to ring. Sod it, she thought, no it ain't. She should have texted me.

She dialled the number and held the phone to her ear. Straight to voicemail. Bugger, where are you? she thought, but decided that she'd try again in a bit.

Marguerite Carlson decided today would be the day to tackle Jade's room. She gathered dusters, polish, window cleaner and bin bags into a bucket and placed them at the foot of the stairs. She put the vacuum cleaner next to the pile. She decided to let Aspen sleep a little longer and returned to the kitchen, switched the coffee machine on and put some croissants in the oven.

By 9am Shazza still had no answer from Sarah and her calls were going directly to voicemail. She knew Sarah would not stay out all night because of the dog. She paced the length of the lounge, no more than five paces, so used the hallway as well. *Where the hell was she?* She'd only had to walk up to Charnwood Road to get a taxi. How hard was that? Oh Christ, she'd not fallen off those ruddy heels, had she? Hospital. Call the hospital, that was the thing to do. What was the number? What the hell was the number?

She rifled in the cubby hole near the front door. She was sure there'd been a phone book when she moved in. If she'd not chucked it. Oh, for fuck's sake! If only she could afford a smart phone like Tina used to own, she could have looked the number up on there.

She looked in the cupboard under the sink and still nothing. Racing to the bedroom she flung a sweatshirt on over the top of her pyjamas and banged on the door of the neighbour's flat.

She called the hospital. Nothing. No sprained or broken ankles. No Sarah Jenkins. She scrolled down her short list of contacts and called someone else.

Marguerite heard her husband's mobile in the hallway. He'd left it in his jacket again. She decided that he could do with a little longer in bed too. The phone rang again. And again. Whoever it was wasn't leaving a message. They wanted to speak to him.

She poured him a coffee from the filter jug, took the mobile out of his pocket and walked upstairs. Who the hell was Sharon? she wondered. He was a DCI now; he didn't have informants as he'd used to when they were young. She'd always found it hard to trust him when he was off to meet some criminal type or another.

She plonked the coffee and the mobile on the bedside cabinet and shook him until he woke.

'Someone called Sharon seems desperate to get hold of you,' she said, and stalked out of the room, pulling the door to, but not closing it.

Carlson, bleary eyed, looked at the coffee and then at the phone as it rang again.

'Ronnie? Ronnie? Is that yow?' Shazza gasped down the phone. 'Something's happened to Sarah. She left me in the pub, but she's not got back to me and I can't get hold of her and she's not texted me and she's not in the hospital, and I can't get hold of her. Ronnie, something's happened.'

'Slow down, slow down,' he said. 'Who's Sarah?'

Marguerite listened at the door.

Who's Sarah? She heard him say. Oh shit, Shazza, what have you done? he asked whoever was on the phone. Okay, calm down, I'm coming. I'll be with you in a bit. Just calm down, okay?

Marguerite heard drawers opening and the wardrobe doors banging, but he opened the bedroom door before she could move. He seemed surprised to see her standing there.

'I have to go out,' he said. 'I'll be back later but I don't know what time.'

He pushed past Marguerite, raced down the stairs and was gone. Marguerite stood on the landing in askance, wondering who on earth Shazza was and why one call from her made her husband race out the door.

Later, when Aspen finally woke and made her way to the kitchen, Marguerite was no longer in the mood for cleaning Jade's room. It would have to wait for another day.

Carlson got into his car and once the phone and car connected, he called Gippingford station.

'Sergeant Dobbs,' he said. 'Good, I'm glad it's you. Can you get me the contact details for the editor of the Gipping-ford Post? Yes, his, sorry her, personal number. She won't be at her desk today. And I need to know the address of a reporter, Sarah Jenkins. Oh, and can you call Poole and get him on standby? No, I'm not sure if I'll need him in or not. Just let him know to be ready in case. Thanks.'

Carlson ended the call and joined the slip road for the bypass. It would be quicker than going through town on a Saturday morning. He slowed for the speed limit on the bridge, which gave him time to think and wonder what the hell the two of them had been up to. How did they even know each other, he thought? Talk about small town. He left the A-road and drove onto the estate where Shazza had her flat. He braced himself for the plod up those stairs but for once the lift was working.

Shazza was at her door waiting for him, wearing socks and a creased baggy t-shirt.

'You'd better tell me what the hell you've been up to,' was all he said as he pushed past her and into the tiny hallway.

Shazza followed him into the lounge and curled up in the chair, pulling the t-shirt over her knees. Carlson paced, although his longer legs made the distance three paces and not her five. She told him of Sarah's original plan, how stupid it was and how they didn't really know who they were after in any case.

'I agreed to take her to meet some of the girls, so she could interview them,' she said. 'You know, get some good background for her story. Anyway, none of them would talk to her, so Sarah changed her mind. Then after seeing one girl go off with a man and the other girls taking photos of the number plate, she kinda freaked out and so we called it a night.

'We went to the pub and had a couple of drinks, then she decided to go home. I told her to walk up to Charnwood Road to get a taxi, not that she could really walk in them shoes. I've called the hospital. She's not been teken in with a broken ankle or anything. I don't know what to do and I'm really worried now.'

'I can't believe you've been so ruddy stupid, the pair of you! After Tina as well. Why didn't you just leave it to us? We are the professionals after all.'

'I —' Shazza began.

'You what?' Carlson snarled at her.

'I wasn't sure you was coping all that well. After yer daughter and all that,' she said.

'And that gives you the right to interfere in a police investigation? To put your lives at risk? How stupid can you be?'

Shazza huddled deep into the armchair. 'I did try to put her off the idea, but she was having none of it. She wanted to get the kind of story that none of the London journos could, 'cos she had me and I knew the girls on the street,' she said. 'Look Mr C, she was gonna do it, with or without my help.'

'Well you clearly didn't try hard enough. Hang on' — he raised his hand to silence her and answered his phone. 'Text me the details,' he said. 'Right, you. Get dressed. We're going to her house.'

Shazza ran to the bedroom and scrabbled into jeans that were lying on the floor. She slid her feet into trainers, grabbed a coat, keys and her phone.

'Ready,' she said.

They drove to Mendlesham in silence. When they reached Sarah's little house, the pitiful howls of the trapped dog made it clear that she was not home.

CHAPTER FORTY

When Poole returned to his flat late on the Sunday evening the last thing he felt like doing was playing on the computer. He poured himself a cold light beer and checked his emails. He saw that there was a notification from the online gaming software. He logged on and there was a message for him from Treallis.

'Missed you this weekend. Hope we can quest again soon.'

He started to type something in the medieval language used by most players in the game but could not think of anything suitable. In the end he typed *'More quests IRL'* and left it at that.

He sat back in his chair and sipped the beer.

'I have quests of my own too — fare thee well' appeared on the screen. Ben frowned at the message. The wording seemed familiar, although in another context, but he couldn't remember where. Although it seemed a little odd, he'd seen worse. People were there to role play. Some used it as an opportunity to step out of their real lives completely and take on a new persona. They could be braver than they were or could be in real life, more foolhardy, weirder. He was definitely used to people being weirder. But then who was he to judge? He had always been told he was odd himself. At university his girlfriend, Penny, told him he needed to open up more. He'd told her he wasn't really sure what that meant.

'I tell you I love you,' he'd told her, but apparently that wasn't enough. Apparently, he had to tell her his every single thought as well. She always looked disappointed when he replied "nothing" to the "what are you thinking?" question. What was he meant to be thinking about? he wondered. He was pretty sure he wasn't supposed to say he'd been thinking about whether the carburettor on his Fiesta sounded dodgy or not. Poole knew he didn't know much about women, but he knew that much. Whatever he did, Penny always wanted more. She left him for the captain of the chess team in the end. Poole tried to be heartbroken, but he really didn't know how. He knew he missed her. He missed the sex, the attention, but he didn't miss the stupid questions and the matching sweaters. He didn't miss those at all. They suited Captain Chess though. Gave him a bit more colour. He needed it.

After Penny there had been other girls; he had no problems attracting them, but he couldn't sustain the enthusiasm or the interest. He grew tired of the arguments that they all seemed to want to have. So much angst, when all he really wanted was the peace and quiet to read a good book. Later, when he got into online gaming, he had all the company he wanted. Well, virtually all. And virtually all virtual company. And if he didn't want company then he could play Player Vs Environment and set his character to be on a lone quest. He didn't need company. He had plenty at work and it was overrated. Although perhaps the company of coppers, criminals and lawyers left something to be desired.

He switched off the computer and allowed himself another beer. He sat in the semi dark, relishing the silence.

Aspen was relishing the silence too. After not coming home at all on the Saturday, her father had returned to the house at Sunday lunchtime in need of a shower, a change of clothes and something to eat. He looked grey; Aspen had never seen him so exhausted. Her mother had made a big fuss of laying out a roast dinner for him but when he'd entered the dining room, she'd thrown it at his head. A blazing row had ensued and whilst her mother screamed at her father, Aspen had arranged to meet Tim and spend some time with him. He'd collected her from the house and they'd had a late lunch at a country pub, then afterwards they'd gone back to his flat where they'd consumed the two bottles of white Rioja Aspen had taken from her parents' house. They'd snuggled together on the sofa, not watching a film she'd chosen, fingers entwined. Tim had leaned in towards her and kissed her, tracing the rim of her lips with his finger and then his tongue. He'd kissed her deeply.

'What took you so long?' she'd whispered.

He'd eased away from her and grinned. She knew the reason. She'd taken his hand. 'Bedroom?' she'd asked, and led him through the door he'd indicated. At first, they'd undressed slowly, drinking in each other's body. Then giggling, they'd met in the centre of the bed and ripped clothing apart. Now, satisfied and exhausted, they lay with legs entwined and Aspen, happier than she had been in some time, knew the last thing she wanted to do was go home.

Bernie Latimer was not having a quiet Sunday evening, although it was quieter than it had been. When Rose had come in from her shift at the call centre on Saturday morning, the first thing she'd wanted to know was why his face was scratched.

'What the hell happened to you?' she asked.

'I was tackling that big bush in the back garden,' he said, 'after I dropped you off. You've been on at me to do it.'

'What, in the dark? You really do think I'm fucking stupid, don't you? What the hell have you been up to, Bernie? I know nail marks when I see them,' she shouted at him. 'Have you been visiting those whores again? I thought we'd discussed this. You promised me you'd not do it anymore. And now with this nutter on the loose, you've been back with those tarts and you've got into a fight with one of them. You know, you're the one who's fucking stupid.' She flung her hands in the air, no longer caring if he hit her or not.

'You know what?' she said. 'I don't give a shit anymore. I've had enough. You're on your own. I've had it with you. I'm going to stay with my sister for a bit.'

She turned to leave, and he grabbed her arm to stop her going. She glared at him and prised his fingers off her wrist.

'That's the last time you touch me, Bernie,' she hissed. 'The very last time.' She went to the lounge door and then turned back.

'One thing you do need to know Bernie, is that when Janice and I went away for that weekend, I didn't lose anything. Not once; not my purse, not my keys, nothing. There's no way I would have left my keys in the flour jar. Janice reckons you're doing it to make me think I'm going barmy. It nearly worked, you know. If it hadn't been for my weekend away.' And with that she stomped out. She'd not even taken a change of clothes, he realised.

Rose reappeared on Sunday and then she did take some clothes. As many as she could get in the dark blue suitcase she'd bought for the trip to Tenerife last year.

Bernie had expected another row, but she'd said nothing. Not a single word. She'd kept the key, so she was coming back. Despite what she said, she was too thick to survive on her own without him. She loved him; she was always telling him that she did, and he'd told her he loved her too. Yeah, she'd be back.

In the meantime, he had to do something with the reporter, and he wasn't quite sure what that was going to be. Still there was no hurry to make a decision. She wasn't going anywhere, and Dave wouldn't be blundering in anytime soon either. He could take his time. Have another beer. She might have died of fright by the time he went back there. That would be the best solution all round. In fact, that would be perfect.

Carlson pushed himself out of his chair and made his way across the squad room for the team briefing. The faces of five young women stared back at him from the photo gallery on the white board.

Ben Poole, waiting to begin, looked at him as he sat down at the periphery of the group. Carlson dipped his head and, as Poole began to speak, a hush slid across the room.

'Okay,' he said clearing his throat. 'We now have the bodies of four young women and a fifth, the reporter who found the first body, is missing. No, this is not a coincidence, as she decided to interview the working girls for a newspaper story and thought dressing up like them would lend her credibility.'

The team groaned again as they had done when the news was first given to them. Poole help up his hands for silence and continued.

'I know, but hush up you lot. Sarah Jenkins gave up on her reporting as hardly any of the girls agreed to an interview, so she went to the Bell for a drink and then left to get a taxi. We also know that she didn't make it into Charnwood Road to get that taxi. We've not got any CCTV from Hanbury Road as they've been smashed again. Yes, again. And CCTV in Charnwood Road does not show her appearing at all that evening. This' — he pointed to the map — 'is the side street she most likely walked up, and you can see that there are cameras here and here, which would have shown her leaving Silent Street and entering Charnwood. However, her mobile phone does leave Silent Street, goes back into London Road and then is switched off.'

'Do we think that she switched it off herself?' Tim Jessop raised his head from his notebook.

'Well, I don't know, Tim,' said Poole. 'That's what we need to find out. That's what detection is all about.'

'No, what I mean is,' said Tim, trying to recover at least some kudos, 'is that we've checked all the dead girls' phones and they all ping in London Road, and then there's nothing. We're not getting any mapping outside of London Road and, thanks to the other working girls, we have most of their numbers. You can see when one of their phones coincides with a punter's — well, except when he's switched it off and is hiding his whereabouts from his missus. But then you see her phone pinging again back in London Road. With our dead girls the phones ping in London Road and then nothing. It's like he makes them switch them off as soon as they get in his car or something.'

Jane Lacey scratched her head with her pen for a moment. 'He couldn't be using a phone blocker, could he?'

All their heads swung in Jane's direction. Carlson stood up. 'That's a really good idea, DC Lacey,' he said. 'Can you follow that up with the techies? If he can buy or make a portable one, then that would explain how we lose their phone signals. Can you also check on the radius of the blocking? It can't be so powerful that it knocks out the radio signals for emergency services, or we'd know about it before now. Thanks, Jane. Really well done.'

'However,' he continued. 'This gets us no further forward with our missing reporter. She was seen in the Bell; she wasn't seen talking with anyone and she left on her own. She was heading to get a taxi and she'd been warned not to get one in London Road. Therefore, the quickest if not the most sensible route would have been to walk up Gipping Street. One of the girls she was speaking with earlier thinks she saw Sarah walk into Gipping Street but she's not sure. She got a customer just after, so she wasn't around to see her come out again. If indeed that's what she did. We need to find her, people, and fast.'

Poole took control of the briefing once more and assigned the various tasks to the team. He came over to Carlson's door-less office.

'Okay, Boss?' he asked.

'It's my fault,' Carlson replied.

'How do you work that out?'

'I told her. Sharon,' he said, in response to Poole's puzzled look. 'I told her all about Jade and from that she decided that I wasn't up to the job of finding who'd killed her friends. And now I'm thinking she and this bloody reporter cooked up a stupid idea to find the guy themselves. It's all my ruddy fault.'

Carlson saw Poole half nod then watched his DS stiffen. He had been about to agree and then probably thought better of it. Instead Poole said, 'You can't take it all on yourself, Guv. We'll find her.'

'Yes,' said Carlson, 'but will we find her alive?'

CHAPTER FORTY-ONE

September 2006

When William Travis let himself into his bedsit, a palm hit him in the back, crashing him through his doorway and onto the floor. The assailant followed, slamming the door shut behind them.

'What the fuck?' Travis tried to push himself up, but he was grabbed by the scruff of his neck, had his arm seized and was frog marched into the centre of the room. Propelled onto the single bed, he smashed his head into the wall. Now that his attacker had let go, Travis rolled over to see who it was. A young man in his early thirties, with light blue eyes and wispy pale hair stood before him, breathing heavily. A small rucksack over his shoulder. He gave Travis a mocking smile.

It couldn't be. Could it?

'Bernie?' his voice came out as a croak and not as firm as he would have liked.

'Yeah,' said the other, waving his hands jazz fashion. 'Surprise!'

'What are you doing here? How the hell did you find me?'

'It wasn't easy, you shit, but I decided you were worth the bother,' Bernie replied.

Travis shifted into a sitting position and continued staring at his visitor. Now that he knew it was little Bernie, he felt a lot less panicked.

'What can I do for you, son?' he asked.

'You can stop calling me son, for a fucking start,' Bernie retorted. 'After what you did to me, and to my mum?'

'Okay,' Travis said, 'I guess this isn't a social call. So, you might as well tell me how and why you've taken the time and effort to track me down. You can start with how.'

Bernie looked around for something to sit on. There was nothing but the bed, a rickety chair and a beanbag. He chose the beanbag. Travis relaxed. The kid had put himself at a disadvantage. Idiot.

'When I was released from care, I went back to where I'd lived with mum,' he said. None of the women who'd known her were still around. A lot were dead. You know what happens to druggies, they don't lead a long life generally, but one of the girls I spoke to mentioned the landlady at the local pub. Reckoned she might have known me mum. Turns out she did, and she knew you. Said you were a nasty bit of work. She didn't know the half of it, I told her.

'Then she told me that you'd had a couple of different names. She had an idea that you were from up north — she thought Liverpool, although she did say that you moved around a bit. Worked the fairs,' said Bernie. 'So that's what I did. I got a job on a fair and I've been moving around the country trying to track you down. I know you like the tarts, so each town we come to, I go to the red-light area and ask around in the pubs.'

Travis nodded. 'I'd heard someone was asking for me,' he

said. 'Never thought it would be you. Police maybe, not you.' He laughed at the look on Bernie's face. Trying to look hard.

'Yeah, I'm sure they might be looking for you for some shit you've done, but they'd not be looking for you because of Mum. It's a cold case. No one really worries about the death of a junkie or a tart, do they?'

'I'm sorry about that,' Travis said. 'It was just an argument that got out of hand. I didn't mean to kill her.'

'And what about me?' said Bernie. 'Did you mean what you did to me? YOU SICK FUCK!'

Travis was shocked at the sudden rage that poured from the kid. There was no warning. Like someone had flicked a switch. The kid went from chatting to an anger Travis had rarely seen.

'I WAS JUST A KID!' Bernie stood faster than Travis could react. The kid was by the bed now. Travis cowered back, raising his hands in defence.

Bernie stopped and tilted his head, almost in puzzlement. 'Oh, for fuck's sake. I'm not going to do that to you. I've had a gutful of shitty little perverts like you.'

'Well, you're hardly here for a catch up, are you?' said Travis, lowering his hands and being annoyed at himself for allowing a tremor into his voice. The kid's rage had scared him. Who could have known little Bernie would grow up so angry?

'No, I don't know why I wanted to find you really. I guess just to ask why you killed my mum and tell you everything that's happened to me because you murdered her.'

Travis was even more surprised when Bernie moved towards the kitchen area and put the kettle on. He made tea and then proceeded to tell Travis all about Mr Dewsbury and Marc, the bastard landlord, at the half-way house. On occasion Travis had to stop himself from laughing out loud at the kid's pathetic attempts to make him feel guilty. The stupid prick would never get it. Travis had nothing to feel guilty about. He had enjoyed every single thing he had done to the kid and his dead whore of a mother and now he was loving the kid's embarrassment and the stories of the humiliations he'd suffered at the hands of others. Little wimp.

As he watched Travis's eyes, Bernie knew he'd made a mistake. Far from looking sorry, remorseful or guilty, Travis was smiling at him. He was enjoying the stories of his suffering vicariously. Bernie noticed that every so often Travis's gaze would move from looking at him to looking at the wardrobe. Bernie turned to look at it too.

'What's with the wardrobe?' he asked Travis.

Receiving no answer, he walked over to it and pulled the doors open. There were half a dozen boxes piled up and marked with the words Lancashire Constabulary.

'What the f—' he asked, looking at Travis.

'It's my little collection. From work,' he said, as if that explained everything. 'Look.' Travis reached under the bed and pulled out another box. 'I'm night security at a warehouse. A few months ago, the firm I was working for was going through a rough patch and I thought I was going to lose me job, but I got told that the police wanted to hire some of the space. I didn't know what for, but a caged area got built in the corner and after that boxes kept arriving and were piled in the cage. As night watchman I had a key to the cage and so I started having a little look see.' Travis sneaked a look at Bernie to assess his reaction.

Bernie smiled at him. 'Carry on,' he said.

'So,' said Travis, 'some of the more interesting ones I brought home, then I could have a longer read. No one was checking up on them and so there was no one to notice anything was missing. I've always liked the true crime stories, and this had loads that never gets into the papers or on TV.' Travis proudly showed Bernie his treasure trove.

'This is one of the best,' he said, and he retrieved a VHS tape and pushed it into a machine on the table by the rickety chair.

As the video played, Bernie found himself becoming intrigued by the film. He had heard of the Lytham Lyncher case and how Patrick Wheeler had terrorised women on both sides of the Pennines for years. Here he was in action. Bernie knew that this was a collection he wanted to possess, to watch again and again and read the case notes. What he didn't want was to share any of it with Travis.

'Is there more?' he asked.

'Oh yeah, loads,' Travis replied. 'No one's around, and even when they put cameras up I knew how to avoid them. So I could take what I needed when I wanted.'

He boasted to Bernie where the cameras were and how he'd managed to move between the spots not covered. Bernie nodded intently, a plan forming in his mind.

'I'll make some more tea,' he said.

Travis smiled at him. The same self-centred, sick smile he used to give him when he'd finished doing what he did in the bedroom all those years ago. The smile that spoke of secrets never to be shared. This time, for the first time, Bernie smiled back. 'Can we watch another?'

Travis laughed and turned around. Bernie quickly reached into his rucksack, stepped close to Travis and slipped the long-bladed knife between Travis's ribs, whilst squeezing his left hand tight over the gasping man's mouth.

Travis wriggled and flayed, desperately trying to get free, but Bernie wrenched the knife out and back in again. Travis still struggled and was becoming more slippery as blood gushed from his wounds.

Bernie squeezed holding his hand tightly over Travis's mouth and nose and, all too quickly, the wriggling stopped. Cursing in case he'd given Travis an easy death, Bernie let him slip to the floor, but his persecutor, the murderer of his mother, was still breathing and far from dead. The rug was covered in blood, and Bernie used it to drag Travis to the bathroom. Heaving him into the tub, he looked at Travis lying helpless, and felt years of pent up rage overcome him. He struck, blow after blow. By the time he stopped, the bathroom looked like an abattoir and Travis had been dead for some minutes. Bernie collapsed to the floor, breathing heavily.

Once he regained his breath, he went back to the main room and from his rucksack took out a carving knife, a large hacksaw and some plastic bags. His work in the bathroom took some time, and when it was complete Bernie was starving. There was very little in Travis's fridge, but after washing his hands thoroughly, Bernie scoffed the pork pie and some bags of crisps from the cupboard.

He shifted the sodden rug and placed it by the front door. On top of it he stacked several full plastic bags, then went back into the bathroom and stripped and cleaned the room and himself as best he could. He rubbed himself dry on a threadbare towel and threw that and his clothes in a bag and onto the growing pile by the door. He took Travis's security guard uniform from the wardrobe and dressed himself in that. It was tight across the shoulders, chest and waist, but it would do.

It was late when Bernie opened the front door of Travis's bedsit. He took the rucksack down to his car. The streets were silent and empty; the whole world seemed tucked up safely in their beds. With each load Bernie looked around, listening for movements, but the area remained still while he took bag after bag from the flat to the car. It was exhausting work. The boot was soon full of Travis and so the boxes from his collection went on the back seat.

Finished, Bernie got into his car, he thought for a moment and drove to a site a few hours away, where the fair had been two years before. It was early when he arrived, and he pulled the car as far into the woods as he could. When he'd discovered the old deserted well, he'd thought then it would be a good place to get rid of someone. He was glad he'd remembered it.

CHAPTER FORTY-TWO

Sarah came to in the dark. Her legs were burning with cramp but when she tried to stretch them she could not move. He'd allowed her to put her clothes back on, but not her shoes. Her feet were bare, and she could feel her fingers against her toes. Unable to shift her position easily, she shuffled around like a beetle trying to right itself. Her head collided with something solid and Sarah realised that she was confined in a very small space. Her jaw ached from the ball gag he'd stuffed in her mouth. She tried not to think how many other mouths it had been in. Breathing was becoming more difficult and the more difficult it became the more she panicked.

Breathe, she whispered to herself, breathe. In, two, three, out, two, three. She repeated the mantra until she regained calm, and breathing, even with the gag, became easier. She tried to rub her head against the floor to see if that would help shift the restraint at all.

Sarah was surprised to be alive. When he'd told her he was going to have to kill her she had fully expected him to keep his promise. She remembered his hands on her throat and his pale eyes boring into hers. As she blacked out, she thought death was coming for her. Her last thoughts were of Danvers, her dog, and of her by-line. She had been on the cusp of a great story. The exposé of a lifetime. The one that would get her back on track, back on a London paper. Even though she wasn't sure that's what she wanted anymore. She'd begun to settle back into this town. Even started to make friends and rebuild her life.

Anyway, Sarah thought, if this was the afterlife, it sucked. Where were the angels and the cups of mimosa and oh, what was the other thing? She couldn't remember. She would have shaken her head, but everything was bound too tightly. Perhaps it's the other place, she wondered. No, you're being ridiculous, she decided. No, she was definitely still alive. But she was not sure why and, more importantly, she did not know how long it would be before the situation changed.

It wasn't the best idea, Poole thought. He wasn't a fan of mixing work and pleasure but, after thanking his contact for the information she'd given him from the Vice team, she'd asked him out for a meal. Except now they were going to eat at hers. She was going to cook for him. He had said that, since he owed her, perhaps he should cook but she insisted. She had fervently insisted, so here he was dressed in smart casual, with a fresh blue shirt he'd got in the London sales and ringing on her doorbell.

She flung the door open and the first thing Poole saw was the low neckline and the clingy skirt. He swallowed, passed her the bottle of red and crossed the threshold.

'Dinner's nearly ready,' she said. 'Turkey, potatoes and salad.'

'You shouldn't have gone to so much trouble,' Poole protested, but he need not have worried.

She bustled into the tiny kitchen and opened a large oven which took up much of the work surface. There was a pan of potatoes on the stove top and Poole noticed that the water had simmered away. She filled the pan with cold water and put it back on the hob.

'Salad?' Poole said. 'Perhaps I could prepare that for you? I'm a whizz with dressings.'

'Oh no, it comes with its own dressing,' she replied. 'But it's in the fridge behind you.'

Poole opened the fridge. It was empty apart from some ready meals, half-empty Chinese food cartons and an enormous tub of coleslaw. He lifted it out held it up questioningly, and she nodded.

'Just bung it on the table,' she told him, and gave him a dessert spoon. For serving, he guessed. He took the coleslaw through to the miniscule lounge and set it on the table. He removed the lid to give it a stir. It was partially frozen, and he stirred it more vigorously. Poole hated coleslaw. He wasn't sure that frozen coleslaw would improve the experience.

'Ta dah!' she said proudly, and he moved aside as best he could to allow her past. She brushed not so lightly against him and placed the turkey roll and potatoes on the table.

'Sit, sit,' she told him, and he did as he was bid.

Cutting large lumps from the turkey roll, she placed it on the plates and dumped three potatoes next to the meat. They thumped loudly on landing. She scooped frozen coleslaw next to the hot food. Poole mentally ransacked his medicine cabinet; yes, he was sure he had both indigestion and diarrhoea treatments at home.

'There,' she said, smiling at him. 'Isn't this nice?'

Poole, unable to answer, poured wine into both their glasses. He raised his for a toast, but Tracy was already gnawing at a piece of turkey roll from the end of her fork. He bent to the task of cutting a potato and, as suspected, it was raw inside. He cut off and ate the cooked tuber and nibbled at the turkey roll. The coleslaw remained untouched.

To his surprise, dessert was acceptable. Supermarket apple and rhubarb crumble with custard. It didn't go with the red wine, but Poole was past caring, his mind solely focused on his escape and how to avoid repeating the entire experience.

CHAPTER FORTY-THREE

The slamming of the front door let her know that, at last, someone was home. Marguerite Carlson looked at the bedside clock. Eleven am — not her husband then.

'Aspen?' she called.

'Yep, it's me. Where are you?'

'Up here. In bed.'

The door opened, and Aspen's head peeked around it. 'Are you poorly?' she asked. 'I thought you were going back to work.'

'I took a day off. They haven't really got much for me to do. It looks like they managed just fine without me, so I don't know how much longer I will have a job.'

'Will they make you redundant?' Aspen asked, although Marguerite thought her mind was elsewhere.

'No, I don't think so. They're far too nice for that. Although I don't think they would worry too much if I put in my resignation. I might do that. It might be nice to do something different. Anyway, enough of me. What have you been up to? I've not seen you since the weekend.'

'The weekend where you threw Dad's dinner at him. That weekend?'

Marguerite had the grace to look a little sheepish. She laughed, 'Yes, I haven't had the courage to tell your father that the dining room will need decorating again. I can't get the gravy out of the carpet either.'

Aspen came and sat on the bed. She smiled and squeezed her mother's hand. 'Perhaps you should have had that wooden flooring in there too.'

'Shussh,' said her mother, conspiratorially. 'I wanted to do that, but your father said it was too expensive. Now when I tell him this, he'll say it was just a ploy.'

'Why did you do it?'

'I was angry. Stupid jealousy. I know, I know,' she said in response to her daughter's amused look. 'Even after all these years. He was just like this when we were young. He'd get a call, on the house phone in those days. I'd answer, and some trollop would sleaze down the phone at me, and off he'd go. Just a snout he'd say, but even then, I wondered.

'With mobiles and promotions, it was less frequent, or I was less aware of it. Then on Saturday it all started again. Some woman wouldn't stop calling. I took the phone to him eventually, he spoke to her and raced out of the house and I didn't see him until the next day. What was I supposed to think?'

Marguerite sighed. 'He tells me it's to do with the missing reporter. The girl calling was a friend of hers. They'd gone out together and the reporter didn't make it home.'

Aspen pursed her lips. 'So, you're friends again?'

Marguerite nodded, reaching out her hands to her daughter. 'And I'd like us to be friends again too, darling. I'm so sorry. I've been selfish. Shut you out. I decided that you were right about Jade's room. I even got all the cleaning things ready at the weekend. But then, well…'

'I'll sort us some brunch,' Aspen said, leaning forward and kissing her mother on the forehead. 'If you're up to it we can make a start after that?'

Marguerite smiled at her. 'That would be lovely, darling. I think just a little toast for me though.

'And not too much butter,' she called at Aspen's retreating back.

Despite her insistence that all she could manage was a little toast and a scraping of butter, Marguerite Carlson demolished three scrambled eggs with half the pack of smoked salmon mixed in. She leaned back from the breakfast bar and drank her coffee.

'Well,' she said. 'I needed that.'

'Clearly,' said her daughter with a wry smile.

'I might need a little rest before we lug that vacuum cleaner upstairs.'

'Why don't you go through to the sitting room and I can make some more coffee,' said Aspen. 'We can just sit and have a natter before we get started. Like we used to do when I was doing my 'A' levels.'

They cuddled together on the sofa.

'Are you going to tell me where you've been for the last two days?' her mother finally asked.

'At a friend's place,' Aspen replied.

'Man friend?'

'Yes, a man friend.'

'Are you going to tell me about him?'

'No, not yet,' Aspen said. 'I want to see where we go before I bother you with meeting him.'

'I'm unlikely to be the problem,' Marguerite said. 'It's your father he has to impress.'

'Dad's met him already,' Aspen said. 'They know each other through work.'

Marguerite pushed her daughter to arm's length, so she could get a better look at her. 'Ah, he's a police officer?' she said.

Aspen nodded.

'Oh, darling,' was all Marguerite said and she hugged her daughter close.

The two women sat together in silence for some time. Eventually Aspen stretched and got up from the sofa. She held out a hand to her mother.

'Ready?' she said.

'No, but then I can't see a time when I will be ready,' said Marguerite. 'My therapist says this is all part of the healing process.'

'I didn't know you were seeing someone,' said Aspen. 'Is it helping?'

'We'll see after cleaning her room up,'

'Jade,' Aspen said. 'She was called Jade. We are going to clean Jade's room.'

Marguerite sighed, but she rose from the sofa and collected the bucket from the under-stairs cupboard. Aspen trailed behind her with the vacuum cleaner. They trod the board of each stair as if it were a step to the gallows. Each in their own way knew it was a good thing to be doing but each wanted it to be over. One of them dreaded the secrets that she might find, but Aspen, having made a thorough search of the room with the guidance of Tim Jessop, knew there was no longer anything in there that her mother could find to cause her pain.

They stood on the threshold, not wanting to cross, and then Marguerite stepped into the room.

'It feels different,' she said.

'Different? Different how?'

'I don't know. It smells different. Not like Jade. It's like someone has been in here and moved things around. I can smell the dust. I couldn't smell the dust before.' Marguerite's voice was rising as she spoke. 'Someone's been in here!' she shrieked.

'Mum. Mum, you're imagining things. No one's been in here. Just family. I come and sit on the bed sometimes. I know Dad does too. No one has been in here. Just us. Just family.'

Marguerite sat scrunched up on the floor; she pulled her knees up and rested her head on them. She sat rocking herself back and forth moaning that someone had been in her baby's room.

Aspen knelt down beside her and hugged her for a while and then she went to the hallway and called their GP. She left a message for her father too.

After Dr Gibson had seen Marguerite he came into the kitchen to see Aspen. 'And how are you doing, young lady?' he said as he put his Gladstone bag on a tall stool. 'I don't suppose a fruit lolly is going to fix this one, is it?'

Aspen laughed. 'No,' she said ruefully. 'I don't think it is. But I do appreciate all the times a fruit lolly did fix something. It's funny,' she continued. 'I never associate the fruit lollies with injections. I always associate them with something nice. I used to munch on them while studying for my 'A' levels and during the exams. I have you and Mrs Gibson to thank for that.'

'Aye, I do miss her,' he said wistfully. 'But enough of me. How are you coping? I can see your mother is still taking it hard.'

'There's not a timeline on these things though, is there?' said Aspen. 'Mum isn't coping. Dad is hiding it all away and focusing on work and I just take one day at a time. Mum thinks we've put it behind us and blames us for that, but we're just managing the best way we know how.

'Jade's death is one of the reasons I chose to study psychology at uni. I wanted to know why she killed herself, but also, I wanted to understand why the people Dad comes into contact with do the things they do. The joke is that I have more questions than answers and I don't even know if I'll go back to uni... Sorry, I'm wittering on. You must have other patients to see.'

'I do, of course I do, but none of them are as important as the wife and daughter of one of my oldest friends. I've given your mother something to calm her down. She should sleep for a few hours. If she wakes in the night and is still shaky, you can give her one of these. But only one, mind.' He handed Aspen a small brown bottle with four caplets. 'She can take the rest over the next few days. Now, do you need anything?'

Aspen shook her head. 'No,' she said. 'I've got someone to talk to. Mum has too, and I'll see if I can get her another appointment. It would be good if you could get Dad to open up and talk though. Take him down the pub, perhaps?'

'A medic taking someone for a drink?' Dr Gibson raised his hands in mock horror. 'Disgraceful! Whatever next? Seriously though, how much is he drinking at the moment?'

Aspen opened the larder door. A large plastic carton sat on the floor, brimming over with empty bottles. More lurched precariously at its side.

'I see,' he said. 'Maybe not the pub, but I will see what I can do, my dear, I'll see what I can do.'

And with that he picked up his bag, brushed off his tweed jacket and headed for the door.

CHAPTER FORTY-FOUR

Chris Albright thought his sister Julie was taking a very pragmatic approach to clearing out her partner's possessions. Dave had only moved in a few months ago but he'd made himself quite at home, so it was no small task. When the police released his body and personal effects, she had been allowed to organise his burial. It had been a quiet funeral, although that creepy friend of his from work had turned up. Julie said she had been glad Chris was there to deter him from coming back to the house.

'He just makes my skin crawl,' she said to her brother. 'I'm sure he's a perfectly lovely bloke. Him and Dave got on like a house on fire. Always out for a drink and a game of pool together, but I wouldn't have him here at the house. Not that Dave asked, you know. He was sensitive like that.'

Chris shrugged and gave a non-committal grunt in response. He was less convinced of Dave's sensitivity. After all, what kind of sensitive bloke got half his face blown off by a shotgun, he wondered. But at least the toe rag was out of Julie's life and maybe she'd find someone else in time. He lugged a couple of black bin bags to the car and threw them in the boot. When he got back in the house, Julie was tossing a set of keys up and down in her hand.

'What do you reckon to this little lot?' she said. 'I can't work out what half of them are.'

He took the bunch of keys from her, removed them from the ring and spread them out on the kitchen worktop. He swivelled them around, sorting them into order by size.

Julie leaned forward and slid a couple to the side. 'These ones are for here,' she said. 'That's a spare for his lorry and I guess that one is his locker at work. I'll need to give those back. But what are these?'

'That Yale one looks like a front door key. Not sure about the Chubb, and these look like garage keys,' Chris said. 'Err, how many garages did he have, sis?'

'He didn't have any. He had one when he had his flat, but he stopped renting that out when he moved in here.'

'And the police didn't ask you about any of these?'

Julie shook her head.

'You sure, sis?'

'Of course I'm sure. Why would they ask? Why would they be interested?'

'Are you not a little bit puzzled over how he died?' he asked, giving her a hug. 'Have you never wondered what he might have been involved in?'

'I've tried not to think about it,' she said, returning the hug and then pushing him away to face him. 'I was hoping whoever it was got the wrong man.'

Chris turned his attention back to the keys. 'And these,' he said, holding up the Yale and the Chubb, 'might he have kept his flat?'

'Why would he? He moved everything in here. I expect he just forgot to return them.'

'Sis, if you rent somewhere and don't give the keys back

they don't refund your deposit.' Chris was becoming more suspicious, turning the keys over and over in his hand. 'Now, I don't want to speak ill of him —'

Julie started to say something, but Chris held up his hand. 'Dave was boasting last summer about the wedge of cash he'd got back off them. Don't you remember? But there's no way he got it back and still had keys. If these are the keys to his old flat then he was lying about the deposit. What's his game?' The look on his sister's face told him everything he needed to know. 'Tell me where the flat is,' he said, kissing her forehead. 'I'll go and check if it needs clearing out. You look at his bank statements and see who he pays the rent to for it.'

'If he's still paying for it,' she said.

'Oh yes, sis. Of course. If he's still paying for it,' he replied. Chris, however, had a pretty good idea what the answer was. One of the blokes in the darts team knew Dave of old and said he was chummy with a lot of the type of people you did not cross. The sort that, if you did upset them, might just use a shotgun to settle a score. Anyway, a trip to the flat might even give them an idea who had shot Dave's face off.

Spring 1992

As his eighteenth birthday approached, Bernie knew that he would soon be able to leave Trablos Grange for good. Even though his sentence had been served and he was now free to go, Bernie had stayed as no foster home could bear to have him for more than a few nights. Denise had vanished from his life long ago. She'd abandoned him like every other woman in his world. Well stuff 'em, stuff them all, he

thought. I don't need any of you. Every time he went somewhere new and thought he might settle in, the whispers
started and he was shoved back to Trablos. It wasn't as if he
did anything wrong, he thought, he just watched. Girls liked
to be watched. They knew he was there and pranced around
half naked on the landings or with bathroom doors left ajar,
just to wind him up. Tarts, they were all just tarts.

He turned as the door behind him opened.

'Ready?' asked the social worker.

'Ready,' he said, picking up the one bag containing all his
belongings. He stepped out of the Grange and into his new
life. He hoped it would be a good one.

Chris Albright swung his ancient Toyota into Bursford Street
and parked up. He looked around at the area before he got
out of the car and could understand why Dave Bradwell had
preferred to live in his sister's neat little three-bed terrace.
He sauntered across the road, glaring at three lads who
lounged on the street corner. The Chubb fitted the lock on
the street door and he made his way up the shabby staircase.
There was only one door and he knocked on the dishevelled
green door of Flat 1 and listened. He knocked again. Still
nothing, so he tried the Yale. He was not surprised when that
fitted the lock too.

'Now, let's see what you've been up to, you little toe rag,'
Chris muttered to himself as he walked down the hallway.
The light didn't work but the one in the main room did. Well
almost. He crossed the floor and pulled back the curtains. He
choked at the dust. Jesus, he thought. Those haven't been
opened in a while. The window looked out over a grimy back
yard. He ran a finger over the glass and a wedge of grime

stuck to it. He wiped it on his jeans. There was nothing in the yard. He took in the contents of the room. Not a violent man himself, he could still tell when there had been a scuffle. The rug was kicked up and a chair was on its side. He noticed that a corkscrew was on the floor by the sideboard. A smashed glass beside it. Chris poked his head into the tiny kitchen, but nothing seemed out of place. The bin was empty. The bathroom was bare and, in marked comparison to the rest of the flat, surprisingly clean. The bath was spotless. The bedroom contained a bed, stripped of all bedding; a dressing table, with no clothing or toiletries; the wardrobe was built in and was empty as well. Only the sitting room showed any sign of life. Chris was puzzled at the lack of paraphernalia if Dave was still renting the place. He had been convinced he was using it for something. An escape from Julie when he was supposed to be driving. Somewhere to bring other women. Something like that, but apart from circulars and junk mail there was nothing to indicate he was using the flat at all.

At least Julie would be pleased that there would be no more of Dave's property to sort out. Chris headed for the front door, only just spotting the cupboard since the hallway was so dark. He opened it. When he spoke to the police later, he honestly could not recall who had been more surprised. Him or the hog-tied woman on the floor.

Superintendent Jim Tasker decided the news he had to impart was so good that he would descend the two flights of stairs to tell Carlson his missing reporter had been found for him. He waddled to the lift and pressed the down button.

He burst into the MIT squad room — Minor Investigations Team, as he liked to think of it. The doors swung back and would have concussed a lesser man. They collided uselessly with Tasker's girth and he toddled down the room with the swaying motion of all heavyset men.

'Ronnie, my man,' he chortled. 'Can they not find a decent office for you? You should come and work for me. I'd find you something better than this pig pen.'

Carlson looked up and considered Tasker's remark ironic given the Superintendent was the one with the piggy eyes. He watched the big man as he regarded the partition walls and stopped short of actually entering into the space. Probably a wise decision as there was a distinct danger the only way he'd be leaving it would be to have the whole thing dismantled around him. Even Tasker's reputation as force hard man wouldn't avoid the jibes that would come from him being stuck in a cubicle.

'What can I do for you, sir?' Carlson asked wearily.

'How are you getting on with finding who killed my snout?' Tasker asked with an air of superiority.

'I think we know who killed him, don't you, sir? Not that we'll ever prove it. Sometimes proof seems to be hard to find, don't you agree?'

Tasker sniffed, and Carlson knew he had got the reference loud and clear.

'We did our best on your daughter's case, Ronnie. It wasn't for lack of trying. We just couldn't prove anything conclusive against the little scrotes, you know that.'

'Some would have tried harder, I'm sure, sir.' Carlson spoke more calmly than he felt. If he'd been allowed to oversee the case, he would not have stopped until he had answers. However, that was not standard process as well Carlson knew.

'Is that a dig at my team?' Tasker snorted. 'You think you should have got this job? You think you could do any better? Next you'll be telling me that you would've beaten me if your daughter hadn't killed herself!' Tasker's face grew red and his breathing heavier as he gripped the partition walls. They rattled in protest. The sentence seemed to reverberate off them and Tasker winced. 'I'm sorry, I shouldn't have said that.'

'I bloody know I would have beaten you!' Carlson stood up and leant on his desk, fists clenched, propping him up like an angry grey-back gorilla. He looked at Tasker, thinking he appeared even more like an English Bull Terrier than usual.

'Careful, Ronnie,' said Tasker, his nostrils flared but he took a deep breath. 'You're flirting with insubordination,' he said softly.

Carlson sighed. He knew he would have got the job if he'd stayed working, but after Jade died nothing seemed worth the effort any longer. He'd finally come back to take up the reins again, but on days like this he was still wondering if it was worth it. 'Was there anything else, sir?' he asked.

'Yes, as a matter of fact. I have some good news for you. I've got something that you've been looking for? A certain reporter?'

'Oh shit,' said Carlson. 'I'd not been told. Where's the crime scene? Is Kilburn attending?'

'It's a bit early for him, Ronnie,' said Tasker. 'Your lassie is still alive. She's at the General. I'm guessing you'll be wanting to see her before you see the crime scene.'

Carlson did not hear the last remarks. He was already out the door. He needed to see that bloody reporter and he'd better let Shazza know she'd been found.

CHAPTER FORTY-FIVE

When Carlson walked into the hospital he had no difficulty working out that Sarah Jenkins was on Petunia Ward.

He seethed at the sight of the crowd, hovering at the entrance to the ward, but being prevented from encroaching into the space by two uniformed PCs.

Most seemed to be journalists. The same bottom feeders that, with their mainstream media coverage, had screwed up any chance of putting a surveillance operation in place to catch Sarah's attacker. Although he reluctantly had to admit to himself that the likelihood of staking out the flat she'd been found in died as soon as the first social media post had been made.

He shook his head and reflected on how quickly news spread nowadays. The first cars had responded to Chris Albright's phone call with the standard "blues and twos" and that had been enough to draw a crowd. When more cars turned up, then plainclothes detectives, then an ambulance, the social media paparazzi had YouTube videos being uploaded in tandem with tweets, Instagram stories, snapchats and Facebook Live. So much for trying to keep things low key. Every passing teenager with a phone was a reporter and they were all looking to sell their footage to whichever news company would buy it.

Carlson nodded at the nearest of the PCs who recognised him and let him through. He eased his way over to a harried looking nurse trying to undertake the half-hourly observations that Sarah's condition currently required. He showed her his ID card.

'Can't you help?' she said, pointing at the large group of people. 'This is a hospital, not a circus. Your officers aren't moving them on. I called security but even they couldn't shift them. I do have other patients to consider.'

Carlson fished around in his breast pocket and pulled out his warrant card once more. He walked back to the ward's entrance. 'Come on, you lot,' he said. 'You are not going to get anything standing here and you are making a nuisance of yourselves. Move along. Let her have some breathing room.' He gave them what he hoped was his sternest glare.

Reluctantly the group dispersed until only two women remained. One he knew, the other he did not.

'I'm Elise Watkins. Sarah's editor. We spoke on the phone,' she said, accompanying him into the ward and over to Sarah's bed. She spoke quietly. 'Thank you for finding her.'

'I wish I could take the credit,' said Carlson, 'but she was discovered in connection with a completely different case. I'm still surprised —'

'That she was found alive? So am I. Surprised, but grateful,' she replied, and held out her hand to shake his.

A small croaky voice sounded from the bed. 'I can hear you.'

If Sarah had been going to say anything else, it was swamped by a small but surprisingly heavy young woman with jet black hair who, now that she could get near it, flung herself onto the bed.

'I'm so glad to see yow,' she sobbed, 'but once you're better I'm gonna kill you for scaring me like that.'

'She's not out of the woods yet, you know,' said the nurse, shooing Shazza off the bed. 'She could still have kidney complications. You do know she's lucky to be alive? If he'd left her on her front, if she'd been left for a day or two more...' she paused, her words hanging in the air like the sword of Damocles.

'When will the doctor be doing his rounds?' Carlson asked.

'*She* will be here later,' came the nurse's terse reply.

'I'd like to speak with her, if I may,' said Carlson coolly. 'I will need to question Ms Jenkins about recent events.'

The nurse ignored him and carried on taking Sarah's pulse and temperature. She noted them on the chart, gave Carlson a sour look and stalked off.

Carlson turned to Sarah, 'I am bloody annoyed with you,' he said, 'but I'm really glad to see you alive. I'll come back later and we'll have a full discussion when you're up to it. But for now, I really need to know, is there anything you can tell me about who did this? A description? Anything that stands out?'

Sarah held his gaze momentarily and then started to cry. The tears came unbidden, but the intensity of her sobs racked her body. Shazza glared at Carlson.

'Leave her be, can't yow?'

'I would Shazza, honestly, if I could, but I can't. We need to catch him and she's the only one who knows what he loo —'

He was cut off by a severe tap on his shoulder. Turning, he found himself eye to eye with a stern-faced young woman, dressed in a white coat and with a stethoscope draped around her neck. Her name badge said "Lazenby, Consultant". Carlson thought she didn't look old enough, but he was more annoyed at the finger jab she had just administered to his shoulder.

'I beg you —' he began, but she cut across him.

'And you are?' she asked.

'Detective Chi —'

'Ah, police. So not a consultant, not a surgeon, a registrar nor even a senior house officer. Therefore, not allowed to talk to my patient without my permission. Kindly leave.'

Carlson mentally ran the whole gambit of the argument he could have with the consultant and knew that whatever excuse he came up with or whatever reason he gave, Dr Lazenby would win. This was her domain and Carlson knew that he would ultimately need her on side to allow him and his team access to Sarah. *Pick your battles, Ronnie.*

'Of course, Doctor. But I'm going to need to talk to her sooner rather than later. I have a guy out there killing women and Sarah is my only lead to him.'

Lazenby held her arm out to indicate the path he should take out of the ward.

Carlson turned to leave. 'Shazza, you talk to her if you can. I need to know.'

'I'll keep yow posted,' said Shazza. 'I ain't going nowhere.'

Ben Poole was at his desk typing up his notes when Carlson returned to the station.

Before he got a chance to ask, Carlson said, 'She's fine for now. We can interview her once she's had the all clear from the ICU doctor. How was your talk with the Albrights?'

'Not very conclusive,' Poole replied. 'Julie Albright says she'd thought Bradwell had given the flat up when he moved in with her. Her brother reckons he was boasting about having got a wedge of cash back from the deposit, so he lied to them both about that. Seems that wasn't all he lied about. Superintendent Tasker wasn't entirely honest with us either when he said Bradwell was his snout —'

'Careful, Ben, can't have you criticising a senior officer,' said Carlson, grinning broadly.

'Yeah, well let's just say the Super played his cards close to his chest. I've been chatting with a DC in his team. Bradwell was in deep with the Gainsborough Boys and had been for several years. Not only did he drive the shit up North for them, he ran the processing and distribution too. He'd worked his way up the ranks and had himself a nice little earner. Not sure why he'd risk it to squeal on them.'

'Yes, that doesn't seem right to me either. I guess we might never know why he decided to break the code, but it wouldn't be the first time Tasker has kept something to himself.'

'Anyway, my friend...' — Poole paused, thinking about the meal she had cooked, and decided she was unlikely to be a close friend in the future — 'she doesn't think they had enough on Bradwell to send him down. All circumstantial, but she's convinced that there's something else going on.'

'Did your friend offer any suggestions?'

'Not really, but it could have been something as simple as someone threatening to let the Gainsborough Boys hear a little rumour that Bradwell was blabbing.'

Carlson nodded.

'Ms Albright was very helpful, by the way.' Poole continued. 'Even brought in Bradwell's bank statements. What there was of them. Apparently, he didn't keep them long.

Tended to burn them once he'd read them. Burned. Not binned. Not shredded. He burnt them, which I thought was interesting. I've run a quick eye over them. Looks like he was still paying for the flat. He also took out a wedge of cash each week. Couple of hundred quid each Thursday. Quite a bit considering that, as far as she knew, he was just a lorry driver. She says he gave her one hundred a week for food and that, but he always seemed to have plenty. He'd told her he was lucky at cards.'

'And the brother?' asked Carlson.

'Ah, now there's a difference in opinion between the siblings. Chris Albright was not at all keen on Bradwell. Reckoned he was dodgy. Too flash and too much money to have been earned legally, or so he thought. The brother also didn't believe the "lucky at cards" story. He couldn't wait to go around to that flat to see what Bradwell had been up to. I think he got a bit more than he bargained for though,' Poole laughed and then checked himself. The look on Carlson's face was not amused.

'Look Ben, we know it couldn't have been Bradwell who tied Sarah Jenkins up and left her there. He was killed before she went missing. So, what do we have?'

'The brother has no idea who could have been using the place if it wasn't Bradwell. Kirsty's got a team going over the flat now. She's emailed some photos back already. It fits almost exactly to the DVD we were sent. So it is the place our killer has been using.'

'That leaves us needing to find the connection to Bradwell,' Carlson said.

'And his name, Guv.'

Carlson rubbed his face in his hands, 'Yep,' he agreed. 'A name would be very useful. Very useful indeed.'

Kirsty Russell's paper suit rustled as she leaned against the wall in the small flat. She'd opened the window with the idea of letting some fresh air in, little thinking that the yard outside had not seen fresh air since the walls were built around it. Motes of aluminium powder from the finger-printing still hung in the air. It was always the last job to be done as the mess made by the powder destroyed all other evidence. She sighed; they were so close to catching this guy she could almost taste it. So close but so far. This had been his killing ground, she was confident of that. She wondered what his next move would be now that this place had been taken from him.

She heard voices at the door and Ronnie Carlson rustled in.

'I hate these things,' he said, looking down at his paper suit.

'You should worry,' Kirsty stood astride, showing him the crotch of her own suit was at her knees. 'One size fits none,' she laughed. 'Anyways,' she drawled the word, 'I wanted to make sure you were happy to release the scene? Everything is on its way to the lab.'

'So I see,' said Carlson, looking at the empty room.

'Well, you can't be too careful. We'll need to go over what you want processed and in what order. I think the carpet and the sofa will give most of the evidence you want. Fibres and bodily fluids. I went over it with the black light. I think we'll get some good DNA off of the sofa...' she paused. 'What?' she asked, looking at him.

'It's all such a bloody waste, isn't it?' he said. 'All those hours trying to find out who he is and then in the end it's just bloody luck that we found this place. Just blind luck.'

'Lucky for the reporter, definitely,' Kirsty replied. 'If Bradwell's brother-in-law wasn't quite so nosey, she'd be dead. As for this place, we would have found it eventually.'

'And how many more girls would have died before then?' Carlson looked at her and she could see the worry etched on his face. 'We've still got to catch the bastard. Just because he hasn't got this flat doesn't mean he'll stop killing, does it?'

'No, but it might slow him down. He'll have to find somewhere new, won't he? Come on, Ronnie,' she said, nudging his elbow. 'This isn't like you. You're usually more upbeat.'

He smiled at her. 'I used to be,' he said. 'I'm not sure that I have the stomach for this anymore. Okay, show me around. Talk me through what you've got. I know you, you won't have missed anything, but let's do the walk.'

'Okay,' she said, 'follow me.' She showed Carlson the rest of the flat and talked through what the CSI team had taken away. What tests should be done first, what could wait. He listened and commented, but all the time Kirsty had the feeling that Ronnie Carlson was very far away indeed.

Bernie Latimer watched the news alone. He saw the incident tent covering the street entrance to the flat with the battered green door. He sighed deeply. He was going to miss that little flat. Still, at least he'd got out in time. Apart from that bloody reporter. He should have killed her. He knew he should have. Bloody women were all the same. Always let a man down, but when he'd had his hands on her neck and stared into her eyes, she looked back at him with such anger and indignation that he couldn't do it. Was he going soft? It wasn't that though, he knew. If she'd shown even a hint of fear, he would have killed her easily. Just because she didn't, it should not have made any difference to him. But it had. He'd tied her up, expecting to go back and dump the body after a few days. She should not have survived. She should be dead. What the fuck was going wrong? That bloody Dave Bradwell, it was all his fault. If he'd managed to keep his nerve he would've kept his head. Bernie smiled to himself over the irony. He'd heard on the street what was being said about Dave's injuries. The stuff that was being kept out of the papers. The Gainsborough Boys did not mess about. Dave would have been lucky to have just had his gob shot off. Lucky and grateful.

Bernie breathed in and released the breath slowly. He went over everything again. Once she was out for the count, he'd put the body suit and the gloves back on, tied her up. He'd put her in the cupboard and then cleared his stuff out of the flat. He should have taken more time. He should have picked everything up. Should have wiped everywhere down. He should have gone back sooner. Oh, fuck, fuck, fuck. It was all that bloody Dave Bradwell's fault. He was lucky he was dead, or he'd kill him himself.

CHAPTER FORTY-SIX

Two days after being found, Sarah Jenkins was propped up in bed with her laptop when Carlson and Lacey walked into the ward at Gippingford General Hospital.

'I hope you're making notes for me and not writing a story for your paper,' Carlson said to her.

'A bit of both, Chief Inspector.' She studied him briefly and pointed to a chair bedside the bed. 'Good morning,' she said to DC Lacey. 'I'm sure no one will mind you taking the chair from that bed at the end. They went home this morning.

'I've actually written down quite a lot that you may find useful, Mr Carlson, but I am also writing up my personal experience of being in the hands of a serial killer. It is, after all, my duty as a member of the media.'

'You can't publish that!' Carlson nearly exploded.

'Not the full story, no, but once you've caught him I can.'

'You'll bugger up any chance of a conviction!'

'Look, Chief Inspector, this is my life and my livelihood,' she said, glowering at him. 'If I don't write it then some other hack out there will. At least I'll have the facts straight! Now why don't you ask me your questions and I can get on with my writing.' Shutting the lid with a slam, Sarah put the laptop on the tall cabinet by the bed.

Scowling at each other like two boxers about to leave the safety of their corners, Carlson went over his queries and Sarah Jenkins filled in the blanks, while Jane noted the responses.

'About one metre eighty, soft spoken but not posh. He wasn't muscly, more sort of wiry, I'd say, but strong. God, he was strong!' She put her hand to her neck where the marks of his hands were clear. 'Big hands, as you can see, weird pale blue eyes. Full head of hair, pale too, not albino but really, really light. As if it had no colour at all, so I suppose almost albino. Early forties.' Sarah allowed herself to flop back against the pillows and blinked the threatening tears away. 'He followed me into Gipping Street; I could hear someone, but I couldn't run because of the shoes I was wearing. He grabbed me from behind. I put up a fight though. I do kickboxing.'

Carlson nodded, as another piece fell into the puzzle.

'I really thought I could fight him off. I assumed it was just some pervert. It just never occurred to me that it would be him,' she said. 'And yes, I know that was stupid of me. Then he put his hand over my mouth.' Sarah gagged at the memory. 'The next thing I remember is waking up in that dirty little flat. He still thought I was a working girl at that stage. He was pissed at me for leaving my post as he saw it. He said I shouldn't have done that. He grabbed my phone off me, but he wasn't worried about it being GPS enabled which I thought was odd. Then he tipped out my bag, found my notepad and recorder and that's when he went ballistic. He slapped me. A couple of times. Maybe more. I didn't count. Then — ' Sarah stopped abruptly. The emotion overwhelmed her. She put her head in her hands, breathed deeply, forced down the cry that threatened to swamp her like a tsunami. Composing herself, she looked at Carlson, shaking her head. 'I'm sorry, I can write it down, but I can't say the words to you just now.'

Carlson gave her a grim smile. 'That's okay, I know,' he murmured.

'Afterwards, he dragged me to the bathroom and he made me shower. I knew I was destroying evidence, but I just had to get the stench of him off me. It did occur to me to try and preserve something, a tissue maybe, but I didn't get a chance. I wondered if this was what he'd done to the others. He gave me a towel to dry myself and made me walk into the bedroom. I thought he was going to do it again. I remember being so angry with him, but that's all I can remember. He either drugged me or hit me because the next thing I can recall is waking up in the cupboard.' Sarah looked up at the ceiling; tears streamed down her cheeks. She rubbed at them ineffectually with the heels of her hands, sniffed, and blew her nose before continuing. 'I panicked, but alongside the kickboxing I've been learning to meditate. I slowed my breathing down and was able to breathe through my nose despite that disgusting thing he put in my mouth. I kept passing out. I was so cold, and I was sure I was going to die there. Then I heard him come back and thought...' She stopped again and once more battled the tears away. 'I heard him moving around, I thought he would do it again and then kill —'

Carlson handed her fresh tissues and waited.

Sarah looked skyward and calmed her breathing.

'I thought if I stayed quiet, he might not remember I was there. Then the door opened. And it wasn't him. It wasn't him. It wasn't him, thank fuck it wasn't him.'

Sarah bowed her head and sobbed. The nurse from the previous day hurried over.

'That's enough. You two need to leave. Now, please,' she said. 'Sarah needs to get better, not relive it all again and again.'

Lacey and Carlson rose to go. Carlson turned to raise a hand and to show his thanks. Sarah Jenkins stared back at him. The hard-eyed look she used to have was gone. Replaced by something else he could not quite put his finger on. Not fear, so much as a guarded wariness she did not have before. Wordlessly, Carlson waved a farewell, trying to convey to her he'd get the bastard if it was the last thing he ever did.

Carlson walked into his house. It was quiet and there were no lights showing in the front rooms. Was it always going to be dark now, he wondered. Would there ever be a time when he'd come home, and the house would be jumping again? Lights on everywhere. Music. Or even just noise. What wouldn't he give for there just to be some noise? It felt as if the house was in constant mourning.

The kitchen door opened, and Tim Jessop walked into his hallway.

'DC Jessop?' he said. 'Fancy seeing you here.'

'Oh, shit. Sorry, sir. Didn't see you there, sir. Just going, sir.'

Aspen appeared in the kitchen doorway.

'Tim, you're not going anywhere,' Aspen said. 'You were popping to the loo. You can still go to the loo. I'll sort Dad out. Come on, Dad. We were in here.'

'Where's your mother?' Carlson asked as he was ushered into the kitchen.

'She's still in bed. Dr Gibson dropped by and he gave her something to calm her down. He did say she may sleep until morning and if she doesn't, then he left these.' Aspen waved a bottle of white pills at him.

'What kicked it off?' he said.

'She wanted to clean Jade's room. She had everything ready. Dad, did you know she's been seeing a therapist?'

Carlson shook his head. 'No, I didn't,' he said.

Tim came back in the room. 'Would you like a beer, sir?' he asked. Carlson nodded, and Tim opened the fridge. He took out a bottle of beer, removed the lid and passed it to his boss.

Carlson declined the glass, still somewhat surprised at how at home his DC was in his kitchen and with his daughter. 'It seems I have rather a lot of catching up to do,' he said, giving them both a wry smile.

'She was really up for it, in a "I don't really want to do this, but I should" kind of way, Dad,' Aspen began, 'and then when we got in the room she just had a meltdown. I called you, I called Dr G and I called Tim.'

'But you still haven't said what happened,' Carlson prompted.

'She thinks someone has been in Jade's room,' Aspen replied. 'Moving things around. She said the room smelt different. She said she could smell someone else.'

'And have you been in the room?' Carlson directed this question at Tim.

'No, sir, I have not,' Tim replied. 'I did —'

'You did what?'

'I did advise Aspen how to search the room, sir.'

279

'And why would you want to do that?' Carlson frowned at his daughter.

'Me?' said Tim, and Carlson saw a look of bewildered terror pass over the young DC's face.

'No hon, he means me,' said Aspen. 'I wanted to find out why she killed herself, Dad. Tim suggested places to look. To see if she had a diary at all. I didn't find it, which surprised me, because I was sure she kept one.'

'She did, but you wouldn't have found it,' said Carlson. He got up from his stool on the far side of the kitchen island and walked to the hallway. Tim and Aspen shrugged at each other and leaned onto the work surface. Carlson returned with his briefcase. He placed it on the countertop and clicked it open. He took out a thick A5-sized leather-bound booklet. There was a long leather cord which tied it shut, enclosing the hand-made paper within. He stood staring at the diary for several moments before he passed it to his remaining child.

'She *did* keep it!' exclaimed Aspen. 'I bought it at the Christmas market in Birmingham. I saw it and it was so her. I was really upset when I couldn't find it. She said she loved it when I gave it to her and then, when it wasn't there, it was as if she'd lied to me and I lost her all over again.'

'She kept it. It was just tucked under her mattress by the pillows,' said Carlson. 'I didn't want your mother to read it. I've been reading it over and over on my own. There are no names. Just initials, and those don't match people she knew at school.'

'No, they wouldn't,' said Aspen, flicking through the pages of the diary. 'She gave them nicknames and then used those initials. Remember when Mum found my diary?'

Carlson bowed his head, recalling the screaming row the two of them had had.

'Well, after that I devised a code, and then when I gave Jade this diary I told her all about my code and she thought it was a great idea.' Aspen bent her head over the book, engrossed in its contents.

Tim and Carlson looked at each other over her head, confused.

'Is there anything to eat?' Carlson said. 'I seem to have missed lunch.'

'Lasagne,' Aspen muttered. 'I made a lasagne. Tim, could you please?'

Tim rose but Carlson waved him back into his seat.

'You don't need to make yourself that at home, Tim. I can still find plates and the oven in my own kitchen. Do you need anymore?' he asked, nodding his head to Tim's beer.

Tim declined, so Carlson piled up his plate and took another beer from the fridge.

'So, come on, Miss Marple,' he said. 'What is the diary telling you that it clearly never told me?'

'Well, first off, Dad, I took the laptop and I gave it to Tim. He gave it to his friend Stuart. Stuart was able to break the password.'

Carlson knew he had involuntarily raised an eyebrow in the direction of "Tim". The DC looked suitably embarrassed.

'I talked with Sierra team, sir, in my own time, of course, and they talked me through everything that they had found on her phone and the anonymous text messages. My friend was able to track down the IP addresses used. Most are in internet cafes, as you'd expect, but one was registered to a boy at Jade's school. I was going to speak with you, sir, but it all kicked off with the reporter and I didn't get a chance. What's in the diary, Aspen?'

'The lot,' she said. 'See here, where she's put TB? That might mean "thick bastard". I'm guessing that's her name for

Peter Reynolds. She told me about him at Christmas. Who he was. What he wanted. How he behaved afterwards. And who took the photos. FC — that could be "fat cow". I think that's Genevieve Butler; Jade told me about her too. Apparently, she was mad for this Peter, but at the time he was crazy about Jade. It's all here, Dad. Everything. How powerless and alone they made her feel. Even scared that we'd not take it seriously. Dad, everything that they put her through, it's here.'

Aspen held the diary out to her father, who took it and started leafing through, seeing it with fresh eyes.

'So *now* can we find the bastards who killed my baby?'

They all turned. Marguerite Carlson stood in the door-way, her makeup smudged, hair a mess. Tears running down her face.

Carlson got up and pulled her to him. 'Yes love, we can find them and punish them.'

'Good,' she said, shrugging him off. 'That smells good; may I have some?'

'Of course, love,' said Carlson. He brought a plate of food to her and she tucked in.

Only Aspen saw the tears he was blinking away.

CHAPTER FORTY-SEVEN

Spring 1993

Bernie lay face down on the single bed. The tears had dried on his face and the salt was making his skin itch. He would have preferred to lay on his back. Better still would have been to curl up into a ball and die, but that wasn't going to happen either. If he was lucky, someone might remember he was there and bring something cooling to put on his back. But Bernie knew he wasn't lucky. He never had been. He sniffed and wiped his nose on the sheets where he lay. No one was coming to help him. In his few months staying at the hostel he had made no friends, preferring to keep to himself and trusting no one. Most of them were too stupid to be a friend of his in any case. Everyone was in competition not to get cornered. The hostel was designated as a place of safety — a half-way house to take him from institutionalised young offender to useful member of society. That was the idea at least. If it had not been run by a friend of Mr Dewsbury, it might even have worked. It had turned out to be worse than the secure home.

Bernie raised his head to listen, but the hostel seemed unusually quiet. No sounds came from any of the rooms. Even the television was quiet. At least he wasn't tied up this time. Once before the bastard had left him tied up all night and the following day. Bernie had soiled the bed and there had to be a new mattress. No questions were asked, of course. They never were. He lay in the dark and fumed silently. There was someone moving around downstairs after all. Bernie recognised the footsteps. They came to the bottom of the stairs and Bernie held his breath. But they turned, paced the short distance to the front door and Bernie heard it open and then slam. With a deep sigh of relief, he realised that Marc, "the bastard" as he preferred to call him, had gone out. Bernie got off the bed. Tears pricked his eyes again as the cuts creaked and bled more as he moved. He arranged a tea-towel on the bed and covered it in Vaseline. Laying on the towel, he eased it into place, wriggling as much as he could bear to make the makeshift dressing cover the worst of the lashes on his back. He placed one hand on the nape of his neck while he gathered up a t-shirt and put it on, tucking it in so that it would keep the tea-towel in place. He put a sweatshirt over the top. Pulling out a bag from under the bed, he put in his few belongings and some cash he'd earned working at the garden centre. There wasn't much. He was pretty sure there was some money in the bastard's room but that was always kept locked. If he damaged the lock now it would spoil the surprise.

He went to the kitchen and grabbed some tinned food and even remembered a tin opener and a spoon. These he took back to his room, then he switched off the light and waited.

He didn't have to wait long. It must have been a slow night in the pub. He went to the top of the stairs and hid in a small alcove near the bastard's room. He had a clear sight of his own room too. Bernie could hear Marc rummaging down below, but finally he lurched up the stairs. He stopped for a moment on the landing and Bernie thought he'd come back to finish off from earlier, but the git made it to his own room. Before he could turn and lock the door Bernie had burst through and brought the steak hammer down with force, but not too much. He didn't want him dead. Not yet. Marc dropped like a stone, dazed but not unconscious, and he tried to fend off his attacker. Bernie gave him a whack on the temples which calmed him down.

He dragged the now unconscious Marc onto the bed and tied him to the finials at each corner. Face down. With the carving knife he'd found abandoned at the back of the kitchen drawer, Bernie cut Marc's shirt and jeans from his body. Whilst he waited for the other man to wake up he took some time to rifle through the drawers and the wardrobe.

He found an instant use for the ball gag and some other toys that would come in handy later. More importantly he found a canister filled with notes. It would be enough to get by on for a few months if he was careful. Bernie took the money and put it in the bag in his room.

When he returned, Marc was just rousing.

'Glad you're back with me,' said Bernie. 'I think you should know I've had enough. I've had it with sickos like you. Tonight, you're going to have a taste of your own medicine.'

He took the cat o' nine tails from where it hung. He whipped his abuser until Marc's flesh was raw and his own arm ached. This is boring, he thought. 'What do you get out of this, you bastard?' he asked.

The reply, like the earlier screams, was muffled by the ball gag. Bernie took another look through the drawers. Perfect. He took the dildo from the drawer and plugged it into the mains. 'Brace yourself' was all he said as he pushed the dry implement into the bastard's anus.

Judging from the wriggling and muffled sounds it must have hurt. At least the battery won't run out, thought Bernie grimly.

He went to his own room, changed his shirt, zipped up the bag and walked out into the night to the bus station.

Several hours and two bus changes later he was outside a front door in a tower block, surrounded by three matching towers. He rang, heard hesitant footsteps and the rattle of the safety chain on the other side of the door.

'Hello Terry,' he said.

At first Terry Hanslope said nothing, but reached out his hand and took Bernie's bag. He turned and walked down the dingy corridor. Bernie pushed the door open wider and walked in. He followed Terry past the room where the bag had been placed and into the kitchen.

Terry turned and faced him. 'Tea?' was all he said.

'Cheers,' Bernie replied.

Terry plonked the mugs on the small Formica table and found an open packet of digestive biscuits. The two young men sat and drank tea, munching the biscuits without speaking for several minutes.

It was Terry who eventually broke the silence.

'You can stay here for a couple of weeks, then I'm moving up north. Gonna try my luck on the North Sea rigs,' he said.

'Shit, Terry,' said Bernie choking on the digestive. 'But you don't like the cold, mate. How are you going to manage?'

Terry shrugged. 'Good money to be made. I met a guy at the pub, he's got me the job.'

'And you can trust this guy? He's not some perv?' Bernie

swigged the last of his tea and went to make himself some more.

Terry laughed. 'You make yourself at home Bern,' he said. 'No, he's okay. He's looked out for me so far. Like you used to before you got sent down.'

'Okay, well I'll need to stay a few nights, you won't mind, will yah? I need to sort some work out, too. I've got enough to get by for a while and I can pay me way here.' Bernie pulled out a battered wallet and peeled off a couple of tenners.

'Couldn't make it thirty, could ya?' Terry asked.

Laughing, Bernie passed him another note without question. 'You always was shit with money, Tel,' he said. 'Okay if I have a wash and then we can go and have a pint?'

'Last door at the front of the flat. There's a shower over the bath if you want it,' said Terry.

Bernie scowled at the thought of his still raw back being exposed to water, but said nothing. Terry did not need to know anything about that. He turned back to the counter to finish making his tea.

Terry stuffed the notes in his pocket. He had not failed to notice that Bernie's wallet was comfortably full and maybe, if he played his cards right and didn't say anything too stupid, more money could come his way. Bernie hadn't always been generous in the past, but he'd given up the extra tenner easily enough. Maybe things had changed.

They hadn't. Terry was much too frightened of Bernie to contemplate stealing his money, but each time he asked for a few quid more over the next couple of days, Bernie laughed louder and longer at him. 'You're shit with money, Tel; shit. I've given you all you're getting, you muppet.'

Ben Poole trudged down the stairs to where the CSI unit had their offices. Kirsty Russell was perched on the corner of someone's desk. Her green blouse was slightly open at the neck and he noticed how pale and silken her creamy skin was. She saw him walk in the room; her eyes were upon him and he felt himself blushing. He was sure she'd read his thoughts, seen him eyeing her up. At least no one would see the blush, he thought.

'Hi Ben,' she said. 'To what do we owe this pleasure?'

He even liked the way she said his name. He concentrated hard to stop himself from grinning like an idiot.

'Hi, I could do with a word in private if that's okay?'

'Sure, I was just heading out to get a coffee. Walk with me?'

'Perfect,' he said.

Kirsty, it appeared, preferred the lift, although he was pretty sure his reason for taking the stairs was more related to putting off the inevitable embarrassment and ridicule from colleagues. All the way up he kept kicking himself for behaving like a fool. Not taking the lift with her and insisting on the stairs had sounded idiotic. It *was* idiotic. He liked her. Why couldn't he just tell her that? They met in the foyer, left the station and headed out towards the nearby independent coffee shop.

'So, come on. What do you need to talk about away from sir?'

'Is it that obvious there's something I don't want the Guv'nor to know about?'

'Let's just say, Ben, that I've worked around police officers for a very long time and you all seem to have a not dissimilar tell. Shall we drink in?' she asked as she went to place her order with the barista.

Ben agreed, and they sat near a window. The spring sunlight caught her hair, giving her a celestial glow.

'Come on, fess up,' she said.

'Okay,' he said, lining up his napkin and stirrer side by side. 'I've got a situation —'

'You've got a girl into trouble.'

'No!' he said, horrified. 'Nothing like that. Jeez, what kind of cretin do you think I am? But, on the other hand, I'm sure I've done something pretty stupid.'

She arched an eyebrow and indicated that he should continue.

'I play online games. PVP, player versus player. Dragon Quest, this one is called, knights in armour versus dragons, elves, orcs, etcetera. You can fight alone or alongside someone else.' He paused, half expecting her to laugh at him. But she didn't.

Her only reaction was to sip her coffee. 'Go on,' she said.

'Recently, I've been fighting with a friend — he's called Treallis.'

Kirsty's coffee developed unseen bones and she choked. 'Sorry,' she said. 'Carry on.'

He scowled at her momentarily, 'Yeah, saying it out loud it does all sound a bit daft. In the game my name is —' he paused. 'Actually, it doesn't matter what my name is for now. Anyway, this guy I'm questing with currently, he said something odd the other night. He said that he too had quests IRL, that's in real life, and then instead of saying goodbye, he said "fare thee well".'

'What's unusual about that? You said it was knights in

armour. I'm guessing a medieval setting, full of fair maidens? Don't you use that style of language?'

'Yes, yes, of course we do. But that's not my point,' said Ben. 'My point is that the letter we got from "Jack" the other day used the same phrase. And it got me to thinking. Is my Treallis actually Jack, and how the hell do we find out?'

'Ah,' said Kirsty, setting down her coffee. 'But presumably players in these games are based all over the world? What makes you think he's local?'

'I have no evidence at all. I just have a gut feeling. All I want to know is can he be traced?'

Kirsty leaned back in the booth. 'Probably,' she said, 'but it'll cost ya. And…'

Here it comes, he thought.

'You are going to have to tell Ronnie.'

CHAPTER FORTY-EIGHT

Bernie Latimer decided that he should go into work as normal. It would look odd if he behaved out of character. He surmised that the police would be hunting for someone acting unusually. Disappearing. Of course, he never thought that it could come to this. It never occurred to him that the police would have been smart enough to get close to him. He'd read all the old case notes. Jeez, that was a great find. Weeks he'd had with all the papers he'd taken from Travis. Weeks to study the leads, the hits and the misses, and to watch the films over and over again. He relished the moments of someone else's helplessness and it helped alleviate the pressure of how he'd felt in his younger years. The abuse from Travis, Dewsbury and Dewsbury's friend, Marc. At least he'd got his own back on two of them. Bernie laughed out loud wondering how long it had been before Marc had been found tied to his bed. There was no way that the bastard would report the attack to the police. There had never been anything in the papers either, he'd checked for weeks afterwards.

From studying the previous cases, Bernie also knew how

long it had taken the police to catch Pat Wheeler. Even then they'd just got lucky in the end. And that was exactly what had happened here. The coppers had found the flat by sheer fluke. Apart from not having done a final wipe down after the reporter, he usually wiped down as he went along, preparing for just such a situation. Yes, he was always careful, he knew he was, so he was confident that there was nothing in the flat which could connect it to him.

Except Dave's missus. Did she know Dave had let him use the flat? No, she couldn't. If she knew that then Dave would have had to tell her why he was letting Bernie use it. No, Dave wouldn't have told her about his side line. Wouldn't have trusted her. It would all be okay. He'd have to find a new place. Maybe a new town; Gippingford was getting old. He could move on. He'd done it before and there was nothing to keep him here now.

That's what he'd do. He'd go into work today and tell them his old mum was ill, and he had to go and look after her. Or maybe his Gran. He couldn't remember if he'd said his mum was alive or not when they took him on. And anyway, if they said anything he'd say he had two mums. Adopted and natural. That happened a lot. They'd swallow that. Yep, Bernie knew exactly what he was going to do.

'Boss,' said Poole, knocking on the partition wall which led to Carlson's desk area. 'I could do with a chat.'

'Come in,' Carlson said. 'Not good news I take it, if your face is anything to go by.'

'No, it's not,' Poole replied. He sat in the chair, took a deep breath and related to Carlson everything that he'd told Kirsty the day before.

'What makes you think it could possibly be the same person?' Carlson asked. 'Presumably these games are universal? There must be thousands of people playing them.'

'Yes,' agreed Poole. 'It's just that — well, the girls have disappeared on a Friday night. The game is usually quite busy then, but I had the impression that since he's been talking to me, he's never been online on a Friday. I've gone back and checked, and I was right — that's the one day when he's never around.'

'That's not conclusive though, is it Ben? There could be any number of reasons. He could work away from home and travel back on a Friday. It might be the night he looks after his kids, he might be in a darts team. It could be any of those, or a hundred more reasons.' Carlson sat back in his chair and tapped his right forefinger against his chin. He studied Poole's face and found the look on it intriguing. He smiled. 'What makes you think this is our bloke, Ben?'

'I'm not exactly confident, sir,' Poole replied. 'It really is a gut feeling.'

'I see,' said Carlson. 'Short of asking him outright, next time he's online, I can't see that it's something we can follow up. Can you?'

Carlson saw anger flash across Poole's face, but he continued, 'Look,' he said, 'I agree it's odd, but unless you've been telling him all about the case, I can't see that it's anything more than a very strange coincidence. What are the odds of a player in this game finding another player? Unless you're suggesting he came looking for you, and if that was the case, how did he find out about you? You think someone inside your circle of friends or within the station is leaking information on your gaming habits?'

Poole gave a slight shake of his head.

Carlson decided not to completely crush his DS. 'I mean,

you can ask Kirsty if it can be looked into without too much cost. If it won't blow the investigation's budget, then follow it up. It's not a top priority though. Okay?'

'Yes, Guv. Thanks.'

As Poole wandered away, he almost put his hands in his pockets he was so distracted. He really wasn't satisfied with the answer he'd got, but he hadn't expected anything else. In Poole's opinion the old boy was past it. The Guv hadn't really got a clue about the computer age. Kirsty had found a contact number for the game's developers for him, and he decided to call them later when America woke up.

Bernie walked out of the building tossing his keys into the air. Easy, he thought, swallowed the whole story about his old Gran. He almost skipped back to the Peugeot.

From an upstairs office at the warehouse, his manager watched him, thinking the behaviour was unusual for someone who needed time off to visit a sick relative. She'd suspected he was lying but was relieved all the same. He'd always given her the creeps. She followed his jaunty steps to his car and thought no more about him as she picked up the phone and dialled the agency's number for a replacement forklift driver.

DC Tim Jessop pulled into the school car park. DI Jennifer Stokes got out of the car and gave him a grim smile. Funny, he thought, it didn't matter how old you were, you only had to go into a school and you were thirteen again. Tim trailed in her wake as she followed the signs to the reception area.

'DI Stokes, and this is DC Jessop.' She flashed her ID. 'I'm here to see Miss Keeble, the headmistress?'

'It's head teacher. Not mistress. But, yes, we're expecting you. If you'll take a seat?'

Tim stifled the feeling of having been told off.

They wandered over to the row of plastic chairs, but Jennifer did not sit. She turned when her name was called, and Tim followed her and the head teacher's secretary to the office.

Miss Keeble's secretary knocked on the door, opened it without waiting for an answer and ushered them into the room. Miss Keeble was sitting at the large oak desk near the window and she was not alone. She didn't stand but introduced the wizened gnome-like man as the head of the governors, Mr Davies.

'Please take a seat, Miss Stokes,' she said, indicating the seat next to where the gnome was already sitting. She said nothing to Tim, but he was not concerned and figured she was trying to intimidate them by her tone and manner. Every school had at least one teacher like the head of Gippingford High School. He sat himself at the end of the table, ready to take notes.

'Detective Inspector,' said Stokes, 'not Miss, Miss Keeble.'

'Of course; my mistake,' replied the other. Stokes inclined her head and sat down. Judging by the look on the DI's face Tim surmised she was under the distinct impression that Miss Keeble rarely, if ever, made mistakes.

'Now, what can we do for you Miss, sorry, Detective Inspector?' said Miss Keeble.

'Could you tell me if these names are known to you, if

they are pupils at this school and, if so, whether they are at school today?' Stokes handed a list of names to the head.

'What is this in relation to?' asked the gnome, in a voice which sounded like a dry fountain pen scratching over parchment.

'If you could answer the question, please, Miss Keeble,' said Stokes, not looking in the direction of the short man.

'Yes, they are all pupils here,' said Miss Keeble. 'I will get my secretary to check if they are in today, but I must repeat Mr Davies's question which you chose to ignore. What interest do the police have in these students?'

'You will recall Jade Carlson?'

'Why, yes of course, very sad,' said Miss Keeble, with a slight shrug of her ample shoulders. 'Nothing to do with the school, of course. We were vindicated in the inquest. Death by misadventure, wasn't it?'

'I'd be grateful if you could tell me which students are in school today and, if they are, I'd like them brought to private rooms.' DI Stokes spoke firmly but quietly. 'If you cannot facilitate that, perhaps the school hall, but they will have to be kept apart. No getting their stories straight. You'll also need to call their parents or arrange a responsible adult for each of them.'

'Detective Inspector Stokes, you still haven't been clear what this is all about. I need to know, immediately!' Miss Keeble was a table thumper. Tim had not expected that.

Stokes eyed Keeble like a hawk surveying a rabbit and Tim was instantly impressed. He'd never worked with DI Stokes before, what with her being Vice, but he was impressed by what he was seeing.

'You've allowed a cyber-bullying network to develop in your school, Miss Keeble,' Stokes said in a strangely threat-intoned, yet calm, voice. 'Jade's parents may ask for the inquest to be re-opened. Your school may not be vindicated should that happen.' She paused just a fraction and Tim knew the power in the room had most definitely shifted.

Stoked continued, 'Now, if you'll collect the pupils whose names are on the list? My colleague will assist you. Those who aren't in we'll pick up from their homes. If you'll excuse me, I need to speak to my boss. I expect you'll want to do the same.' Without waiting, Stokes rose and made for the door. Tim stayed put.

It took only a few minutes for the secretary to return with the list. He took it and found the DI in the hallway, gazing out of a window onto the empty playground.

Jennifer Stokes counted the number of ticks, flipped open the cover on her mobile and called the station.

'Hi, Boss,' she said. 'I'll need four separate cars at the school. Two are off sick, apparently. I'll drop by their homes. I reckon they're not as sick now as they are going to be.'

Superintendent Jim Tasker laughed, 'Well done Jen,' he said. 'We'll see you in an hour then?'

'Yes, Boss,' she said.

CHAPTER FORTY-NINE

With much coughing and shuffling of feet and chairs the team settled in the squad room facing the white board displays.

Carlson looked around at them and then at the boards, pleased with what he saw.

'Thanks, Ben,' he said, and sat down whilst Poole stood at the head of the room.

'Morning team,' said Poole. Carlson noticed that he seemed unusually chirpy and wondered what the cause was. Kirsty Russell or the DC from Vice.

'We've had some overnight developments that will really move this case along. First off, the e-fit from Sarah Jenkins, our intrepid reporter' — several of the team groaned — 'has got some hits already. Some came in via Crimestoppers, so nothing that we can go back on and ask further questions, but we also showed it to Julie Albright. You'll remember it was her brother who found the reporter at the flat. She recognised it immediately. Apparently, her late partner and our man were friends. Also, we got a call from a woman claiming to be the guy's manager, which means we have a name and a place of work. Unfortunately, he's still one step ahead as he told his manager that he needed to take some time off to look after his old Gran.'

Several of the team said 'Ah'.

'Exactly, bless his poor old Gran,' said Poole. 'Forensics are starting to come in as well. Nothing on DNA for a few days but we do have a match on a partial found under the kitchen sink. Kirsty, would you like to take us through that?'

'Thanks, Ben,' said Kirsty as she rose to her feet, flicking toast crumbs to the floor. 'In fact, several partial fingerprints have been found at the flat. A couple over the bath where he must have leaned against the wall while he was cleaning it. He wiped down afterwards but wasn't careful enough. If he'd used a spray cleaner then he would have been home free.' She shrugged. 'Still that's not my favourite. Our man bought a box of latex gloves to probably wear whilst washing and disposing of the victims. However,' she paused, 'he wasn't wearing gloves when he put them under the sink.'

'But those could be anyone's prints,' piped up one of the young PCs.

'True,' said Kirsty, 'there are a lot of smudges, as you would expect of anything that you'd buy. However, there are clear prints like this,' and she posed her hand as if grasping a box. Carlson passed her a box of tissues, so she could complete her demonstration. 'This is where the prints we found were. Nothing overlaying them. Therefore, that individual is highly likely to have been the last person to have handled the box. That name is in our system. Petty theft a few years ago. It's a name which also matches the one we got from Julie Albright, from the man's manager and from a couple of the Crimestoppers calls. So, ladies and gentlemen, we have a winner. Bernard Latimer, or Bernie to his friends.'

Ben Poole rose to his feet. 'Bernard Latimer drives a black Peugeot 306, but he also has a grey van registered to his name. He could be using either vehicle. His details have been passed to Border Control, but we need to find him, people, and soon. He's proved he's dangerous and now that he's on the run it could make him more dangerous. Approach with caution, but find him!'

Ben handed out tasks to the team and then came back to where Kirsty and Carlson were talking.

'We'll get him, Boss,' he said. 'I still can't believe he was so careful to wear gloves for everything except the box he kept them in.'

'No cure for stupid,' Kirsty said, 'but the truth really is that he probably never expected us to find his killing field. Prints on the outside of the box, therefore, should never have been a problem. He did a good job of cleaning up at the flat. A bit panicky, mind, but a good enough job.'

'At least with him on the run, he's unlikely to kill again for a while. He'll be more worried about his own skin for the time being,' said Carlson. He fished around in his jacket pocket for his mobile and held it to his ear.

'Yes, Tim,' he said. 'Well done, lad. I'll be up in a moment.' He replaced the phone and looked at the other two. 'I'm just going up to SOCIT. Tim went out with one of their DIs this morning. They've pulled some kids in. I want to see their miserable little faces.'

He strode off towards the lift. Poole looked curiously after him and then at Kirsty.

'What's that all about?' he said.

'His daughter,' Kirsty replied. 'You know she killed herself?'

'Yes, of course.'

'Well, SOCIT were investigating the cause. We all knew it was cyber-bullying but Tim, or at least his friend, has managed to crack it. Carlson let Tim be in on the arrests this morning. Now,' Kirsty said, with a concerned expression, 'how about your own cyber stalking? Did you discover who your gaming partner is?'

'No, it's a pain but they wouldn't release any information without a court order and that could take months.' Poole folded his arms and huffed. 'The Guv told me to drop it, but since I thought it would just be the effort of a couple of emails and a phone call I thought I'd give it a go. I'm still sure my gut instinct is right. I'm convinced it's him. If I'd figured it out earlier though, it could have saved at least one life and the journalist wouldn't have been raped.'

'None of that is on you, Ben,' Kirsty said putting her hand on his shoulder. 'You acted as soon as you'd made sense of it. If you'd realised the connection and said nothing it would be a different matter. You're not Supercop you know. You're a good man and I am going to let you buy me dinner.'

'Oh, are you?' said Ben, grinning. 'Best I catch me a bad guy first.'

He looked around the room to make sure no one was watching them and then, uncharacteristically and with the sure knowledge she wouldn't mind, kissed her lightly on the cheek. She grinned at him and he sashayed to the stairs and his car.

Since the attempt to hunt Treallis down via the app's developers, Poole pondered one last idea of trying to contact his online companion. He opened the boot and collected his personal laptop and made for the nearby café, deciding not to risk using the police HQ's intranet to connect to the web. Even if he ended up catching the killer, there were still rules about connecting non-standard build laptops to the network.

He sipped his coffee and logged on to the game. The Wi-Fi was slower here than his superfast fibre connected home, and he sat with his chin in his hands.

'Need some company?' Poole looked up to see the familiar shape of Carlson looming over him. He shifted over to let his senior officer sit alongside him. The two men sat shoulder to shoulder, hunched over the screen.

Ethereal music blasted from the speakers and Poole speedily hushed the sound, looking around the café as he did so. He clicked on the list of regular quest companions but Treallis's name was greyed out. Poole right clicked and read from the details in the pop-up box that Treallis had not logged in for three days.

'Can you message him through the game?' Carlson was squinting at the screen, watching the ghostly images of quests and battles in the background.

'I suppose so,' said Poole, surprised that Carlson had heard of messaging. 'I've never needed to before. What do you want to say?'

'I know,' Carlson said. 'May I?' and he reached over and typed just one line.

'Treallis, we need to talk. IRL.'

Poole looked at him, but Carlson winked at him and simply said, 'I used to game when my daughter was alive.'

'Thanks, Tim. Thanks for letting me know,' said Aspen. 'Will

I see you later? No, I understand. I am a policeman's daughter after all.' She kept her voice light, but she was still hurt that the job would come first.

'That's what it will always be like, you know.'

Aspen whirled around. Her mother had walked into the sitting room behind her and she'd not noticed.

'Excuse me?' she said.

'The job. The job will always come first. Before you. Before children. Before birthdays. Christmas,' said Marguerite harshly. 'You name it, the job will always come first.'

'Why do you stay then?' asked Aspen. 'Why do you put up with it if you hate it so much?'

'Why? What a strange question. I do it because despite everything that's happened, I still love him. I always have.'

'But you've been so horrid to him. Ever since Jade killed herself you've been such a bitch to him.' Aspen paused, deciding what to say next. 'Mum, it's like… well, it's as if you blame him for what happened. He couldn't have stopped it any more than you could.'

'I know,' sighed her mother. 'I know it's not his fault. It's just that he seemed to get past it so easily. I couldn't.'

'You're wrong. He didn't get past it. Not at all,' Aspen could hear the barely suppressed anger in her own voice. She had reached breaking point with her mother. 'He was just trying to be strong for us all. Like he's always done. He took Jade's diary so you wouldn't find it and take all the blame yourself. He protected you from that. You've no idea how much he protects you from things.'

'Oh, I know he likes to present himself as the hero. The saviour.' Marguerite looked at herself in the mirror over the fireplace.

'Mum, can you hear yourself? Can you hear the things

you're saying? You are so wrong. How can you say you love him when you treat him like a pariah and you push him away and blame him for everything? Do you know how much you hurt him last night when you shoved him away? Have you got any idea?' Aspen rose from the sofa and stood behind her mother, glaring at the reflection.

'My therapist says that it might help if both your Dad and I came to see her. She thinks that it will help us both to talk things through with a... well, a referee, present.'

'Good,' said Aspen. 'At least someone is talking sense to you. Just make sure you do that, or you are going to lose him. I saw his face last night when you pushed him away. You didn't. I've never seen anyone so broken. I can't tell you how much I hated you then.'

Marguerite looked stunned. She turned away from the mirror and stared at her daughter. Tears came again, and Aspen felt a deep regret. Children weren't meant to see their parents cry. Let alone be the cause of those tears. Yet she had needed to tell her mother what she had seen. How much her father had been hurt.

Marguerite's face took on the look of a child in despair. 'What have I done?' she said, opening her arms. 'What have I done?'

Aspen, suddenly the parent, rushed to her and held her tight. 'Nothing that can't be fixed Mum, but you need to let him in. You need to forgive him, and you need to forgive yourself. I'd like to come and see this therapist too. I think it will help us all. Will you do that?'

Marguerite said nothing, but the hug she gave her daughter showed her affirmation in a way that words could not.

CHAPTER FIFTY

Shazza stood in the middle of the ring. Blood ran from her nose and she wiped it away with the back of her left hand. Her right was raised high in the air by the referee. Her opponent, with an eye already swelling and showing every sign of being the perfect shiner by morning, bowed and touched gloves with her.

Shazza bowed in return, then turned and strolled back to her corner. Every atom of her being wanting to cartwheel or do a back flip. Bo might frown about that though, she thought, and since he was waiting in the corner for her, she'd probably save that for later.

'Well done, girl,' he said, hugging her tight. 'I'm so proud of you.'

Shazza hugged him back and then the tears came. No one had ever been proud of her before. Never. This wasn't just her victory, she knew that. She owed it to everyone who'd had faith in her, but she'd had faith in herself too. That's what getting clean had done for her. She'd got her life back.

Squatting on the small stool, she was still sniffling as Bo wiped her face and took out her gum shield. She drank the water he squirted in her mouth and held out her hands for him to remove the gloves. Sitting with her head down, so no one could see her tears, her eyes misted again, and the drops fell onto her shorts. When the right glove had been tugged off he handed her the box of tissues and simply got on with the job of releasing her left hand, as if sitting sobbing in the corner of a boxing ring was the most normal thing he'd ever seen.

'Thanks Bo,' Shazza said, blowing her nose. 'I couldn't have done it without you.'

'And me,' squeaked a voice at the side of the ring. 'You couldn't have done it without me, either.'

Sarah hung onto the lower rope. Her face was healing, though she'd probably always have the scar across her right cheek bone, but she was getting her old confidence back. She'd written her story as she'd told DCI Carlson she would. She'd not published it yet and Shazza wasn't sure that she ever would. Writing it was enough for now. As good as therapy, she'd said.

'Bloody cheek,' said Shazza, laughing. 'What bloody help were you? I spent all of my training time running back and forth to the hospital and walking that monstrous dog of yours. What help was that?'

For a moment Sarah's face dropped, until she realised Shazza was teasing her.

'You cow,' she smirked. 'Danvers gave you all the fitness you needed to win this bout. When she swung that crescent kick I thought you were a goner. I've never seen anyone duck so fast. And that right hook of hers. How did you avoid it?

'She has a tell,' confided Shazza. 'Bo spotted it in the first round. Just before she goes for a big punch she flicks her hair back.'

'This is why I tell you girls to tie your hair up before you get onto the dojo,' said Bo. 'No loose bits, no flick, no tell. Am I right, or am I right?'

Both women laughed at him. 'Yes, Bo,' they chorused.

'What are you going to do now, Shazza?' Sarah asked.

'Well, Bo and I —' she began.

Sarah looked from one to the other, her eyes wide in surprise.

'No, nothing like that. Don't be daft. Bo's offered me a job at the gym and I'm going to take it. I don't think I could ever settle to working in an office or nuffing like that, but the gym? That'll work for me I think.'

Sarah saw the look that Bo was giving Shazza. She was confident that, despite the age gap, it wouldn't stay a working relationship for long. She hoped she was right.

Bernie Latimer pulled off the motorway into the services. Scotch Corner was the last big station before the road became quieter in Northumberland. With more people in the busier service stations he hoped the chances of his being recognised were reduced.

He'd shaved his head to alter his appearance as his photo was on every front page and every news broadcast he'd seen. Normally he would have avoided the A1 like an outbreak of zombies, but if he was going to get to Aberdeen it was the best way. Most of his journey from the south had been on the M1. Busy services again, although the risk of getting picked up by automatic number plate recognition was negated as he had dumped the black Peugeot, set light to it and picked a small van instead. He liked vans. The grey one had been fantastic for moving the bodies, but it was registered in his name, so the police could search for that too. The other advantage of a van was that he could sleep in the back, saving money on a room, further cutting down the chance of being spotted. He'd paid cash and given the seller Travis's driving licence for the V5. The seller hadn't even quibbled that it was an old style of licence and even possibly illegal. It bought him some time. He wasn't sure if the DVLA would pick up that the licence holder was dead but, even if they did, by the time they got the change in ownership he would be long gone. Possibly even out on the rigs already. For now, it was a risk he was prepared to take. Bernie knew he had few friends now and so he was heading for the only one he had left. The only person he could still trust. Terry Hanslope. Terry had moved to Aberdeen to work on the rigs. He'd met and married the landlady of his onshore digs and when she died, from natural causes of course, Terry stayed ashore and ran the B&B. Bernie's plans currently went no further than that. Realistically he guessed it was only a matter of time. But if he kept his head down long enough the manhunt would be scaled down and eventually ceased. He scratched the stubble on his face. It too would help with the disguise.

Bernie decided to spend as little time as possible at Scotch Corner. It had taken nearly eight hours to get there and the van wasn't the speediest vehicle on the road, but he opted to head further north before finding a place to kip for the night. Terry had suggested he find somewhere in Northumberland's Kielder forest as, although it would take him off route, it was enormous, Terry said, and he could even stay and rest for a day if he needed to. When Bernie looked at the road map, however, it seemed too far a diversion and he chose to stay on the A1 and find somewhere to kip outside one of the villages.

Bernie took his Big Mac, large fries and diet coke back to the van and ate there. He slid down in the seat as the traffic police Range Rover glided into the car park and parked three bays away. They got out and stretched their backs. One looked around the car park, catching sight of Bernie staring. He froze for a moment and then quickly picked up some fries and popped them in his mouth. The police officer's eyes continued roving the car park. The officers walked away from their vehicle, but Bernie waited until they had walked up the steps to the building before he started the van up and drove off. Once back on the A road he ate the rest of the now cold fries. He passed signs for Alnwick, Craster, Ellingham. He saw a sign for Bamburgh. A long-forgotten memory came to mind. Denise had had a postcard of the castle on the fridge. Her favourite castle in the world, she'd said. Her husband had taken her there on honeymoon and to a little place called Seahouses. From the beach there, she'd seen the castle for the first time. It was magical, she'd said. A smooth pink castle rising out of ragged grey rock. Although the marriage was never destined for success, she'd never forgotten the castle. It was as good as place as any, he thought. It was nearly midnight when he drew into the small town. Little more than a village, he thought. Close to the sea front he found a car park, parked up and prepared to sleep in the back of the van. As he was getting ready to roll himself in the blankets, he saw a light in one of the bungalows opposite. He peeked out of the van's rear window. A curtain was pulled back, draped around a shape, and the person was having a good nose out the window. Bernie realised his was the only vehicle in the car park. Swearing softly about nosey neighbours, he got back in the front and drove around for a while longer. He eventually found a garage and pulled the van in between two cars in the MOT bay. After checking the opening times, he settled down in the back.

He woke early and was on his way before the garage staff

arrived. The miles trundled by and he allowed himself lunch, then another rest and kip in a lorry park on the outskirts of Dundee. When he started the van, there was an ominous click. He turned the key again. Still nothing. Cursing loudly, he thumped the steering wheel. He popped the bonnet and looked under the hood. After a few minutes of staring and moving wires around, Bernie had to admit he knew absolutely nothing about cars.

'Problem, mate?'

Bernie stepped back from the van to see a short dumpy man picking his fingernails and wiping the result on his jeans.

'Battery's flat, I think,' Bernie replied. 'But I don't understand how with all the miles I did yesterday. It should be fully charged.'

'Most likely the alternator then. Yer fan belt's not been slipping?'

Bernie shook his head.

'Come back in the caff. I reckon the owner can tell you if there's a garage nearby.'

Bernie pulled his cap down low over his eyes and followed his new acquaintance back into the café. The owner proved to be a font of all knowledge, but it was going to be a long walk.

Bernie set off, walking close to the A90 as the sound of the traffic reverberated around him, making his body vibrate as the noise shook him. Following the instructions, he found an underpass and walked down another road until he found the garage. Having explained his situation and shown that he had enough cash for a repair they got the recovery vehicle and drove him back to collect the van.

Back at the garage once more, the mechanic found the defunct alternator and quoted Bernie for fitting a new one. It would take every last penny he had, but he had no choice. He just hoped he had enough fuel for the last part of the journey. While waiting for the part to be delivered and fitted, Bernie did not know what to do for the best. If he walked around the streets there was a chance he could be recognised. His picture was on the front of both the Sun and the Daily Mail newspapers in the garage waiting room. He decided to stay hidden in the garage; at least that way he hoped he would see if anyone had spotted him, but where he would run if that happened, he had no idea. He pulled two chairs together, sat in one with his feet on the other and pulled the cap over his face. When the mechanic came to tell him the van was fixed, Bernie was surprised to discover that despite everything he'd slept. He set off again into the evening's rush hour traffic, not knowing if they'd squealed on him or not. He was too tired to care any longer.

At around 8pm he rolled into Aberdeen and the back street where Terry's B&B was located. He was impressed to see that it was an imposing double-fronted building. The large bay windows surrounded an ornate wooden door with glass panels. More windows, dormers, burst from the roof. Making the most of every inch of the property, Bernie thought.

As agreed with Terry on the phone two days beforehand, he pulled into the tiny driveway beside the guest house. He exited the van and stretched every muscle he could think of. Grabbing his bag, he walked through the unlocked front door as Terry had told him.

'Terry?' he called.

Bernie heard voices at the back of the house — a mix of Scottish and English accents, although he could not make out the words. Rough necks came from all over the country and even farther afield, he knew, but he had hoped to see Terry alone, at least for a while. He made his way to what he guessed was the kitchen. His old friend Terry was seated at the table with a familiar-looking tubby, grey-haired man, a younger black man and two middle-aged men in cheap suits. As soon as he walked in the room, Bernie realised his mistake. Terry looked at him. Apologetic and shamefaced.

'I'm really sorry, mate,' was all Terry could manage.

'But why, Tel?'

'When you came to stay that first time, before I came up here, I begged you for a few extra quid, but you just laughed at me. I've never forgotten it. Never forgiven it.'

Bernie was dumfounded. The event, if he could remember it, would have been nearly twenty-five years ago. Had Terry really held a grudge all that time?

The young man was already standing up. He had very few words. 'Hello Treallis,' he said.

'Da'anarth?' Bernie asked.

The young man nodded and, at a signal from the older man, pulled out his handcuffs and said, 'Treallis, you're nicked.'

EPILOGUE

Once again, the house was silent when he returned. He went to the kitchen and rummaged around in the fridge. The oven was on. A casserole bubbling away in the clear dish. It smelt good and his stomach rumbled.

Ronnie wandered up the stairs. He opened the bedroom door and looked around it. He saw his wife standing by the window. Hands on the ledge, head bent. She was crying. Again.

'Mags?' he said.

She turned. 'You're back early. Is it over?'

'Yes, it's over.'

'Good,' she said.

'I was thinking —'

'Again?' she sighed.

'Yes, I was thinking that perhaps we could hold a memorial service for Jade,' Ronnie said. 'Remember her life. What she still means to us.'

'Would anyone come?' Mags replied.

Ronnie thought back to the day of the funeral and the morass of mourners by the graveside, standing in the rain as

Jade's coffin was lowered into the earth's gaping wound. He'd looked up at the titanium grey sky and the drops had grown heavier. It seemed to him as if the sky was crying too. Yes, people would come. To remember her short life, to stare, but people would come.

To his wife he simply said, 'Does that matter? You'll be there. I'll be there. Aspen will be there. Anyone else would be —' he hesitated — 'just extra people.'

He pulled Mags closer and held her in his bear-like grasp.

Marguerite sighed. 'Thank you,' she said, hugging him back.

Recompense (DCI Carlson book 2)

Synnöve: The King's Cupbearer

Old Haunts and other stories

DCI Carlson and the team will return soon in Perdition - the third novel in the series. To keep unto date with their adventures and my other work, please join my mailing list here - https://contact.carolinegoldsworthy.com/contact

I do hope you enjoyed Tangent it would be lovely if you could leave me a review either on Amazon or Goodreads. It helps other readers find my work.

Thank you.

AUTHOR'S NOTE

The idea for Tangent festered and evolved rather than sprang into being through some inciting incident. I moved to Kesgrave on the outskirts of Ipswich in September 2006. One morning, just before Christmas, I was walking my dog and a man told me that I was the first woman he'd seen out on her own for some weeks. It occurred to me that perhaps I was placing myself in danger and, as Pippa my Doberman and I reached the Millennium Field football pitches, that realisation became clearer as, clad in bright yellow jackets, police officers were carrying out a linear search of the arable field on the other side of the hedge. It was a day or two after the discovery of Paula Clennell's and Annette Nicholls' bodies. Fortunately, no more young women were to lose their lives at the hands of that man, as he was captured, charged and imprisoned. However, it did make me wonder what led people to take so many lives. I came up with my own theories, as you will see, but this in no way reflects the life or upbringing of the man who became known as the Suffolk strangler.

This story is a disturbing read of the dark world which is

the undercurrent of many towns and cities. When first starting out on writing a novel, the debut novelist is always told to write what they know. This was a problem for me because I wasn't sure what I did know or indeed, if people would be interested in hearing it. The more I thought about it, the more I realised that there are aspects of life that I know quite a bit about.

When I was 14, a man followed me from the centre of town where I had been at a disco (yes, they were still called discos in those days), all the way to the end of my street. I walked more quickly, but he got nearer and nearer, and I knew he meant me harm. I could hear his breath getting closer and closer to me, becoming faster as he did so. I was terrified. And then something changed. I was still scared, but I was angry too. Angry that he felt it was appropriate to frighten the life out of someone who was little more than a child. When he did grab me, I was lucky in that he put a hand on my shoulder and didn't try to grab me in a bear hug. He was unlucky, because I was ready, and I was angry — very, very angry. I basically just beat him off with my handbag. Again, I was lucky, because he just ran off into the night. I saw him again a few days later, as he was coming out of his house. He looked at me, stepped back and hid behind his front door until I'd gone. Much of the fear and anger that I experienced in that event has come out in this story. But it's not the only experience I used.

When I was 25, my father committed suicide. As you can imagine, it was a terrible time for myself and for my sister. For a long time after the event, I held in all the emotions that one goes through when a family member takes their own life. Thirty years later, using that experience has been as good as therapy for me, working through those emotions and the trauma that a family undergoes when one of them has just suddenly gone.

I'd also like to express my deepest thanks to the people I met whilst volunteering at Iceni in the summer of 2010. You all gave me considerable insight into the world of addiction and recovery, and I hope that I have given my characters as strong a voice as that of the women I encountered at that time.

Dear reader, I hope you have not been too disturbed by this book. Indeed, it is my fervent hope that by experiencing these lives vicariously, it might encourage you to either volunteer or contribute in some way to your local drug outreach centre, women's refuge or night shelter.

Thank you,
Caroline
Suffolk
2018

ABOUT THE AUTHOR

Caroline Goldsworthy describes herself as an Essex girl living in Suffolk. She was born in Chelmsford and moved to Colchester aged three. Going to university in her early thirties, Caroline graduated with a BA in Spanish Language and Linguistics and won a full scholarship for an MA in Language Acquisition. It was during this time that Caroline discovered she really liked writing.

For the last few years she has been working as a programme manager for a large telecommunications organisation which was the reason for moving to the outskirts of Ipswich. She still lives there with her ageing Doberman, Pippa, and, when not working out how to kill off her characters, she's either reading, knitting jumpers with large needles or continuing cross-stitching a samurai warrior.

Tangent is her debut novel and the first of the DCI Ronald Carlson series of crime thrillers.

facebook.com/CarolineGAuthor

twitter.com/CarolineGolds63

ACKNOWLEDGMENTS

If it takes a village to raise a child, it certainly seems to take one to write a book. The act of writing itself is a very lonely business, despite the number of people who visit daily, share their stories and then sit on the side-lines again. Some are more persistent, wanting a larger part of the story as a whole, and Dave Bradwell was certainly one of those, since, initially, he had a very small part indeed! But he persuaded me he had a story of his own to tell.

As a writer, you don't manage to retain any sanity without your friends and acquaintances. So this is a short note of thanks to mine.

To my fellow students on the Arvon Crime and Forensics course whose reaction to my readings showed me I had a story worth completing. To Margaret Murphy and Helen Pepper, the tutors on that course, whose support and guidance have continued far beyond the week at Lumb Bank.

To my beta readers, Graham Waddingham, Lesley Byrne, Simon Cowdroy and Anna Caig for the feedback and a special thanks to Graham and Lesley for keeping me on track with the telephone tracking. Any mistakes left are my own.

Thanks also to Petra McQueen of The Writers' Company, my first editor, as well as Janet Laurence and the anonymous CWA reviewer whose feedback help me polish the manuscript.

Thanks as well to Anna, Gem, Helen, Kelly, Ruku, Stacey and Tim of the Saturday morning and virtual writing groups who kept me writing and got me out of the house. Thanks also to Grant and the staff at the Forge Kitchen, Ipswich, for allowing us the space to write together on a Saturday morning.

I'd also like to thank my colleagues for their massive support, especially Carl Sproston who read out some of Shazza's words for me, so I could use his lovely Black Country accent.

Finally, I'd like to say a huge thank you to Ian Hooper and his team at the Book Reality Experience who helped take Tangent from manuscript to the completed paperback or e-book that you have before you.